The
Flour Mill
Girls

Anna Cliffe is a former journalist. She lives close to the sea on the Kent coast. *The Flour Mill Girls* is the first of three World War I novels about the Graham sisters.

The Flour Mill Girls

ANNA CLIFFE

ZAFFRE

First published in the UK in 2022 by
ZAFFRE
An imprint of Bonnier Books UK
4th Floor, Victoria House, Bloomsbury Square, London, England, WC1B 4DA
Owned by Bonnier Books
Sveavägen 56, Stockholm, Sweden

A CIP catalogue record for this book is
available from the British Library.

ISBN: 978-1-83877-933-7

Also available as an ebook and an audiobook

1 3 5 7 9 10 8 6 4 2

Typeset by IDSUK (Data Connection) Ltd
Printed and bound in Great Britain by Clays Ltd, Elcograf S.p.A.

Zaffre is an imprint of Bonnier Books UK
www.bonnierbooks.co.uk

For Josie and Louis

Prologue

It was a winter morning that promised fair weather but at that moment Daisy felt wretched.

This once vigorous man slumped before her had been so handsome and full of life. Now, mere months later, he was broken and dependent.

It was most upsetting to see, and Daisy felt as if all the colour in the world around her had leached into dull grey tones, leaving her tender and raw.

Five young men she knew had volunteered to go and fight the Hun the second they could.

They were so bonny and bright as the train carried them away for training that Daisy had a swell of pride that almost burst through her chest as their shouted goodbyes mingled with those of all the other volunteers. It was a bittersweet farewell that climaxed in a crescendo of brave-sounding echoes reverberating the whole length of the station platform as friends and families shouted back.

But it wasn't long before Daisy found herself certain that no one, whether at home or abroad, would survive the war unscathed.

She couldn't stop wondering whether it was better for a soldier to suffer terrible physical injuries but to keep a strong mind, or to evade bodily harm but be terribly damaged within their head by what they had experienced. And what about if one or more of the five she knew had both physical and mental damage? Daisy never could decide which would be better, or worse, no matter how long she spent wondering.

She couldn't often bring herself to think about the very worst outcome of all. Death. Corpses being left to rot, forever lost in a foreign land, although if anyone had asked her – which nobody did – she would have said that the shadow of death had begun to loom over everything she knew and held close.

What would this war mean for all those left at home? In a matter of weeks, young women of Daisy's age had had to wave goodbye to nearly all the marriageable young men.

As far as Daisy could tell, the cost looked to be a very high price to pay for a war that had its genesis a long way away. Try as she might, she still couldn't quite understand how the hostilities had begun, or why so many British men had been desperate to fight, or really what any of it was supposed to achieve.

The newspapers gave little away, obviously set on keeping up morale and making sure that those at home felt that things abroad were tip-top. Although those around her took what was said in the broadsheets as gospel, Daisy was more suspicious.

And casualties had started to come home. But at least this offered some hope.

The telegraph girls – and they mostly were girls – were a sight that made everyone shudder, with their news of confirmed deaths or loved ones missing in action.

Still, this early morning, Daisy tried to shrug these worries aside as she shook out the rug in her hands.

But the dark shadows at the edge of her vision seemed insistent, the raspy breath of the poorly man echoing in her ears.

She looked around at where she had grown up, a picturesque spot accompanied always by the inevitable creaks and whistles and whooshes of the turning sails of the smock mill that had been built just across the yard, and she could see a multitude of subtle signs of a decline in what she had always held dear.

Her parents were riddled with worry, Daisy knew, terrified her brothers wouldn't return.

Asa and Clem's absence had been cruelly felt, and meanwhile all three older Graham girls, and Cynthia too, and cousin Olive, had to help Jared in the mill, and pull together to try and keep their bakery and the tea room in business.

It was exhausting, but the Grahams knew that they were fortunate compared to other families in the area, as many harvests had been left to rot where they grew now that most labourers had signed up.

Those early summer months of 1914 had promised fun and larks.

But as the year ended, fun and larks were a distant memory.

∽

The Grahams had once been a family full of happiness and with a strong trust in what the future might hold for them, a lively household with sisters and brothers who joshed each other certainly, but nearly always in fun. Sharp words and deeds were rare, and life had felt good.

How foolish they had all been back then in those months of June and July, Daisy thought now as the year began to wither, to believe that the manner in which they had lived from day to day, counted out in celebrations of harvest festivals, Yuletides and Easters, and maypole dancing and first kisses, would go on for ever. A time that would stretch but was always made rosy with the promise of husbands and babies to come.

Daisy now felt this younger self to be shallow and naive.

Looking up at the morning sun again and then down, she couldn't shake the sense of bone-weariness beyond her years.

Gently, she tucked a wool blanket around the lap of the man in the wheelchair. His right hand attempted to pat a thank you on the lower part of her arm, the tremors overtaking his body making it hard for him. He didn't say much these days.

Daisy manoeuvred his wheelchair to better catch the best patch of early-morning winter sunlight and then she made sure to smile as she said in as cheerful a voice as she could, 'Do you want me to fetch you a scarf or a cushion?'

He shook his head and closed his eyes, carefully lifting his chin as if to enjoy the sunshine on his face, his cheeks desperately wan.

To think he feels he got off lightly! thought Daisy. *It's a crying shame, and a disgrace.*

What was really eating Daisy was that she knew without a doubt that, worse than the morning ritual with the wheelchair and the blanket, after helping her patient with what were sometimes quite shameful ablutions, when she went to bed and was lying on her own, she would be plagued with sleeplessness.

It was a restless, anguished time each night, broken with occasional short snatches of sleep plagued with visions of marching enemy soldiers wearing their spiked Pickelhaube helmets, well-heeled boots drumming a beat that sounded more than a match for the British Tommy Atkins.

In these moments of lucid dreaming, her loved ones stood to silent attention in a row as they watched on with dark eyes and furrowed brows, and Daisy would waken with a gasp, feeling panic-stricken at the sight of both sides squaring up to each other within her dreams.

What she dreamed never altered, although sometimes she would awake with a cry on her lips and her cheeks tear-streaked.

Before

Chapter One

'Oi, you rascals! Get your mitts away from those jam tarts, else there won't be any left for your birthday party later and then where will we be?' cried Daisy, as she gently slapped away the offending hands and then shooed Senna and Tansy out of the kitchen with a firm wave of a tea towel.

But Daisy couldn't help smiling to herself as her twin sisters didn't give up without a fight, standing outside the open kitchen door, giggling and making silly faces at her before putting their hands up to their chests as if they were puppies begging for treats.

She pretended not to notice though, as she certainly had no intention of giving in to their beseeching looks.

'Ach, not you too now, Asa! You'll burn yourself,' said Daisy as a few seconds later she had to flick the tea towel really quite sharply at her eldest brother's hand, which was hovering over the tarts cooling on their ancient wire rack.

But he was too quick for her.

'No matter. Them that works hard deserve rewards,' Asa announced with a slightly too proud nod of his head as he backed away. Or at least that was what Daisy thought he said as he'd crammed in a whole tart with one fleet move.

'Oi, give over, you great lummox – you're lucky you didn't blister your mouth. I've been in the kitchen since first light this morning, mind, so watch what you say about work, Asa. And, truth to tell, all you're doing right now is sorting out a few tables and chairs.' Daisy's words were curt.

'Well, I'm dealing with Mother, who can't make up her mind where everything is going, *and*—' her eldest brother looked coy, his neck going very red suddenly '—I'm up to my ears with keeping Joy placated too as she's having trouble resting and it's not doing much for her good temper. So it feels like I've been at it since the dawn chorus too.'

Daisy grimaced in understanding, and then she passed Asa another tart.

Brother and sister stood for a moment side by side, their shoulders lightly touching, as – Asa having to dip his head as he was tall and the top of the window was low – they stared out of the small kitchen window at all the activity on the sizeable patch of grass that took up most of the free space outside the mill house.

This was a square of green still shiny from the night-time dew, and it prettily separated the family's white wooden smock mill from the small but sturdy mill house where the Graham children had been born and raised. The shadow of the windmill and its four turning sails would move reassuringly across the grass during the day, Daisy knew.

Right now, the sails were spinning around evenly at a gentle speed, accompanied by the familiar repetitive pounding from the components of the mill's engine with the accompanying harsh grating of the huge, heavy grinding stones against each other as their father Jared kept up with milling the grain that local farmers brought to the mill by cart to be made into flour.

Brother and sister could see that their mother, Cynthia, known for being a stickler where order and tidiness were concerned, was staring crossly at her daughter-in-law Joy, Asa's wife, and wasn't paying any heed to the mill behind her.

Actually the mill was so much part and parcel of everyday life for each member of the Graham family that it was rare that anyone, other than Jared or his sons, noticed it standing there, or stood back to look properly at its sails slicing through the air, and so in itself this wasn't in any way unusual.

Instead, Cynthia, with a firm pointing of a finger, was busily directing – there was no other word for it – a harried and extremely pregnant Joy as to exactly how the trestle tables on the grass should be set with their plates and cutlery upon the red-checked tablecloths.

Privately, Daisy had always felt Asa's wife was mis-named as she was definitely a glass-half-empty sort of person, known far and wide in Crumford for never holding back if she thought Asa had stepped out of line, which he seemed to do with alarming frequency if his wife's complaints were anything to go by.

But watching now, as Cynthia interrupted her own instructions with a sharp rap of a knuckle on the table, in case there could be any misunderstanding, Daisy thought Joy appeared to be setting the tables perfectly well already.

Cynthia's new directions seemed to demand that Joy reposition the chairs and their cushions, and Daisy felt more than a twinge of sympathy for her sister-in-law as Cynthia could be very hard to please at times.

It was ironic that Daisy's mother ruled the Old Creaky roost with an iron hand that everyone had to obey, her husband Jared most of all, as Cynthia often preached to her daughters and their cousin, Olive, that a woman's role was to do as her husband bid (although these days when Cynthia said as much, Daisy and Jared would catch each other's eye in a jokey way about this irony) as what Cynthia wanted, went.

Although Daisy's sister-in-law kept any sharp comments to herself, judging by the dramatic rise and fall of her shoulders, Joy clearly gave a deep sigh of frustration as she straightened up and then rubbed her back in a very obvious manner, moving her jaw from side to side, as though biting back what she'd love to say to Cynthia.

Quickly, Daisy poured some cool water into a glass and thrust it into Asa's hand. 'You'd better give this to your wife pronto and make sure she drinks it sitting in the shade; if you're quick, you'll get to Joy before she gives Mother as good as she's getting. And then make sure you distract Mother by asking where the tankards should go before they are needed, as she'll never want those on the tea table until after the men have had their cup of tea and some food. If you're lucky Mother might forget about Joy for a little while.'

'Good idea,' agreed Asa, and they grinned.

They were in the midst of a spell of relentlessly sunny summer weather, and all indications were pointing to it being yet another unseasonably warm June Saturday that would pass with barely a cloud in the sky. It was going to be a long day, with their guests arriving from five o'clock in the afternoon in order that those who needed could do more or less a full working day.

Asa's hobnailed boots sounded their distinctive clatter across the stone flags immediately outside the back door to the mill house, and then his footsteps were silent on the grass as he made his way towards his wife.

Daisy turned and surveyed her baking. She'd better prepare some more jam tarts, she decided, as she reached for her hessian bag of flour and another jar of last year's bramble jam that Cynthia had made.

∞

Rather unexpectedly, this forthcoming tea party had grown into quite a big do, much more than the simple birthday party for the seven-year-old twins Daisy had first imagined. And luckily the weather seemed to be obliging them for an outside affair, as although the cloudless sky was a clear blue, fortunately there was enough of a breeze blowing in gently from the nearby English Channel that the heat wasn't going to feel too oppressive.

Aside from the fact it was the twins' birthday (something Senna and Tansy had for weeks been excited about), the family's grain mill was doing reliable business these days. So in part this get-together had grown into a thank you for the local inhabitants of the historic Kentish town of Crumford that was half a mile or so from the mill.

Some of the pretty Crumford buildings dated from medieval times, while others had the steep pitch of Dutch roofs, with gable ends swooping down in alternating curves and right angles from the pediments at their apex. Over previous centuries a lot of Dutch people had crossed the sea to live locally, and their evidence could be seen everywhere, if one knew what to look for in the buildings they had constructed.

On a clear day, France could easily be seen across the English Channel if one stood on Crumford's easterly shingle beach that was a fair way from the main drag of the market town, across some scrubby marshland and sand flats that were a paradise for many species of birds.

Daisy had anticipated the party's timing would be fortuitous, as the local farmers weren't as busy yet as they would be in the coming couple of months, when all hands would be needed on deck to bring in safely the various local harvests of hops, grains of many sorts, as well as hay and straw, at the same time as all the summer vegetables, salad and fruits that would constantly be cropped and packaged for sending to London.

As always, the Graham family felt very appreciative of the support and patronage thrown at their mill by all sorts of local people, and they wanted their customers to know this.

While milling had been for centuries integral to the community, it was a trade in which shysters sometimes operated, and the fact that the Grahams' mill was widely known as being honest as the day is long, and well run too, had meant that over many years they'd built a sizeable and loyal clientele.

All the same, there were several other mills within a mile or two, all eager for their business, and so every Graham family member appreciated that theirs was a clientele who must never be taken for granted.

Their smock mill, officially called Graham Mill, had been in the family for generations. But rather than Graham Mill, it was known affectionately to all and sundry as Old Creaky as the four arms carrying the sails could make a real racket in windy weather if Jared hadn't adjusted its head in time so as not to catch too much of the blow.

When Jared retired, the family accepted that Old Creaky would pass down to Asa, who was Jared and Cynthia's firstborn, with slightly younger brother Clem as deputy. Really the mill was too much for any one man, and so both Asa and Clem had left school as soon as they could to help Jared in the family business.

The brothers worked hard each day learning as much as they could. Asa was better at the milling side of things, such as keeping the flow of grain steady into the large circular grinding stones, and making sure that everything was ticking over mechanically inside the compact wooden structure between the frequent visits of wheelwrights and journeyman mechanics. Clem, on the other hand, had more of a knack for dealing with the local farmers with wit and cleverness, and in drumming up new business.

Still, Daisy and her younger sister Violet, split by just a year between them and being only a tad younger than Asa and Clem, had proved over the last year or two to have solid business heads on their shoulders too, and they were now really beginning to add to the family's income, despite neither young woman yet being twenty.

Daisy ran her small but busy tea room from half of an old barn tucked away on the opposite side of the property. Asa and Clem had renovated it for this purpose the previous autumn. Violet had set herself up as baker with a range of delicious loaves, some made from unusual flours or dotted with seeds. Her bakery was walled off in the other half of the barn, with the whole of her side of the dividing wall taken up by an elaborate arrangement of iron ovens that had been cast especially for the space. Violet had designed all of this ironwork, and these new ovens were her pride and joy, one even having a hotplate that extended through the wall to Daisy's side, so that she could make tea and griddle toast.

Violet had even included a further two small ovens surplus to her own requirements that could operate from the main ovens when she was baking or else have their own source of heat if it were later in the day and she was finished. These were kept for local people, who'd bring joints of meat or home-made pies for Violet to cook, a service for which she charged a peppercorn fee.

Their other sister Holly, nearly eighteen, divided her time between assisting Violet with knocking back the early-morning rises as the bread proved (not always completely harmoniously, as Holly wasn't renowned for being the sunniest of souls at daybreak, a quality that always irked Violet, who was more a lark than an owl) and in making sure the fire stayed in until all the loaves were ready.

Then occasionally Holly would nip next door to lend Daisy a hand in the tea room by bringing in Violet's loaves when they were ready and helping prepare the orders. Sometimes if it was busy, Holly would help with serving seated customers with their victuals in the tea room, which aside from the bread, also sold tea towels, pillowcases and napkins that had been neatly embroidered by Cynthia, as well as pots of preserves and chutneys their mother endlessly boiled up when local produce was in glut. And then finally Holly, who had a very nice writing hand and was always trying to come up with ideas to expand the family business as she was also very commerce-minded and always had been, despite being so young, would spend an hour with Cynthia in the afternoon after dinner-time, making sure all the various account books were up to date.

Over the years, Holly had led her two older sisters in various schemes for making money, although Daisy always tried hard not to remember the rock cake debacle one market day in Crumford, when they'd been not that much older than Tansy and Senna were now, when unruly big boys had stolen the cakes the girls had made to sell, and then pelted the three sisters with them. As

Violet said as they limped home, 'Those rock cakes had the right name – it was as if we were hit with actual rocks.'

But in spite of Holly's obvious financial nous, and Violet's clear capability, Daisy always liked to think of herself as being the sister with drive, imagination and know-how, as well as being the sparky sister who was the most fun.

In Daisy's eyes, Violet was the steady sister, being neither terribly good nor terribly bad at whatever she did, while Holly was the pert one who was something of a noodle (although if asked, Daisy would have been hard-pressed to say why). But as Holly was probably the prettiest of the three older Graham girls, Daisy thought, then she was likely to make a good marriage and then that would be that.

As children, the three older Graham sisters had been close, although not so much in recent years, and Daisy wasn't sure why this was the case, other than suspecting it might be due to her rather than them. She'd tell herself she should make more effort, but then something else would catch her attention and somehow she would forget her good intentions.

When Daisy was at school she had been told by sometimes exasperated teachers that she was imprudent and rash by nature, and so it had been easy to imagine herself leading an exciting life once she was out in the big wide world as a grown woman, maybe a life even a little madcap at times.

However, life so far had refused to play ball with these expectations, and Daisy sometimes worried that the spontaneity – or as she liked to call it, vigour – of her younger self was becoming dulled.

Running her tea room didn't quite cut the mustard in terms of thrills. But it would have been unbearably churlish of her not to contribute to the Graham family coffers, especially as she'd been gifted her half of the old barn for the tea room, and she wanted to support Violet with her bakery. Violet was as happy as a clam these days, and Holly seemed content too. Daisy envied them both, slightly too many days with the tea room routine predictable and dull.

When she was like this, she would set off on a long walk down near the sea, where she could wander the flat coastline accompanied by the calls of different sorts of seabirds, with the shadowy rise of the cliffs of Ramsgate to her left and those chalky rises of the Dover cliffs to her right, and with the dove-grey outline of France directly across the Channel in front of her. Or she would walk into Crumford to window-shop.

There was another young woman living at Graham Mill, and she was almost the same age as Daisy, being only a month younger. This was Olive, who had lost both parents, her mother Iris – Cynthia's sister – having died while birthing Olive, and father Thom following a silly accident in which he had too much to drink one evening in an alehouse near Margate, after which he had stumbled into the street and right into the path of one of the very first automobiles in Kent. The accident was reported by all the local newspapers.

Olive had been only five when she had come to live at Graham Mill, and Daisy could barely remember a time without her there. She and Olive had always been as thick as thieves, as Daisy enjoyed spending time with Olive rather more than she did with her sisters.

Olive was a real character – her booming laugh well known in Crumford – and at over six feet tall, she towered over most local men and took delight in staring down imperiously if any of them were taking liberties. Few of them dared to do so more than just the once.

The powerhouse of the Graham family was Cynthia. Husband Jared took, sensibly, the path of least resistance by letting Cynthia get on with things her way, escaping to the mill if any sort of family friction was brewing; this was a strategy that had served him very well during his twenty-five-year marriage.

Cynthia was always ready to step into the yard as adjudicator should any farmer claim the flour being returned after grinding was inferior to what they had grown and therefore was clearly not the product of the grain previously delivered.

It was hard for a farmer to stand up in public against a woman over disputed business dealings, Cynthia knew, and although she would never let on, she enjoyed insisting that whatever was wrong, it would be most definitely the farmer's mistake. If anyone dared not to capitulate immediately, the next stage was Cynthia calling for Olive, who would come to stand beside her aunt with the type of sigh that told the errant man he really wasn't thinking this through, was he?

Daisy thought it marvellous how even the gruffest farmer buckled before the impassive stares of these two impressive women.

⁓

Just after this past Easter, one Sunday afternoon Daisy had floated her tea party idea when most of the family were squeezed into the tiny parlour to relax with cups of tea after their roast beef lunch, and Holly was shuffling a deck of cards for a game of rummy.

Daisy knew she must take good care nobody twigged her ulterior motive as that would be the best way to put the kibosh on her plans.

She'd already encouraged the twins to play outside, and before the card game started, Daisy mused, 'Wouldn't it be fun to have a lovely birthday party for Tansy and Senna? It's not long now until they are going to be the grand age of seven, and I remember having a party at that age. Mine was such a lot of fun, and I've often thought back very fondly on it. The twins have many friends and I'm sure they'd love to come.'

Nobody said anything immediately in response, although Jared gave a small grunt.

22

Undeterred at what to an untrained eye might seem a general lack of enthusiasm, Daisy waited before adding casually, 'I was thinking that perhaps various of our patrons could come too, so killing two birds with one stone as this would show our appreciation . . .'

Daisy knew this meant that a prominent local family, the Brewers, could be invited – and thus offer a perfect opportunity for Daisy to get to know a little better the eldest Brewer son, Ren, heir to the very profitable family brewery, which was her real reason for suggesting the party.

While there were occasional balls at the Guildhall in Crumford, or the town's great and the good would gather at outside revels such as May Day dancing around the maypole, Daisy was convinced that a more personal celebration at Old Creaky was likely to be more productive in nudging things along between herself and Ren. On those other occasions she was in competition with all the other eligible young ladies for the attentions of local single men.

But over the last year Daisy had begun to think she and Ren were the perfect match, at least on paper, and she longed to give these thoughts the chance to progress to the next stage.

Both she and Ren came from successful business families who enjoyed good social standing.

Ren's strong jawline, manly physique and abundant head of hair would be admirably complemented by her lively but light-hearted personality and distinct flair for witty repartee (qualities Daisy liked to think she had in excess), and if they were to unite as a pair, then they could go far, she was convinced.

Ren had a strong physical presence, and Daisy thought he always seemed to be moving somehow, even if he were sitting still. Her brother Clem always called Ren his best friend and a decent chap, and Daisy, who looked up to Clem, thought this meant that Ren was a good egg.

In fact, quite often when Daisy tried to recall what Ren actually looked like, it wasn't his face that came to mind, but more the sense of someone strong and decent, a man with nearly always a good-natured crinkle around his intelligent eyes that suggested he had either just laughed, or was about to.

As Daisy saw it, Ren's wealthier background would add to her status (and consequently nudge all the Grahams up the social scale) while her own quick wits would wash across Ren in an equally favourable manner. And the fact that Ren had two younger brothers, Alder and Rosen, of appropriate ages that meant they were perfect matches for Violet and Holly, hadn't escaped Daisy's attentions either.

'I should think the Brewers might like to be invited,' Daisy said in a low voice as she picked a bit of fluff from her skirt.

Olive's smile suggested she knew exactly what Daisy was up to.

Daisy ignored the twinkle in her cousin's eye, and instead turned towards Holly to say in a companionable way that the playing cards probably needed a bit more of a shuffle.

'Hm,' muttered her father at last in a non-committal manner.

'Do you know, Jared, I think Daisy might be on to something,' said Cynthia thoughtfully, signalling to everyone that Jared's 'hm' was definitely a yes.

Jared didn't much enjoy social gatherings of any sort, beyond a pint or two of ale of a Saturday night in the nearest public house, and so his answering 'Hmmmn' took longer this time and was accompanied by a defeated sigh.

The forthcoming party was a done deal.

∞

The alacrity with which Cynthia added names to the guest list told Daisy that a possible public romantic alliance (or even three, if the stars were fully aligned!) between the largest milling family in Crumford and the wealthy brewing family hadn't gone unnoticed.

The trio of Brewer lads would undoubtedly be snagged as husbands very soon. It was no secret that Crumford was awash with mothers eager to do the best for their daughters.

Indeed, Cynthia commented more than once while walking home from church, with a slight snap to her voice, how some mothers with marriage-age daughters were scrutinising the Brewer boys and then pushing their girls forward in a most unbecoming manner. It wasn't at all the done thing – albeit this was said in a slightly envious tone at the audacity of these other mothers. And then she would add, 'Aren't some people absolutely shameless?'

Once Olive dared to say, 'Well, at least no one could ever accuse the Grahams of such behaviour, could they?'

'Certainly not,' agreed Cynthia, apparently oblivious to any irony in Olive's comment.

As the plans for the party began to take shape, Daisy thought that Cynthia had forgotten her earlier words.

Daisy had to resort to having a quiet word with Jared, begging him to rein her mother back. Daisy couldn't bear the shame if people outside the family followed Cynthia's lead and began to think of it in this way too, and then Ren spurned her on the day.

Jared said, 'Leave it with me,' and at breakfast the next day he handed Daisy a revised list of names to whom invitations could be sent, including several eligible young ladies, although thankfully not too many but just enough to divert claims of being obvious.

Chapter Two

It wasn't until lunchtime on the day of the party that Daisy could at long last scrutinise with satisfaction the mounds of food she'd prepared, which were now under domed nets to keep the flies off, or on plates on marble shelves to ensure the food stayed cool, and allow herself a quiver of butterflies at the thought of what the afternoon – or, more precisely, the evening – might bring.

These thoughts largely revolved around flirting and very possibly even kissing.

Daisy had been kissed before, obviously.

Indeed nearly all of the local girls took advantage each summer of the influx of hop-pickers and casual labourers who travelled to the south-east coast from all parts of the country for the seasonal work bringing in the various harvests as, with no strings attached, there was always an abundance of young men who were simply ripe for the taking if the girls were so inclined.

The Crumford young men behaved similarly as regards the female casual labourers.

It could get very complicated as to who was after whom, and it was a surprise to nobody when tempers got frayed, and fisticuffs occurred.

Daisy and her sisters were quite willing to watch when this happened, but they took care never to get involved themselves.

All the same, it was easy pickings during the long summer days, so much so that Violet had once described it as like shooting fish in a barrel, and Daisy had known exactly what she meant as a young lady would have to be very strange indeed not to be able to find a beau during the picking season, if she so wanted.

While the Graham girls might not be the most beautiful of all the young ladies in Crumford – their hair was probably a bit thick and unruly for that, and their eyebrows too heavy – each of them was certainly more than presentable.

And when the sisters were walking side by side down the road there was something incredibly strik- ing about them, as together they radiated health, per- sonality and good humour in a manner that turned heads, and consequently the girls had got used to being whistled at admiringly by casual workers to the area.

Most of the local lads weren't so bold as far as the Graham sisters went, but of course they did have the advantage of knowing, Olive aside, that Daisy could be very sarky and/or sharp-tongued if the mood were upon her, and that she seemed to have a long memory if anybody stepped out of line or said anything crass.

Daisy saw it slightly differently, of course. She was just looking out for her own and her sisters' best interests, and if any of these young men were too gauche or forward, then they deserved being pulled up.

But with this abundance of young men, lusty from time spent out in the sunshine, Daisy had made sure to be a good girl always, and so no matter how curious she felt about the act of sexual congress, she firmly rejected anything further than mere kissing.

Still, in recent months Daisy couldn't deny the gnawing impression that time was slipping by. Many of her school friends were long married, with babies already.

While she couldn't imagine life without hearing daily the screeches and groans of Old Creaky, Daisy felt she didn't want to be living in the home where she'd grown up for much longer.

There were still eight of them squashed into their modest but comfortable house, which was better than before, admittedly. And when Asa and Clem had each married and moved into their own cottages near the entrance lane to the mill, the house had definitely felt more spacious. But this feeling had only lasted briefly, and with the twins growing apace, again the house was coming to feel as if all the Grahams were playing a rather relentless game of Sardines.

And so Daisy's aim was, ideally, to be walking out regularly with a young man by the end of 1914, with a marriage the following spring, and then a baby coming early in 1916. She liked to have a plan, and this one seemed a very sensible one, and a plan to boot that she could achieve, with a fair wind blowing in her favour.

And if Ren were obliging, then, Daisy reasoned, she could well be ringing in the New Year that would herald 2015 with Ren on her arm as they raised a glass in celebration.

As she slid the latest batch of tarts for the party into the oven, Daisy wondered if Ren had an inkling of what she was thinking.

She couldn't quite make up her mind if she wanted him to, or not.

The truth was that she found him rather hard to read, probably because she only saw him occasionally at church or on market day, when they would do little more than nod a greeting to each other.

If Ren were of the opinion he should soon have a wife, then maybe they could even race ahead a Christmas wedding!

But if he wasn't, Daisy rather relished the thought of the fun of a chase, she realised.

Deep in these pleasant thoughts, Daisy started in surprise when suddenly a head was poked around the back door.

'Ho there, Miss Graham! Good day to you,' it said cheerfully. 'Dropped off some crates of beer for later as our contribution. I've put them inside the forge across the yard as it's not lit today and it is the coolest place according to Clem. Father told me to make sure the sunlight doesn't turn it.'

Daisy felt herself colour the brightest pink, the pie-crust collar and frill at her neck suddenly feeling almost unbearably tight and uncomfortable. This sensation was promptly heightened when she realised she couldn't think of a single thing to say in response, not now that Ren – *Ren!* – was standing right before her. In person. And looking very well honed and chiselled, with his tanned skin, perfectly even teeth and lustrous curls.

She heard the ear-click of herself swallowing.

Her awkwardness seemed to rub off on Ren in a trice.

His expression flattened, and his eyebrows pursed in what was probably confusion.

After a pause in which neither could quite meet the glance of the other, the first time this had ever happened between them, they both caught each other's eyes, and had to turn swiftly away from one another as if embarrassed.

Then Daisy felt rather than saw – she didn't dare look – as if Ren had nodded cheerio in her direction before he backed away across the yard towards where she guessed his horse and cart would be.

Bother. *Bother.* Indeed, damn and blast!

She'd been caught off guard and then shown herself up as pretty hopeless, Daisy admonished herself.

Then she rallied with the thought that Ren's eyes definitely had had a glint of amusement about them, hadn't they, even when he'd been frowning? Well, she hoped that was what she had seen, as long as it meant Ren was laughing with her, as opposed to laughing *at* her.

A shadow loomed, and Daisy turned to see that Ren's spot in the doorway had been taken by Asa, with Olive staring at her in an amused way over Asa's shoulder.

'Cat got your tongue?' enquired her brother with a too-innocent expression. 'Eh, Daisy?'

'Really?' said Olive, echoing Asa's demeanour.

Daisy closed her mouth, having discovered it gaping, such was her surprise still at having seen Ren precisely as she was thinking slightly lascivious thoughts about him.

And flustered at being caught out in this way by Asa and Olive, a fresh wash of heat coursed through her, although whether this was because Ren had sparked something dormant that was already deep within or because she felt foolish for being – for the first time in her life that she could remember – lost for words, Daisy couldn't tell.

What she did know though was that she wouldn't be wearing this pie-crust bodice again in a hurry, as it was far too constricting for challenging moments like this.

Chapter Three

Mid-afternoon, before they expected anyone to arrive, there was the sound of a car horn from out in the lane.

Cynthia and Daisy raced the family outside to see what the commotion was about.

It was Basil Brewer and his three sons, who were manhandling a picnic hamper of goodies, some more beer, a few cushions and rugs, and a suitcase.

Daisy and her sisters looked at each other, mystified as to what the suitcase could have inside it.

'Ren thought you might need some extra rugs etcetera,' explained Basil. 'I know we're early, but we thought we could make ourselves useful.'

'Daisy, can you guess what is in here?' asked Ren, as gingerly he carried the suitcase.

'No, I can't,' she answered. 'What is it?'

'Hold your horses – all will become clear,' laughed Alder.

'A hint,' Rosen said. 'Wear comfy shoes, ladies!'

The sisters were none the wiser.

It wasn't long before the surprise was revealed.

The suitcase was opened up, once it was on a sturdy table in the shade, to reveal a Decca portable gramophone, complete with a copper horn.

Daisy had never seen anything like it.

Basil showed Jared the handle for winding it up, and began to explain that the records had to turn at exactly seventy-eight times a minute for the sound to be true.

'Have you got something to play on it?' Daisy asked Ren. 'We don't have any records.'

'Yes, in the motor car. Let's go and grab them. I know the piano is outside now, but I thought that the gramophone could come into its own later on when everyone is bored of having to play music, and it means we can dance to the latest tunes.'

'What a treat,' Daisy told him.

Daisy and Ren went back to the car, and Daisy felt much more comfortable than she had when he'd surprised her earlier.

She stood near to Basil's Rolls-Royce for the very first time, as Ren lifted from the rear of the car a wooden box of gramophone records, which he placed on the verge.

At close quarters she could see the brand new open-topped car was immaculate and very swish, and for the first time Daisy appreciated that the Brewers were *much* better off than the Grahams.

She gently touched the smooth paintwork of the motor. 'What a humdinger,' she said quietly, as if to herself.

'Isn't she?' Ren laughed.

'She really is,' Daisy replied.

'Stay there, Daisy,' Ren said, and quickly he trotted the box of records over to where the others were as Daisy stared at her reflection in the newly washed windscreen.

When Ren came back, he showed her carefully around the car, even lifting the bonnet so that she could see the engine, explaining the electric lights at the front of the car were a special feature Basil had requested. Very patiently, Ren answered Daisy's questions about what the various bits of the car were.

Daisy loved the feel of its leather seats, which were soft in a luxurious way that she was unfamiliar with, although they smelt a little similar to the new leather harnesses that carthorses would sometimes have when they pulled their carts to Old Creaky to drop off or collect sacks of grain.

'If you want, hop in and try the driver's seat,' Ren offered.

Daisy grinned at him.

Once in the car, she sat there with her hands clasping the steering wheel.

'Is driving easy?' she asked.

'Oh very,' said Ren. 'Me and my brothers have been doing it since we were quite small, and there's nothing to it, I promise. Both Clem and Asa have been driving around our land for ages as well.'

'Yes, I suppose your hop fields cover a lot of ground, and to have you all driving must be very helpful to your father.'

'Exactly,' said Ren.

'I'm so envious,' said Daisy. 'Young men have so many advantages. Asa and Clem have kept schtum about being able to drive, probably so as not to make me jealous. I think I'd have liked being a young man with all the opportunities it offers.'

'Your life's not bad, is it, Daisy?'

'Oh no, it's not – I didn't mean that. But we don't have a car, and even if we did, I think Mother would take a very dim view if any of us girls wanted to drive it. I doubt that you, or my brothers, can imagine what it feels like never to have the option of being the slightest bit independent. In fact, Mother might not even be especially keen on Asa and Clem being behind the wheel either.'

'Well, let's not tell her then.'

'Agreed,' said Daisy, but she couldn't quite keep a tiny note of jealousy from her voice.

There was a silence, and then Daisy looked at Ren, and said, 'I'm sorry. Don't pay me any heed. It's been a busy day and I probably need a cup of tea.'

'Actually, I think what you need is to drive this car,' Ren said very matter-of-factly.

'Ren! Have you lost all sense of reason? I couldn't possibly do that,' squeaked Daisy.

'Oh, Father won't mind, and I'll tell you what to do. It's very easy.'

'Really?'

Daisy felt excited, almost giddy, at the thought of being so daring.

'Yes, really,' said Ren, and after he had given her a run-though of how everything worked, he jumped out and cranked the starting handle, and the Rolls's engine purred into life.

Daisy's eyes shone as Ren got into the passenger seat and then helped her turn the steering wheel so that the car could get onto the flinty road from the grass verge.

They went very slowly but soon Daisy had driven almost all the way to the nearby market town of Deal.

She loved the sensation of being in the driver's seat and she quickly got the hang of the steering wheel and how to keep the engine going, even though Ren kept a hand near the steering wheel and made sure that they weren't travelling much faster than walking pace.

There were few other motor vehicles, but each time they met one the other driver pipped his horn or gave a cheery wave. Daisy didn't dare take her hands off the steering wheel to do either of these things, but Ren raised a hand in acknowledgment each time.

'I love this!' shouted an elated Daisy. 'It's wonderful.'

'Clem said exactly the same the first time he drove, but he's never driven the Rolls as I taught him in the brewery vehicles, and so you're one up on him.'

'Excellent!' cried Daisy. 'You've no idea how difficult it is to do things my brothers haven't already done.'

'You're doing very well,' said Ren.

Daisy could have spent the rest of the afternoon in this way but then, suddenly, she remembered the party. The party that she had done the lion's share of the work for.

She had quite forgotten all about it in the excitement of driving!

'Oh my goodness, Ren, we must get back. Everyone will be wondering where I am, especially as the whole blessed shindig is my idea.'

Ren laughed, and said, 'Yes, I can see that not to have the host there would cause a to-do.'

He helped Daisy drive around several streets that roughly formed a square, so that she didn't have to work out how to turn around, and soon they were on the way back to Old Creaky.

As they drew close, Ren said, 'Slowly now, Daisy.'

But Daisy could see Cynthia standing on the verge peering up and down the road, obviously looking for her. It was the last thing she wanted to see.

Her mother didn't look best pleased.

In fact, Cynthia looked downright irate, and with that clunking realisation, immediately all of Ren's previously carefully explained instructions that she had been following as sure-footedly as a duck takes to water quite left Daisy's head.

'Brake, Daisy, brake,' Ren called a bit more insistently.

But Cynthia's and Daisy's eyes were locked upon each other now, Cynthia's mouth a moue of surprise.

And Daisy found she was unintentionally turning the car in the direction of where she was looking, but was quite unable to do anything about it.

'BRAKE, DAISY, GODDAMN IT, BRAKE, WOMAN!!' Ren yelled in her ear, making Daisy flinch and half close her eyes.

And just before they crashed into the hedge that separated Old Creaky from the road, which they did with quite a wallop and jolt, the last thing Daisy noticed was her mother having to jump out of the way of the car's bonnet. Daisy hadn't known Cynthia could move so swiftly.

The engine stalled, and Daisy and Ren sat there in stunned silence, both staring at the still-shaking foliage spilling over the bonnet of the car as a ticking sound came from under the bonnet, and then they looked aghast at each other as Ren pulled a piece of sticky grass from his jacket.

'You blithering idiot, Daisy, you impetuous, er, *oaf*,' said Cynthia in a withering way to her daughter. 'This is so like you and I am beyond angry. But I'll deal with you later. Right now you'd better go and change into your party dress, while I get the men, and we can see what damage you've caused out here. After, that is, I have a nip of brandy to calm my nerves.'

'I think I need a nip of brandy too,' said Ren glumly, clearly not relishing the conversation he was about to have with his father. 'Maybe two.'

As quickly as she could, Daisy made herself scarce before either of them said anything else to her, and she scampered inside the mill house, pounding up to her room, where she stood trembling for a few minutes, feeling exhilarated and shocked in equal measure.

What a prelude to a party!

Chapter Four

'And so, without further preamble—' Jared Graham ignored the squeals of his overexcited twins and their similarly aged chums, as well as the pounding of pewter tankards and thick glass tumblers on the trestle tables at his words by the older male contingent '—and now the sun is towards going over the yard arm, let's raise a glass to family and friends and good times, and long may these last. And I want especially to wish a very happy seventh birthday to our young Tansy and Senna too. Now, what are we going to do?' Putting a serious look on his face, Jared lifted his eyebrows as he stared at the twins. 'Any idea, girls?'

The twins knew very well – it was the moment of the party they had been itching to get to, and they wriggled about in anticipation.

Daisy had made each of the twins a birthday Victoria sponge, which she'd sliced in two horizontally and sandwiched together with whipped cream and a generous slather of that year's first batch of raspberry jam as the hot weather had meant that some of the varieties in their netted-off fruit cage had ripened early.

Having two cakes meant that the youngest Graham sisters would each have a candle to blow out to make a wish. The cakes had been the very devil to keep secret from prying eyes but somehow Daisy had managed it, and now she and Violet bore them across the green so that their mother could light the candles in the middle of each cake, and then slice the cakes up once the girls had made their wishes so that everyone could have some.

That morning, as Ren had noticed, Cynthia insisted Asa and Clem lug the ancient piano across the garden from the room that doubled as Jared's office and the sleep-over spot for the visiting journeymen to the mill.

This was so that Cynthia could accompany the cakes with a rather raucous version of 'Happy Birthday to You' that everyone belted out to the sounds of their old Joanna, only very slightly out of tune from having spent a couple of hours in the full glare of the sun.

To Daisy's surprise, Clem's rather energetic new wife Marguerite leaped up to stand beside Cynthia. It was a surprise to Cynthia too, judging by her mother's rather shocked glance towards her daughter-in-law who was keeping distressingly poor time on a tambourine that she banged and shook away with her eyes beatifically closed.

Daisy, Olive, Violet and Holly, who were sitting in a row nearby, as once the singing stopped they would be giving the twins their very gentle seven birthday bumps, initially exchanged elbow nudges and amused looks, and then girls began to mime under the table to each other shaking a tambourine, taking care of course that neither Jared, Cynthia nor Marguerite could see what they were up to.

It was at this point Daisy had to pinch her thigh quite hard in order that she didn't give a loud guffaw as it was clear that a totally oblivious Marguerite felt her accompaniment when she played with the Salvation Army each Sunday had given her exceptional skills on the tambourine front. This was a mistaken belief.

Daisy caught Ren's eye, and he clearly knew what she was about as, keeping his face very straight, he slowly raised his eyebrow comically high, made his eyes as big as they could go, and then crossed them as he puffed his cheeks out.

It was too much, and Daisy snorted unbecomingly, causing Cynthia to give her a hard stare.

It was no good.

Daisy had to drop her napkin on the ground and spend a little time wrenching it from under Olive's foot as her pal had stamped on it on purpose with lightning speed, and then folding it carefully before she was suitably composed and able to join in the very last of the birthday hurrahs that, as was tradition, followed the singing. Daisy was sorry now that she had missed out on the wishing bit as when candles were blown out she liked to make her own wish, even during others' birthday celebrations.

Her wish, naturally, had she been able to make it, would have been to do with Ren, and to judge by their faces, Daisy was convinced, Violet and Holly had probably wished similarly, regarding Alder and Rosen. Quite what Olive would have wished for, Daisy wasn't nearly as certain.

∞

Everybody looked to be having a good time, Daisy concluded half an hour later as she stared about her to take a careful inventory of who was doing what.

Violet and Holly seemed to be making good progress with Alder and Rosen, Ren's two younger brothers. The four of them were lounging together on Cynthia and Jared's bedspread, which had been strategically placed on the grass a little way from the trestle tables, with Daisy pretty certain it wasn't lemonade they were sharing out between them, even though everyone knew Holly was only seventeen.

Olive had organised most of the others who were about their age into a lively game of cricket in the field next door, and judging by the laughter from the players, both male and female, the cricketers were getting on like a house on fire. Daisy fully expected the odd embrace and kiss to be exchanged by the time the game wound up with the setting of the sun.

Daisy turned to see Jared and Basil sitting close together with their heads almost touching as they were deep in conversation, only glancing up now and again as they packed tobacco into their pipes to cast a look in the direction of one or other of their daughters or sons.

Earlier in the party, aside from her hostess duties, Daisy had kept Ren pretty much at arm's length so that he didn't fall into the trap of believing that she was *too* interested in him.

This strategy meant she spent time talking with some girls she'd known at school, making sure she was laughing in what she hoped was a tinkly, attractive manner should Ren happen to be passing by, rather than giving in to her more normal honk of amusement when she found anything funny.

Then Daisy had spent quite a while organising an epic hopscotch tournament for the twins and their friends, although fortunately Asa had eventually taken over the kindergarten duties and was now crouching down alongside the youngers so that everyone could learn how to play jacks properly, or knucklebones as he and Clem had always called it.

With her party duties more or less over, Daisy felt it was time she enjoyed herself properly.

Now, where was Ren?

Daisy realised she'd not seen him for a while.

She stared about but he wasn't anywhere to be seen. This was unbelievably frustrating as they had barely spoken two words to each other since she had got out of the Rolls, and her plan of enticing Ren by almost ignoring him required him actually to see she was so busy/popular/otherwise engaged that she barely had time to flick a glance in his direction, and now he really wasn't keeping up his end of the bargain.

All right, poor Ren didn't know any of this, Daisy accepted, but it was irksome all the same.

To distract herself, and with rather more noise than was required, Daisy cleared some side plates and cups and saucers that were no longer needed, and took what was left of the twins' birthday cake inside before she topped up the fruit punch with some cider.

Just as she was polishing off a small glass of cider she'd saved in the kitchen, she heard Jared's loud voice above the dance tunes someone was bashing out on the piano (Marguerite's tambourine mercifully silent). These days Jared was getting to be really quite deaf from working so close to the noisy machinery in the mill, and now he always spoke correspondingly emphatically, but he was calling for Daisy to fetch some more bottles of beer from the forge.

'Oh hello there!' Daisy said to Clem, as she met him and Ren coming out of the forge a few seconds later, each burdened with armfuls of bottles, 'You must be mind-readers. Father wants to make sure everyone has all the beer they want.'

Clem smiled at her and kept walking, but Ren stopped beside Daisy, asking Clem to come back for the ones he was carrying.

Her heart gave a small lurch, and then Daisy felt glad she'd only recently drunk the cider, which had been so strong she'd felt the alcohol race around her body from what felt like the very first sip, as it was definitely a confidence-giver.

'Have you had a nice time, Ren?'

'Very good,' he said with a smile that she couldn't quite interpret, and then he suggested, 'Shall we sit down together awhile, Daisy?'

This was more like it.

Setting four bottles aside, and as no Clem had reappeared, quickly Ren took the remaining bottles he'd been carrying across to the trestle tables.

Back then at Daisy's side at the bench outside the forge, which was set slightly behind the white wooden boards that walled Old Creaky, although still in clear sight of the revellers on the grass and with the music easy to hear, Ren loosened the knot of his tie very slightly and hooked a finger inside his collar to pop undone the top button of his shirt.

Daisy felt her pulse quicken when she noticed the jut and flex of his Adam's apple as he moved his head from side to side to stretch out his shoulders, almost as if he had been doing a hard day's work.

In response, she risked undoing several of the buttons at the bottom of her sleeve, and folding her cuffs back so that her wrists were clearly exposed, promising to herself that she wouldn't let Cynthia see her dressed so provocatively.

Ren was sitting in a relaxed, inviting way, and correspondingly Daisy didn't feel she had to be prim and proper in the manner her mother always insisted upon, her back ramrod straight and legs neatly crossed at the ankle, a pose insisted upon even when they were relaxing in the parlour.

In the lengthening shadows of the summer evening, at last Daisy sat down, her body angled companionably so that she faced Ren, her elbows on her knees and her face angled up towards his.

He fiddled with the top of a quite large bottle of beer and there was a satisfying pop as the air released. He passed that bottle across to her with his voice dipped to a conspiratorial but light-hearted 'Don't let your mother see.'

Daisy raised her eyebrows, in part to join in his playfulness, and in part to acknowledge just a little that if the mood was upon her, Cynthia could be a harridan. If she and Ren were to become serious, it wasn't much use pretending her mother to be other than she was, Daisy reasoned, and it was certain that Cynthia would be a formidable mother-in-law for any future spouse of Daisy's.

Daisy had never drunk beer straight from the bottle before, and undeniably there was a lovely frisson about doing so that made her feel she was kicking over the traces, although she made sure to wriggle about on the bench so that her back was pretty much turned towards the other revellers so they couldn't see what she was up to.

Ren popped the top off a bottle for himself, and they clinked their drinks together and looked at each other for what felt like a long while before they took care to take their first glugs at the same time.

It felt naughtier that way, Daisy realised.

She glanced towards where she thought Cynthia would be, but she couldn't see her mother.

Clem had taken Asa's place with the young kiddies though, and Daisy noticed that Asa and Joy weren't anywhere to be seen. Both Jared and Basil had their backs towards Daisy and Ren. It seemed as if nobody was paying any attention to what Daisy and Ren might be up to on the bench outside the forge, and that was perfectly fine as far as Daisy was concerned.

'I'm so sorry about the car,' she said.

'You've got the luck of Old Nick. Aside from a crack in the glass of one of the headlamps, there wasn't a scratch on it,' Ren said.

'Really? It was quite a bump.'

'Father saw the funny side, much to my surprise. After my brothers, Asa and Clem and your father and I pretty much lifted the motor out of the hedge, and he could see it wasn't damaged, that is. Your mother kept apologising, but he told her not to be daft, and that accidents happen.'

'I'm such a fool,' said Daisy.

'I expect you'll get over that.'

'After many hours of serious contemplation!' she joked.

By now the piano music had given way to some unaccompanied sea shanties being sung by the men, a pewter mug keeping the beat as it slapped the table-top. These were traditional songs from the area, many mournful, and seemed very fitting somehow as everyone in Crumford was always aware of the sea nearby and that this part of Kent enjoyed a rich maritime heritage.

The manner in which Ren was nodding as his fingers tapped on his knee in time with the singers' words told Daisy he was probably thinking similarly.

'I like this singing. It feels part of us all, but fresh somehow. Actually, I think this might be my favourite bit of today, after driving the car, before the crash that is,' she said, breaking their companionable silence.

Ren stopped nodding his head in time with the singing.

He looked at Daisy and raised his eyebrows and slowly grinned, then gently he touched his beer bottle against hers once more. They fell to chatting about this and that, and soon Daisy was applauding herself privately over her previous assessment regarding Ren's ready smile and desire to make her laugh. She was certainly seeing all these traits in abundance, and she liked the way that she seemed to be able to make him chortle as well.

By the time they were each deep into their second bottle, Ren suggested, 'Shall we go for a walk?'

'I was hoping that you would say something like that.' Daisy smiled, standing up so quickly she felt her head spin, although only for a second or two – a sensation she immediately put down to a combination of cider and strong beer, rather than that she had been guzzling the ale quite hastily through nervousness. 'I just need to do something quickly.'

Before they left, now that she'd got some Dutch courage, Daisy made her way up to Jared and Basil, and said, 'Mr Brewer, I must apologise to you. What I did in your lovely car earlier was very reckless, and I am very sorry. It was out of order. Of course I will personally pay for any repairs.'

Basil looked at her sternly.

And then he let out what Daisy could only describe a guffaw and said, 'Be off with you, lass, and enjoy yourself. It does my heart good to see a young lady with a bit of spirit. My dear Ivy was a bit like you, you know.'

'Make haste, Daisy, while the going is good,' advised a ruddy-looking Jared. 'Cynthia was asking where you were a couple of minutes ago.'

'Noted. And thank you for being so understanding, Mr Brewer. I don't deserve it, I know. Now I'm going to make myself scarcer than Mrs Scarce of Scarce Street,' said Daisy, making a funny face.

To judge by Basil Brewer's answering laugh, he was as much in his cups as the obviously tipsy Jared was.

⁓

Keeping the coast away to their left, Ren and Daisy strolled through the fields, all very flat, still clutching their beer bottles, and then, as Daisy perched on a stile, at last Ren cupped her face in his hands and kissed her.

It was a short kiss that felt chaste and, if Daisy were being honest, more amateurish than she remembered from her previous embraces with other lads.

But a kiss was a kiss, and this had definitely been a kiss, and it had arrived almost exactly as she had planned.

Daisy told herself she mustn't criticise Ren for very likely being a bit less experienced in this sort of thing than Daisy believed herself to be.

Her breath bubbled in her throat for a moment when she saw how Ren was smiling at her, with the setting sun behind her flaring the topaz flecks in the irises of his eyes most seductively as he looked down at her.

Gently, Ren leaned forward and tucked a flyaway strand of hair behind Daisy's ear, his fingers grazing softly the delicate skin of her neck for an instant. It felt a gesture more exciting and intimate than their kiss, and for a moment her breath felt snagged somewhere deep within her chest.

Slowly, she breathed out, taking care she didn't gasp in his face.

She rather wished that Ren would find another piece of hair that would need carefully hooking behind her other ear, and that he would then kiss her with passion.

After all, wasn't she the sort of young woman who these days risked wearing her skirt *above* her ankles in the way that the illustrations and advertisements for London ladies' fashion was dictating in the press? If this didn't announce her own capacity for passion, then Daisy wasn't sure what would.

For, eager to be ahead of the other young women in Crumford, Daisy had been quick to follow the pictures she'd seen in fashion magazines, with Violet and Holly also shortening their skirts within the week, despite Cynthia's pantomimed horror at the sight and thoroughly not amused claims that she'd raised a trio of harlots with her eldest daughters.

Daisy smiled at Ren, who held her stare. He took her hands in his, but even though Daisy tried to angle her mouth provocatively, even licking her lips to draw his eye to that area, he didn't move to kiss her again.

Flustered by the unerring way he was looking at her, Daisy couldn't tell if he were braver with a little physical distance between them – even if only a matter of inches like this – and was therefore just shy when really close to her, or if he had just kissed her purely because she had obviously expected him to do so.

'What are your plans for the future, Ren?' Daisy thought this a relatively safe comment unlikely to make things awkward between them now they had turned a corner with one another.

'Oh, I don't know. Father wants to expand the brewery and I suppose I'll get caught up in that.'

'Goodness, it's a big business already.'

Then Daisy paused, before dropping her voice to whisper in order that Ren had to incline his head towards her, 'I wasn't necessarily asking just about work though, you know, Ren.'

'Ah, I see,' said Ren, and he stuck his lower lip forward in a manner that told Daisy he did indeed understand. 'Well, of course Father is hoping that all of us Brewer lads get married and go on to have lots of children, a cricket team ideally, and probably sooner rather than later – he's very fond of the words "legacy" and "inheritance", and the next generation is a big part of that, so he leads us to believe. I believe Father thinks this is what Mother would have wanted.' His eyes dimmed for a moment on the word 'Mother'.

This was more along the lines of what Daisy had been hoping to hear, although she thought *lots* of children a bit forward, and moreover she didn't want to risk the conversation turning melancholy as Ren's mother Ivy had died just the previous summer, succumbing to a long illness, and she could see that Ren had been very fond of her.

'And how do *you* feel about what your father wants?' she said, making sure her voice was kind.

'I'm not sure, Daisy, if I'm honest. To get married feels a large step, bigger than I expected, and I've never really thought what it would be like to be a husband or father, or a businessman. And us Brewers aren't that used to having women around, as Mother was laid up in her bedroom for a long time before she passed and so we didn't spend much time with her in recent years. If I'm honest, I'm not sure I'd be very good at any of it, including Father's latest ideas for the business. His other favourite words there are "expansion" and "profit". And I'm not sure I care very much about expansion or profit.'

Daisy said, 'Maybe you just need to get a bit more used to all of Mr Brewer's ideas. You'll inherit the brewery, and so you'll need a son and heir pretty quickly as that's just good business sense, in order to ensure the family ownership continues. You'd need to choose a wife who is an asset to the business, and who will be appreciated by those you do business with.'

Daisy hoped she hadn't gone too far, but she needed Ren to think of her as possible wife material, and she couldn't afford to let this opportunity slip away too easily as goodness knows when she'd next have his undivided attention like this.

'Yes, Father has always said to me that as the oldest I need at least one heir and a spare, or to be like him and have an heir and two spares,' said Ren as he let out the tiniest of beer belches, and then gently slapped his belly once or twice. 'And I know I'm of an age when I should be thinking this way.'

'Your father sounds very wise.'

'Hmm. I'm not so sure about that. Anyway, it does all feel a bit different talking to you now as I think you're helping me make sense of things.'

Boldly, Daisy leaned forward with her eyes closed. And when Ren didn't instantly respond, she took the initiative and kissed him, making sure she was holding him in such a way that he could feel her chest pressing against his.

She was pleased he reacted by putting his arms around her and pulling her tight.

Then a loud cheer from the cricketers carried to them all the way them across the flat farmland, presumably to announce that one side had won, and Ren pulled away first from the kiss, holding up his empty beer bottle as he said, 'Time to get back for some more grog, eh, Daisy?'

On the way back, they stopped briefly at a gate to watch the dying embers of the sun slip down beyond the horizon at the same time as a nearly full moon began to rise behind them.

It was a magical sight and felt the most perfect of romantic settings, so much so that Daisy risked leaning her head on Ren's shoulder, nodding in appreciation when he slid an arm around her waist, although mere seconds later he removed it and said, 'I wonder who won the cricket. And what everyone else is up to?'

Chapter Five

Quite a lot, as it turned out.

For, when Daisy and Ren got back to Old Creaky, it was to find all hell was breaking loose. Joy had dramatically gone into labour and was now upstairs in the older girls' bedroom where everyone could hear from outside that there was quite a hullaballoo going on.

Poor Asa had fallen over in a faint with the shock of realising that very imminently he would be a father, giving himself a nasty gash on the head.

And generally it seemed that the guests were now as one in the decision that the party had quickly been brought to an untimely but necessary end.

Clem and Jared announced they were off to the nearest public house to avoid the birthing shenanigans, and of course anyone was welcome to join them, while a helpful neighbour had already spirited away Senna and Tansy for the night so the young girls wouldn't hear too much of the uncomfortable noise.

Ren looked at Clem and Jared, and then across to Basil Brewer, who seemed to be marshalling his sons together, and said, 'Not this time, eh?'

'That's a pity, Ren,' said Jared, and Clem nodded in agreement.

Daisy liked how considerate Ren was, although she was sorry that her own evening had been curtailed.

As a midwife arrived and was quickly bustled inside the mill house, just as Joy was heard to loudly exclaim a profanity, the Brewers raced to pile into the Rolls. The engine lurched into life once Alder had vigorously cranked the starting handle, the Alpine Eagle's dark-green paint almost black in the fading light. Holly stood nearby, smiling coyly. Daisy looked at Ren, who gave her a wave and what Daisy hoped was a romantic nod, as he followed his brothers aboard. Then, jerkily and not quite in a straight line, the car set off down the road and Basil let out a merry toot-toot on its horn.

Daisy hoped the jerkiness was to do with the haste with which the Brewers were making themselves scarce, rather than anything she had done to the Rolls earlier.

And then with a much less happy look on her face and a muttered, 'Just when things were getting interesting – darned babies!', Daisy went to organise Violet, Holly, Olive and Marguerite so that they could all work together to do the big clear-up, and then undertake the

Herculean effort of hoisting the piano back inside the mill house.

Asa they left to it. He smoked pipe after pipe as he sat in the garden – his head now sporting a white bandage that Olive had helped him with – and glanced repeatedly up towards the room where Joy was bringing their first child into the world.

Once all the tidying and washing up had been done, and everything put to rights, Marguerite returned to her and Clem's cottage and the three older Graham sisters and their cousin drank cocoa. Speaking softly, they compared notes on the party as they sat around the kitchen table, their words sometimes obliterated by the sound of Cynthia upstairs telling off a huffing and puffing Joy for making such a ridiculous fuss about what was only natural after all.

'So . . .' said Daisy.

'What a wonderful party,' announced Holly.

'I had a bit too much of the punch,' confessed Violet, rubbing her brow. 'Alder was very naughty in topping me up. Thank goodness you made him go to bat, Olive, otherwise I'd be sleeping it off under a tree somewhere.'

'Drink some water,' Olive advised. 'I've just had about a gallon as it was thirsty work umpiring the cricket. Those Brewer lads made it a real contest.'

'Didn't they,' Daisy agreed, although she wasn't really talking about the cricket.

Violet looked as if she was about to ask what Daisy had been up to with Ren, but was interrupted by Cynthia moving to a different part of the bedroom upstairs, to a spot where her voice clearly carried down to the kitchen through the floorboards, pronouncing that if only Joy relaxed a bit, then it would all be much easier. Joy snapped back in no uncertain terms that she hated Asa and she was never going to put herself through this again, and frankly she didn't really appreciate anything that Cynthia had to say on the subject. And if God was a woman, he would have made sure there were buttons in the appropriate places that could be undone easily to get damned babies out.

Everyone in the kitchen below had to stuff their faces behind tea towels so that their laughter didn't travel upstairs.

And despite the responding calm hum of whatever the midwife was saying to smooth the troubled waters upstairs, the three sisters agreed with Joy about the buttons, if this palaver was what being married led to.

As Joy's puffs and groans turned into yelps of abject pain, certainly courting and marrying hardly seemed worth this outcome, thought Daisy, although when her thoughts drifted back to Ren, she felt a tingle inside that was new to her. What Joy was going through had graphically reminded Daisy that before she got to that stage she would have the pleasure of revelling in her husband's naked body.

Then Daisy and her sisters and Olive confessed to each other that none of them had ever seen a completely unclothed man before, and nor did they understand fully what went on between husband and wife when they were alone. Although they spent their time amongst farmers, they hadn't picked up too much about the birds and the bees.

Cynthia obviously should be the fount of this knowledge, claimed Olive, with a glinty eye, and perhaps she should be questioned.

But Daisy and her sisters quaked at this thought, saying that their mother would be the *last* person they could ever ask about what being married was like in the bedroom sense.

'We'll have to speak to Marguerite,' said Holly impishly, 'as I'm sure she and Clem are very practised by now.'

'Holly!' said Daisy primly, before adding, 'Well, at least Marguerite isn't Joy, as I doubt that she'll be thinking favourably of it right now.'

And they all hooted with laughter when Violet added, 'But if Marguerite claims that a tambourine is in any way crucial to the marriage bed, then I fear that I'm going to stay a spinster.'

∞

Several hours later and all remnants of laughter having very much died away after a tense-looking Cynthia came down with some crumpled linen to put to soak, the young women downstairs were feeling totally done in after such a busy and long day, yet none felt inclined to go to bed or to even sit on the softer chairs in the parlour.

As Cynthia went back to Joy's side, Olive looked at Daisy with a twinkle in her eye. 'There is an upside. Aunt Cynthia is so caught up in the arrival of the baby that she's forgotten to berate you further about crashing Basil Brewer's car.'

Daisy smiled, and said, 'That thought hadn't escaped me either.'

Time ticked by.

Increasingly, Daisy wasn't in the mood for jokes. She found the sounds of what Joy was going through to be much more anxiety-making than she had previously, and she put her head on her folded arms on the kitchen table, trying and mostly failing to nap. She couldn't remember how long Cynthia had been in labour with any of her siblings, not even Tansy and Senna, but who knew it took this long?

It wasn't until it was fully light the next morning and the dawn chorus of birdsong had been and gone, that the high bleats of a newborn were heard, with Violet waking Asa and him running up the stairs to his wife, with Cynthia coming downstairs noisily not long afterwards to pronounce that Joy had had a very easy time of it for her first birth, with a quick and simple labour and a healthy baby girl at the end of it.

The three oldest Graham sisters and Olive couldn't stop staring at each other with their eyes wide in disbelief at Cynthia's words.

Daisy couldn't help unconsciously crossing her legs, and then she noticed her two sisters had done the same.

Chapter Six

It was later that same day, after everyone had had a chance to catch up on a bit of shut-eye, that news filtered down from London that was hard to make sense of at first.

Headlines screamed Archduke Franz Ferdinand, heir to the Austro-Hungarian throne, had been assassinated in Serbia along with his wife.

Daisy wasn't sure what this fuss meant as she had never even heard of the archduke, or his wife, although it was disconcerting for her to see the reaction of others around her, many of whom seemed shocked at the announcement.

As she reread the headlines to see if she was missing something, Daisy couldn't help but feel as she listened to the healthy lungs of her baby niece, bawling lustily away upstairs, that what had happened all those miles away in Sarajevo seemed inconsequential somehow, and very distant from her own life.

She said as much to her sisters and to Olive, who all nodded back in agreement.

Daisy added, 'I mean, what has happened to the arch-duke and his wife is awful, I'm sure, but for us doesn't what went on upstairs last night and the birth of Asa's baby feel much more important?'

'I'm sure this fuss over Austria will soon die down,' said Holly.

Violet nodded, and said, 'It's likely to be more of a storm in a teacup, the headlines merely being a means of selling more newspapers.'

Olive looked more circumspect but she kept any thoughts to herself.

∽

Inconsequential the news of the archduke and his wife's slaughter certainly was not however, and it wasn't long before Daisy and her sisters found that they had to eat their words.

For, within a month, Austria and Hungary had declared war on Serbia, and Britain made its Declaration of War only days after that in early August.

The newspapers shouted Horatio Nelson's rallying cry from the eve of the Battle of Trafalgar of 'England expects that every man shall do his duty', and within a fortnight the press carried chilling headlines announcing the first British forces had already arrived on French soil in support of France and Russia.

King George V gave the following address to the nation which was widely reported: 'At this grave moment in our national history I send to you and, through you, to the officers and men of the fleets of which you have assumed command, the assurance of my confidence that under your direction they will revive and renew the old glories of the Royal Navy, and prove once again the sure shield of Britain and of her Empire in the hour of trial.'

Suddenly everyone seemed galvanised into action by the King's statement.

Immediately there rose a nationwide surge of moral duty and pride at being British. To show the extent of public support in what the King had said, huge crowds gathered outside Buckingham Palace in London.

Even down in sleepy Crumford, previous concerns spoken in Daisy's tea room about unrealistic complaints across the nation regarding low wages and poor conditions from a vociferous workforce, and the disgusting demands from the women's suffrage movement for the vote, all seemed a thing of the past, swept aside so that everyone could concentrate on the defeat of the British Empire's enemies.

This groundswell of patriotism spread quickly, and the result was that, as was happening throughout the land, all three Brewer sons, and Asa and Clem too, volunteered to go and fight the very hour the recruiting office opened in Crumford.

To them, it seemed an honour to fight for one's country.

An absolute honour.

It was hard for anyone to disagree with this sentiment, although Daisy did wonder if Asa was doing the right thing as he was such a new father to Rose, who was still only days old, and it seemed tough that he could spend so little time with his baby and Joy.

Nobody else though said anything to this effect, and so Daisy decided not to rock the boat as in any case Asa had already volunteered, and so what would be the point of her saying anything now that he was committed to leaving Crumford to fight?

Those who would stay behind felt immensely proud of these gallant young men; it was the accepted view that it was right they had volunteered.

They wouldn't be away long, and would return as heroes, everyone told one another.

Nobody had time for doubts to start creeping in as it was just a few days before these new recruits had to leave for their preliminary training, each one promising faithfully to their loved ones that they'd be back home in time for Christmas.

Before they left, Ren, Alder and Rosen drove over to Old Creaky one evening, and Daisy felt a rush of pleasure at the sight of Ren.

'Good evening, Daisy,' he said as he came to stand somewhat bashfully before her. 'How are you?'

'I'm well, thank you, but it seems incomprehensible how quickly our world is changing,' she said. 'One minute you and I are watching the sunset, and the next you're about to go and fight for our country.'

'I know, Daisy—' Ren reached for her two hands '—it doesn't make sense to me either. But I know that if I don't go, then I will always think badly of myself. Don't Clem and Asa feel the same?'

'I expect they do. But it is hard for us who will be left at home and—' Daisy's words were interrupted by Clem calling for Ren to join him and the others as all the young men were just about to walk to the nearest public house.

Daisy saw Ren's eyes crinkle at the corners with a cheeky smile, making it obvious that he wanted to go carousing with the others. She realised that despite Ren being pleased to see her, really he and his brothers were there at Old Creaky to talk to Asa and Clem, and although she felt sure that if she insisted, Ren would stay talking to her, he quite probably would have been doing so merely to make her happy, rather than because he wanted to. And she knew she would feel bad subsequently about him not spending one of his last nights at home out enjoying himself with his pals and his brothers.

Daisy understood, really she did. What these young men – and many, many others across the land – were about to embark on was deadly serious, and it was natural that they were going to want to talk about it with each other and let off a bit of steam while they still could.

But knowing that any time she and Ren could spend together was very short too, Ren's fingers still clasping hers seemed something of a poor return.

Still, she made herself say, 'You go and have a good time with the others.'

Ren smiled broadly as she paused, trying to pluck up the courage to ask him outright to write to her. But she wasn't brave enough, and so the best she could do was to drop a very broad hint with, 'I'm not going anywhere, Ren, so you'll always know where to find me', although it got a bit muddled with Ren thanking her for sending him on his way out for the evening with the others.

He pressed her fingers firmly again in a warm goodbye as he stared intently into her eyes for a moment. And then as he trotted over to his friends, Daisy's fingers felt the rush of cool air as he no longer held them.

∽

Two days later, the Graham women – or at least Cynthia, Daisy, Violet and Holly – and a damp-eyed, wilting Basil Brewer, who looked as if he were carrying the cares of the world upon his broad shoulders, gathered together to see the lads off from the local train station on the very first train bearing the Crumford volunteers away.

The female contingent tried their utmost to look as cheery as possible as they furiously waved their hankies, which was difficult as it was impossible not to feel upset about the seismic change to their lives, especially for a cause that nobody pretended to fully understand.

Not many of the women wholly shared the collective feeling of jingoism and long live the British Empire that those going to fight and the press espoused.

A stony-faced Joy didn't even try to pretend as she stood beside the Grahams looking on, with a late-arriving Olive adroitly relieving her of a grizzling baby Rose to gently bounce the little one on her hipbone.

Standing beside Joy, Olive and Rose, was Clem's glum-looking wife Marguerite, now obviously in the family way herself. She twisted her hands this way and that in unhappiness; it was as if news of the war had been mirrored by her and Clem's news of their imminent arrival.

While Daisy was interested in waving off Ren, most of her thoughts were to do with her departing brothers, she discovered.

She realised that she was really going to miss them. In the intellectual sense, she had known this to be the case from the moment they had volunteered, but it was only now that their departure was a reality, with nobody knowing when they would all be together again, that she felt their impending loss in every cell of her body.

She felt Violet reach for one of her hands, and Holly the other, and Daisy realised her sisters were feeling similarly. She pulled each hand up for a kiss, and then the sisters stepped so close to each other that the whole length of their arms were touching in recognition of how at sea the three of them were feeling as they tried to cope with these uncharted emotions.

Daisy glanced at Cynthia, as it would be worse being a mother in this situation, and she was pleased to see that Olive was now standing beside her.

Jared had made his farewells earlier with Asa and Clem, and at this moment would be hard at work in the mill, Daisy knew.

Her father had said that morning at breakfast that he wouldn't accompany them all to the station as he knew he was going to be busier than ever. If there was one thing needed during wartime, it was good food, as an army marched on its stomach. And the flour he was making in Old Creaky was very much part of the war effort.

Daisy suspected that while this was true, the real reason Jared wouldn't accompany them to wave off his sons was that he hated goodbyes.

And maybe he was right not to be there. For a few yards away, Ren and his brothers tried, and failed, to comfort a distressed Basil Brewer.

Ren turned to look at Daisy.

Their gazes met and for a few seconds it seemed that time stood still.

Daisy felt a maelstrom of feelings, at once happy that Ren sought her eyes out on Crumford station when she was sure there were many other young ladies there who'd have thrilled to his stare, but uncertain over whether there was anything between them that they could build upon.

It was complicated, seeing how friendly Asa and Clem had always been with the Brewer boys, their relationships linking the families.

And Daisy knew she shouldn't read too much into what had gone on between her and Ren. They'd never said anything to each other about what they wanted from their relationship, and Daisy felt now she understood what Cynthia meant when – in one of her favoured sayings she often repeated – she'd claimed one tended not to regret what one did do, but instead what one *didn't* do.

Sighing acceptance that it was too late to attempt to clarify how the land lay between her and Ren, Daisy took the easiest option and smiled at him.

She wanted him to leave for war knowing she thought warmly of him.

His eyes softened as he stared at her for several seconds, and then he turned his attention back to Basil.

Daisy thought maybe that was enough for now.

It wasn't the best, but it certainly wasn't a disaster.

With a bit of luck, Ren would make the next move and write to her, and at the thought of this, she felt a tiny stab of excitement somewhere deep inside.

∽

The last thing Daisy saw of those leaving aboard the packed locomotive was Clem and Ren squashed together as they leant out of one window with some friends waving from behind them as, everyone laughing and calling, they blew extravagant and theatrical kisses back towards the train platform. Asa, Alder and Rosen were doing the same from the window of the following carriage as the train's metal wheels clattered deafeningly on the shiny rails as their slow turns started to pick up speed.

The train whistled ear-piercingly as it left the station, and once it had gone, people looked around at each other, as if not quite certain what they should do next.

Daisy was deeply touched to see the tender way in which Cynthia, noticing a rumpled Basil looking quite undone, stepped over to comfort him, speaking softly and then gently laying a gloved hand on the arm that was clutching his straw hat.

The pair stood together as people began slowly to make their way around them, heading in the direction of the station exit. The blue, white and red bunting that decorated the station fluttered high above and the Salvation Army band played to the end of the song, sadly without the benefit of Marguerite accompanying them on her tambourine.

Indeed, Cynthia didn't leave Basil's side until a couple of minutes after the Salvation Army had made its way off the station platform, by which time Basil had blown his nose into a freshly laundered handkerchief he had shaken loose of its stiff folds, and replaced his hat on his head.

Daisy thought she could feel Basil's upset keenly herself.

As she trudged along with her family back to Old Creaky, Daisy realised she felt as if she'd been left dangling, with her plans of finding someone to be walking out with officially by the end of 1914 having gone up in a puff of smoke.

She knew she wouldn't be alone in having thoughts like this. The other single young ladies in Crumford would also be concerned as practically all the men between the ages of eighteen and thirty-eight had signed on the dotted line at Crumford's recruiting office. But this knowledge didn't help.

Then Daisy felt bad about reducing what was happening to them all merely to how she was feeling about her own situation, quickly admonishing herself for being ridiculously small-minded and egotistical when there were much more important things afoot in the world.

'I wish with the whole of my heart that those whom we've waved off today all come back to us soon, each one safe and sound,' Daisy mouthed fervently to herself in atonement.

She looked around her as she found herself shivering, despite the hot weather, and could see through the gauzy thin weave of her blouse that her arms had goosebumped with a sudden and unpleasant chill.

It seemed her very bones knew already that the shortening days of summer, although spiked with patriotic optimism, were but a prelude to more serious business about to take over their lives.

Next

Chapter Seven

Those next few weeks, the absence of the men who had gone to fight was cruelly felt by those left in Crumford. People didn't say so exactly, but everyone regarded everyone else with sympathy as they were all pretty much in the same boat.

It seemed as if a cold wind was blowing through the familiar streets and Old Creaky too. The weather was sunny still, but this seemed a travesty, being far too cheerful-seeming for the jittery mood of the town.

All three Graham girls, as well as Olive, and Cynthia too, had to help Jared in the mill, and pull together to try and keep the bakery and the tea room in business.

Small jobs in the mill were even found for Tansy and Senna, usually weighing flour into small cotton sacks for the farmers that wanted it made ready for shops.

At first they all found this new routine exhausting.

'I can't ever remember feeling so weary,' said Violet one evening as they were all eating their dinner after a long day of physical toil.

Everyone nodded in agreement.

'I suppose in part it's the worry over what will happen,' Daisy replied, 'as we're just not used to it. And we're not used to going to bed tired, and then waking up weary, knowing that all we've got to look forward to is more of the same the next day.'

'Oh come on, let's show a bit of backbone!' cried Holly, always the most boisterous of the girls. 'We'll get used to it. We'll have to. And then it won't seem so bad, I'm sure. Eventually Father won't mind us chivvying him around, and soon we'll know the best way of doing things. Don't you agree, Mother?'

Cynthia looked at Holly. 'Well, I hope you're right, Holly. I do think we'll get used to working more, but I doubt it will ever seem normal not having Clem and Asa here with us.'

'I think Holly's right and that we should be as positive as we can,' said Olive. 'I know it's difficult, but we're not going to do anybody any favours if we remain resolutely down in the dumps. Everyone is missing their old lives, but Asa and Clem and all the others wouldn't want those of us back in Crumford to wallow in the pain of their absence, would they?'

The conversation moved on to other things, but what had been said set Daisy thinking. It was easy to fall into the doldrums, especially as everyone in the land felt uneasy and fearful, but this wasn't a helpful attitude.

Daisy decided that from this point on she would try to seek out the good things, and not dwell too much on what was upsetting. And, being the eldest Graham child at home, she would try to lead the others by example. It might not always be easy to do this, but she would try her best.

∽

Despite their long hours, the Grahams at Old Creaky knew that they were fortunate compared to many other families in the area, as some harvests had been left rotting where they grew since so many farm labourers had signed up. There wasn't a subsequent drop-off in turnover in the mill's business, as they had some new customers from further away.

It wasn't long before summer was in the process of surrendering abruptly to the crisper, shorter days of early autumn, and one afternoon it took Daisy four or five attempts until she was completely happy with what she had written in her letter.

She found it devilishly hard to strike the right balance between making sure she gave Ren a get-out (should he require one), but also being inviting enough at the same time as being not unpleasantly soppy.

Daisy had hoped that Ren would have written to her off his own bat by now, but he hadn't.

She told herself not to allow her feelings to be hurt, as training must be keeping the lads busy. Asa had sent only two very basic letters home, and Clem hadn't sent anything at all – and that was in spite of his wife's interesting condition.

Daisy hoped that the fact she had waited long enough before putting pen to paper demonstrated to Ren she wasn't a clingy sort of person, nor one who was reading too much into their situation.

And now she had something concrete to ask him, a genuine request, so she'd thought it a good time to write. She wanted Ren and his brothers to take photographs for Basil. Daisy had noticed how upset he had been at the sight of all three of his sons going off to war, and was trying to find ways to help him feel less isolated and alone.

All the same, to get herself into the right frame of mind for writing her letter to Ren, after her first woefully poor start had had to be abandoned at only four or five lines in, Daisy distracted herself by scribbling notes to Asa and Clem suggesting that they also should have pictures taken to send to Joy and Marguerite, and Cynthia and Jared.

Daisy knew that photographs of her brothers in uniform would be deeply treasured by the Graham family, and although she was sure that Asa and Clem would be very busy, she hoped they would take note of her suggestion.

At last she felt equal to the challenge of writing her final version of Ren's letter.

Dearest Ren,

I hope you don't mind me contacting you so soon after those of us you've left behind stood on the station side by side and waved you all away on your adventures. What a wonderful sight — so moving and truly patriotic. We are <u>so</u> proud of our young men of Crumford, and were honoured to be part of such a joyous moment in our town and families' histories.

However, it wasn't long before I was thinking, as Old Creaky beckoned us homewards, that before you left I should have asked you if you cared for me writing to you.

Naturally, if you have no free time or you don't think it appropriate, I shall understand, and it will be the end of the matter with no feelings hurt.

Regardless of your answer to that, though, I have a request I would be most obliged if you could think seriously about.

Seeing how upset your father was after you three Brewers had departed, I felt I should write to tell you that it might be a nice idea if, should the opportunity arise, you could organise a photograph of you and your brothers all in your uniforms, perhaps even on your parade ground, to be sent to him so that Mr Brewer would feel for an instant as if he were there with you.

If you also each had photographs taken of you individually, I know I would like to have one of you, should you want me to have it, and I think so would Violet and Holly too if you asked Alder and Rosen to send photographs to them.

Perhaps we could even send back small photographs of ourselves?

Anyway, I enclose a clipping from the local newspaper that has a story and also a photograph that shows your train leaving. If you look closely at the windows you can just about make out yourself and your brothers, and of course our own Asa and Clem.

You won't be surprised that there's not much other news here, aside that it was my birthday yesterday, and Violet's too – we are now the grand age of twenty and nineteen. Crumford has never been big at news, and it's certainly not beside itself over our celebrations.

No parties of course, as we're all so distracted now with much more important things, but Cynthia stood in for me for the first couple of hours in the tea room yesterday, and Holly managed on her own at the bakery, so that Violet and I could have an extra hour or two in bed – it might not sound like much, but we agreed last night that our lie-ins felt like a treat of the first order and were an excellent birthday gift indeed.

We're all feeling a little more tired than usual, as aside from what we usually do, we're all having to muck in to help Father in the mill (even the twins — and their birthday party seems a long time ago now, does it not?), while your own papa is also teaching Holly all about proper double-entry book-keeping in order that she can spend a few hours over at the office at yours in Alder's place helping keep the Brewer's accounts shipshape, and of course the experience she gets there will help us too. She cycles over there every day, looking very grown up and as if she is a woman about town.

Violet is finding herself very busy too, as some of the local ladies are now forming themselves into various committees aimed at helping behind the scenes, and are not doing as much of their own cooking as previously, so even though we don't have the number of menfolk here we're used to, Violet is finding demand for her loaves has risen, and the use of her roasting ovens, even though she had expected to be less busy.

Incidentally, you might be amused to know that Holly tells us that your father isn't much liking training up the last batch of summer workers down from London. They're all women or youngsters still wet behind the ears, with not an ounce of gumption between them apparently — and that's when he's being nice about them!

To be honest, Mother is equally disparaging about the general workers that the farmers we deal with at the mill are having to make do with (probably because Mother had to reload a cart herself the day before yesterday after one of the temporary workers managed to rip the sack and quite a lot of the flour inside got spilled – Father said he didn't realise he was married to a woman who can swear like a navvy!).

I hear on the grapevine too that the Betteshanger mining company is having difficulty as well since they've lost many of their men to volunteering, even though mining is a key industry – they are trying to pull miners out of retirement, but many have various stages of emphysema and so although they are all keen to do their bit, sadly few of the returning miners are able to complete a full day's work.

So let's hope this war is over soon, although not before you chaps have seen just a little bit of action, as it would be a shame for you to go through all your training and then not have the chance to take a potshot or two.

At home we've all got our fingers crossed for an end by Christmas, as the powers-that-be are promising – just think of the riotous celebrations there will be if you all arrive home on Christmas Eve!

Still, to tide us over until then I think we're going to have to find a strong man from somewhere to help out in the mill, and I am pretty sure your pa will be thinking similarly. Goodness knows where we'll find these men, but I'm really hoping they won't have already volunteered.

I will close now, and I am hoping all is well with you meanwhile, Ren, and that you are enjoying your training — we all talk about you often, and the japes you Brewers are probably up to, very likely leading our Asa and Clem into bad ways. I hope that's the case anyway, and not the other way around!

Do let me know if there is anything you'd like me to send you. And by the time you write back, I think the twins may have wheedled out of us quite what Mother said over the split sack that shocked Father so . . .

Sincerely yours,
Daisy Graham, Miss

∽

As she arrived back from posting the letters to Ren and her brothers, Daisy heard raised voices.

Immediately she felt a rush of worry.

But after a moment she realised that her mother's shouted words sounded furious rather than distraught, and although Cynthia could be sharp, she was rarely roused to anger in the manner that she clearly was at this moment.

Daisy's interest was piqued, and she couldn't stop herself going to see what was happening.

It wasn't what she expected.

'Olive! This is simply dreadful news. It's extremely misguided of you, and I cannot believe you have just said what you have. Indeed you cannot mean this. It must be a horrible joke at our expense.' Cynthia's voice was caustic in the extreme, and very loud.

'I'm afraid I am most serious, Aunt Cynthia.' Olive sounded much calmer, if a little clipped.

'Well, I tell you right now, young lady, that it's just *not* going to happen,' insisted Cynthia.

It was teatime and Cynthia was standing stock-still in the kitchen, with the tea caddy poised in her hand, Daisy saw, as she walked through the back door.

Olive, who was usually the most easy-going of souls, was standing in a manner most resolute and as if she were really digging her toes in about something.

Daisy thought this was incredibly unlike her as Olive was the sort of person who was usually very amenable to what other people wanted. Right from when she had very first arrived in the Graham household, she had displayed a real knack for dealing harmoniously with Cynthia, and so Daisy found it perturbing to think that Olive's usual affability was clearly going by the by.

She was eyeing her aunt with daggers as she exhaled an audible sharp huff through her nose.

Still, it wasn't this that took Daisy most aback, but instead Cynthia's response, which was to back off.

Daisy had never seen the like before, and it was almost as if her mother wasn't quite as certain of laying down the law as she normally was.

And if Cynthia, who was usually so sure of herself, felt uncertain, then what could this mean for the rest of them?

Daisy couldn't convince herself that it boded well for anybody.

This didn't mean though that Cynthia's eyes weren't furiously boring back at Olive's as the two women stood mirroring each other with their legs apart and their hands on their hips as they tried to stare each other out. Cynthia then attempted to up the ante with a small but firm shake of her head to winch up the sense of 'no' exuding from her.

Olive's expression darkened and she blinked slowly, her face screwing up briefly.

When she opened her eyes, her chin was jutting in confrontation, and it was clear that she was regarding Cynthia with what was now real bad temper, rather shocking Daisy.

Cynthia snapped at Olive in response, 'My dear sister – your sainted mother Iris, Olive, should you be forgetting – would be turning in her grave if she thought for a second that any one of us here would condone something like this.'

'Frankly, Aunt Cynthia—' began Olive, two high spots of colour springing to her cheeks and her voice insistent as well as quite a bit higher now.

'What on earth does Olive want to do?' interrupted Daisy, who couldn't imagine a single thing that could merit a squabble like this.

'This discussion is pure bunkum, and irrelevant, Aunt Cynthia. It's not simply a question of me wanting to do this,' said Olive very firmly, completely ignoring Daisy. 'It's that I *am* going to do, whether I have the Graham family seal of approval or not.'

Jared, who had been standing in the passage doorway watching proceedings, opened his mouth as if he were going to chip in with his two ha'p'orth.

But Cynthia halted her husband in his tracks with a flick of the palm of her hand held up close to his face for a few seconds, clearly determined to have her say. 'Olive, what you want will happen over my dead body, make no mistake about that. You simply must reconsid—'

But Olive didn't wait for Cynthia to finish, and nor was she paying any heed to the idea of her aunt's deceased corpse. 'We'll never know what my mother would have thought about this, will we?' Olive pointed out over the top of what her aunt was saying. 'But if I take after my mother in any way, I like to think she'd have been behind me, and that she would find your feelings on the matter to be antiquated, unpleasant and nothing more than mere poppycock. I've thought about this for weeks and I know that it's what I must do.'

'What's perfect? What must you do, Olive?' shrieked Daisy, the suspense of not knowing what was going on getting too much.

Cynthia sighed angrily, and gave a little stamp of a foot.

Olive paid no attention, instead taking a moment to breathe deeply to calm herself before saying in a much more conciliatory tone in her cousin's direction, 'What all this fuss is about is that I intend to train as a nurse, Daisy, with a view to going to the front, should we still be at war by the time I can actually be useful. And if I can't go to the front in time, then I am sure there will be other nursing opportunities for me looking after wounded servicemen upon their return.'

'What a splendid idea,' blurted Daisy, the words out of her mouth before she could stop herself.

Olive's daring intention was so heady that Daisy couldn't help but feel a prick of jealousy at the same time as feeling delighted and thrilled in the wake of her cousin's boldness.

It was too late now to placate Cynthia though, who was angrily swiping at a smut from the oven that was on the back of her hand, and so Daisy reasoned that she might as well be killed for a sheep as a lamb.

'Dearest Olive, I simply can't think of anyone more likely to be a wonderful nurse in difficult circumstances than you. How proud we shall all be,' Daisy dared. And she thought just for a second that she glimpsed an approving expression on her father's face before it quickly reverted to one that was unlikely to further fuel the flames of his wife's ire.

'Tsk!' snorted Cynthia, sharply turning her head to glare furiously towards her eldest daughter.

Daisy held her mother's eye as she did very much stand by what she had just said, and to her surprise it was Cynthia who buckled and was the first to look away.

This rattled Daisy, as it had never happened before.

Her first instinct was to immediately apologise to her mother, but something held her back, as even though Daisy understood Cynthia's point of view, she just couldn't support it.

She knew that in her mother's eyes it was perfectly all right for the Graham girls to take up positions within the confines of the family business as she, Violet and Holly already had. But these were stop-gap fillers contingent on being only relatively short-term, as they would end upon their marriages. They were clean and respectable roles, genteel to the core, hefting of the occasional sacks of grain aside.

Daisy knew instinctively that Cynthia would have preferred that none of her girls work, not least as the income from the mill could support the Grahams in this scenario, provided they were all reasonably frugal.

But the mill house was small, and Daisy had pointed out just before she left school several years previously that arguments and upsets would be a dead certainty if the sisters didn't have something concrete to do and were left with too much time on their hands, and the same was true for Olive too.

It wouldn't need to be too much or for too long, Daisy had said back then, really just until the wedding rings were on her own and her sisters' fingers. But it was unrealistic to expect them all to sit around prettily doing nothing until their knights on huge white chargers galloped through Crumford ready to sweep them off their feet in the name of true love.

Daisy had been very convincing in her arguments, and so Jared and Cynthia had discussed the situation carefully.

And then on the eve of Daisy leaving school, the offer of the bakery and tea room had been forthcoming, and Olive had been allowed to volunteer at the school. The sisters, and Olive, had been delighted at the prospect, and it had been a happy year or two getting everything ready and then up and running, and for all four young women to settle into their new roles.

This flurry of activity hadn't detracted in the slightest from Cynthia believing wholeheartedly that it was demeaning and untenable for a young lady from a respectable, middle-class family such as the Grahams to seek any sort of work outside of the family, or – shock – anything remotely resembling what might be thought of as a career.

Marriage prospects could be ruined this way, Cynthia was convinced.

And her mother wasn't alone in these feelings, Daisy knew.

Even in 1914, and with the Suffragettes encouraging for years now cosmopolitan young ladies to feel differently about independence and their future than their own mothers had, in a deeply conservative Kentish town such as Crumford, awash as it was with traditional values, society combined in myriad ways to exert pressure on young women like Daisy and Olive to toe the universally accepted line.

This was an unspoken assumption that stipulated that all young women of a certain social standing should understand unequivocally their main reason for being on this earth was to bring the next generation into the world, and in this and all other things that they should follow what their elders and betters, which was usually taken to mean the Crumford menfolk, deemed best for them.

Daisy and Olive had never been particularly respectful of the calibre of opinions of the men whom they knew (even those of Jared, and certainly not Asa and Clem) when it came to understanding what was best for young ladies.

But to suggest otherwise too publicly, seemed to Daisy to be a large and unwinnable battle, and one that promised to be every bit as challenging as what the British Tommies would be facing in Flanders.

Furthermore, now was a tricky time to be upsetting the old assumptions and ways of doing things. Stability back in Blighty was needed as everyone focused on trying to win the war.

But what *was* so wrong with someone like Olive wanting to be a nurse?

Abso-bally-lutely nothing, that's what, Daisy was convinced, even if it meant that some of the Crumford mothers would make the odd snide comment to Cynthia over headstrong females in the younger generation.

A loud crash interrupted Daisy's musings. She couldn't stop herself jumping at the sound.

For, reinforcing the sense that Daisy had that a change was happening in the old order of how the household operated, with an inexorable shift away from Cynthia's previously all-encompassing influence, a livid Cynthia had bashed the tea caddy down on the table in temper, not caring an iota that she had crumpled up the corner of the tin and left a quite deep dent in the tabletop, such was the force of the bash.

Audibly grinding her teeth, Cynthia swept from the room, refusing to look at anyone, but banging the back door so hard behind her that Daisy fancied she heard a rattle of the small panes of glass in the door's window. Of course, the panes hadn't really been shaken loose, but Daisy had to check to make sure.

It was clear that Cynthia was fuming but also that she was at a loss for how to handle what Olive had said.

Nobody who was left in the kitchen said or did anything for several heartbeats.

Then Jared sighed deeply and wearily before crossing the kitchen as he went to find and placate his wife, stopping only to slip his stockinged toes into his outside boots, then shuffling outside with them moving uncomfortably on his feet as the laces were still undone.

Immediately after he'd gone, Violet and Holly crept into the kitchen from their hiding place in the passageway with eyes glittering from the excitement, as they had never heard any family member stand up to Cynthia before.

'We couldn't believe our ears, Olive, at what you said to Mother,' said Holly breathlessly.

'Nor how you said it,' Violet added. 'Nursing – just think! To be doing exactly what you want, dealing with blood and gore. Precisely what Mother doesn't think any of us should be doing, and especially if there's a risk of having to clean and care for men's bodies. I'm sure Mother is worried to death that to be a nurse might mean a potential future husband would be put off. And I expect too that she believes it would give us ideas above our station, if we were to believe we could be independent and even able to earn enough to look after ourselves decently. How brave you are, Olive.'

Daisy couldn't tell if Violet thought Olive brave because she wanted to be a nurse, or because she had well and truly stood up to Cynthia, in a way that Daisy, Violet and Holly had never dared.

'Blast my marriage prospects then, but it's not as if I have a queue of men waiting for me to give them the glad eye as a come-on. And Violet, I'm not sure I could believe my own ears either – I'm not proud about how I spoke just now to Aunt Cynthia, although I did mean what I said,' admitted Olive, who had now gone very pale. 'I don't think I've ever had a properly cross word with her before. In fact, it has quite given me the jitters.'

'Oh my goodness,' said Daisy, who noticed suddenly that her cousin was indeed looking distinctly wobbly. 'Sit down, Olive, before you keel over, as that would really be playing into Mother's hands. Lordy, I'm so envious of you though. You'll be able to do something brave and wonderful, and that really matters, and those opportunities don't come along very often. You must grab it with both hands.'

'Well, why don't you think about coming with me, Daisy?' Olive replied as she gingerly rubbed her brow. 'Many young women are doing it, don't you know, with some of them hailing from much more respectable and well set-up families than the Crumford Grahams.'

Daisy drew in a large breath; such a thought was new.

She pondered briefly, and then admitted, 'I'd love to, but I'd be a simply awful nurse, and I know I'm needed here. And you are strong and wise and clever, Olive, and you are going to be just what is needed, much more so than I could ever be. In fact, you must do your nursing for both you and me.'

'Thank goodness you don't want to go, Daisy – I think Mother would quite literally burst with anger if you ran off to become a nurse as well. And we'd all miss you so much.' Violet sounded relieved, and Daisy smiled at her. She knew what Violet meant.

Violet was a placid person, and easily the most cautious of the older Graham sisters, Daisy knew, the sort of person who never really liked to rock the boat if she could help it.

The result was that Violet was universally liked. Everyone enjoyed being around her as she was always pleasant company and nearly always much more interested in what others were doing than what she might be up to herself. She hated arguments and had always tried to get everyone quickly on affable terms again, and Daisy loved this quality in her sister.

Then clearly Violet realised her comments might be taken by Olive to mean that the family wouldn't miss her too, and hurriedly she said, 'Of course you're going to leave such a huge hole in our lives though, Olive . . .'

Holly then butted in with a much more controversial comment. 'Yes, yes, Violet. But, Daisy, if you did leave Old Creaky in order to go and be a nurse, then Mother would have to lump it. She can't live our lives for us, can she? Or choose what we do, or who we spend our time with? Or at least she won't, if the war goes on for a while.

Us women, we're just not going to put up with it. And we all might decide to do things Mother won't approve of, don't you think?'

The young women looked at each other. Holly's words dealt with suffrage attitudes that felt simultaneously exciting and trepidatious, and very daring for those brought up in the sleepy environs of Crumford.

'Yes, I think you might be right, Violet, as Mother would most definitely not be impressed if I left along with Olive.' Daisy nodded soothingly in her middle sister's direction.

Daisy then looked sternly at her younger sister Holly with her eyebrows raised as an attempt to halt any further outbursts, before she added, 'I understand what you say, and why you say it, Holly, but I am not sure about any of it.'

Holly made a little indefinable noise at the mention of her name, but then she took her cue from the look in Daisy's eyes that seemed to say that while the place of women in the world was a very interesting topic and certainly one well worthy of further discussion, now really wasn't the time as this was Olive's moment in the spotlight.

And so Holly said on cue, 'Come on then, Olive, tell us what happens now, although not until I've made us all this cup of tea that Mother was in the midst of.'

Olive didn't need asking twice, and immediately fell to describing the two choices she had, which were training properly to be a nurse, or becoming a VAD, which was a volunteer with the Voluntary Aid Detachment, the organisation that provided nursing assistance to the qualified nurses. She could perhaps even go on to become an ambulance driver, should the British Medical Military services relax their current stance on not wanting female nurses and VADs in their field hospitals and base hospitals behind the front, the BMM claiming women would be unable to cope.

Daisy and her sisters murmured their agreement with Olive's assertion that if anything, in the psychological sense, women were generally the stronger of the sexes, being naturally very dogged and resolute in how they did things, and often much less squeamish or prone to fainting at the sight of blood than men were.

'Personally, I think I'd be best suited to some sort of medical role right behind the front line,' said Olive, 'but for now I'm assuming it's likely I'll be kept in England. Our wounded lads are already beginning to come home, and so I'm sure I can train quickly if I want to be a VAD, and then immediately be helpful in one way or another. I didn't expect Aunt Cynthia to be quite so upset and angry though, and I am sorry about that because as we all know, she and Uncle Jared have been so good to me.'

Daisy reached over and clutched both of Olive's hands in hers. 'Mother will get used to the idea, you know, dear. It's impossible that she'll stay as cross as she was, not least as she's very fond of the kitchen table and she won't want to harm it further. She did seem to forget she was cross very quickly about me crashing the Rolls-Royce.

'She's worried about Asa and Clem, and so you want ing to push outside of the safety of the family confines will have picked the scab from the wound of them being away. The world is changing and that scares her. Where us girls are concerned, in part she's worried as she can't throw herself into marrying us off as there are no suit- able men around. If we can't marry quickly, what on earth will happen to all of us? Nobody knows, and we all just have to get used to this idea.

'If the war goes on too long or we lose too many young men, then there'll be an undignified scramble for those that are left, and I expect that thought scares her as Asa and Clem aren't going to want to have to help support us all into our dotage. We're going to need to get married.'

Olive nodded to show she appreciated all that Daisy had just said, and that Cynthia's reaction was under- standable, albeit vexing.

'Even you'll need to find a husband one day, Olive,' Daisy added.

'I'm not so sure about that,' Olive replied, 'after all, who's going to want someone tall and awkward like me?'

Daisy made sure her reply had a confidence about it, even though at times she had wondered the very same as far as Olive were concerned. 'Any number of men, that's who. Just you wait and see!'

'Harrumph,' replied Olive. 'And, Daisy, Ren is the one for you?'

'Ren might not know it yet, but yes. Well, um, I think so anyway.' Hearing herself say it out loud so blatantly to her cousin and sisters, Daisy found she felt less certain about this than she had expected.

Olive didn't look convinced either, although she decided not to grill Daisy further, saying instead, 'Well, if he is what you want, and he wants you, then I hope Ren makes you very happy, and you him, of course.'

'When the time comes and you find someone, Olive, I wish for exactly the same for you both,' Daisy replied sincerely, as neatly she sidestepped considering further Olive's lacklustre comments about herself and Ren.

She and Olive looked deep into each other's eyes, and Daisy found herself the first to break away.

And then to lighten the mood, Daisy made sure everyone's attention was diverted away from Cynthia by asking Olive lots of practical questions about nursing, and soon all of those sitting around the kitchen table were debating how it might be in practice, even laughing at times when things such as the probable practicalities of giving a bed bath were considered at length.

Despite the joviality, Daisy was sorry to note that Cynthia made herself scarce for the rest of the evening, making an excuse not to join them for tea and then spending a long time giving Senna and Tansy a bath before reading them a bedtime story, after which she slipped unnoticed into her and Jared's bedroom and went to bed.

And when Olive made Cynthia a hot drink at the end of the evening, Jared stepped in to take the cup and saucer out of his niece's hand, saying softly, 'Probably best I take it, Olive.'

Olive and Daisy exchanged looks.

Jared didn't normally offer to take a drink to his wife and so Cynthia's feathers must still be ruffled, and it looked like it was going to take more than cocoa to restore equilibrium within the mill house.

Chapter Eight

The next morning, as Daisy ate breakfast with the rest of the family, she couldn't quite shake a feeling that there was an undercurrent of something unusual bubbling away beneath the surface, even though at first glance everything seemed to be exactly as normal, as if the argument over Olive and the nursing had never happened.

Precisely what this undercurrent might be wasn't clear, but the more Daisy's antennae twitched as thoughtfully she drummed her fingers on the tablecloth, the more convinced she became that it was there all the same.

And if whatever it was needed to be kept secret, then it probably wasn't heralding the best of news, Daisy reasoned.

It couldn't be anything to do with Olive and her nursing plans though, Daisy knew, as that had well and truly been wrenched out kicking and screaming into the open the previous afternoon. And right now both Cynthia and Olive had calm expressions on their faces.

Daisy thought her mother had got over the upset of the previous day because of Jared's steadying influence. For, as she lay in bed, Daisy had heard the hum of her parents talking in low voices in their bedroom for what felt like hours late into the night, with her father doing the bulk of the talking and the rough-edged timbre of Cynthia's voice gradually easing in response.

And then Daisy had seen first thing that morning a much more sanguine Cynthia announce to Olive as the pair of them placed the crockery and cutlery upon the breakfast table that although she didn't care to discuss it further, and while she hoped still that Olive would come to her senses, far be it for her to stand in her way.

Immediately Olive's shoulders dropped to a more relaxed position. She drew a rather stiff Cynthia towards her into a hug, as she whispered a heartfelt 'thank you' to her aunt.

'I've so very much to be grateful to you and Jared for, as you have loved me as my parents would have over all the years I've been here,' Olive added, 'and it was horrid and mean of me making you so angry and I hated to do so. But nursing is where I see my future, and I think I will be needed. I realised last night though it is important to me that I leave Old Creaky with your blessing, and so I am thankful – I know it can't have been easy for you to find those words, dear Aunt Cynthia.'

It was a moment filled with warmth, even though Daisy thought her mother didn't look thrilled. Her back and shoulders refused to be anything other than ram-rod straight and very stiff.

Then Daisy noticed Cynthia, from deep within Olive's hug, move her head infinitesimally over to one side so that she could glance around Olive's arm (being too short to look over her niece's shoulder) towards Jared with a resigned expression, which seemed to intimate 'see?'. Her husband responded with a small nod back, which looked very much like a signalled 'well done, missus', provoking Cynthia into the tiniest smile of her own that nobody but Daisy could see.

The moment passed without further ado and in Daisy's eyes it was almost exactly like a thousand breakfasts previously, with them saying more or less the same things (the weather, work to be done and the latest news, exactly in that order), and some people swapping their boiled eggs so that personal preference for either runny yokes for dipping bread and butter soldiers into, or a firmer yolk, could be satisfied.

Still, as she looked at her family, Daisy was increasingly convinced that something definitely felt a bit different. What could it be? Wary of unexpected changes these days, she felt the wiggle of a worm of concern.

She stared in turn at everyone as they were seated around the table, even Senna and Tansy, although Daisy thought they were too young for any subterfuge, but she couldn't detect anything out of the ordinary, and nothing further to denote if what she was feeling actually related to something that was good or ill.

Daisy's brow wrinkled in concentration, but it was no good; she just couldn't put her finger on what had changed. Maybe it was herself who was different?

All such contemplations were rudely interrupted by a shout from outside and the sight of a huge cart piled high with bulging sacks of grain pulling up on the other side of Old Creaky.

The cart's arrival meant Daisy had to set her ponderings aside, as the whole family was needed to muck in. They rushed outside to help get the sacks into the raised granary so the grain wouldn't be contaminated by rain should the weather turn, as the days were distinctly autumnal now and the sky at that moment grey and threatening, the odd plump raindrop landing heavily as the farmer jumped down to the ground.

His carthorse let out a big sigh, and slowly dropped his head down to the level of his front knees, with his eyes closed, his ears flopped to each side of his massive head and one spectacularly hairy hind leg tipped on to the toe of his hoof. It looked for all the world as if the horse were taking the opportunity for a quick forty winks.

The granary was raised quite a long way off the hard standing, having been built on brick pillars, and there were metal shields standing proud of the pillars and the steps to the close-fitting door to the granary, all carefully designed in such a way that rats couldn't clamber up and over these obstacles and get into the granary and contaminate or eat the grain.

Unloading the cart didn't take long as there were so many willing hands ready to help, although this didn't stop it being back-breaking work, and distinctly unladylike.

Daisy couldn't help but think that nursing would be a walk in the park for Olive when compared to hard physical graft such as this.

She glanced jealously over to the resting carthorse, who slightly opened his nearest eye to look at her before promptly closing it again, dropping his head even lower and changing his hind legs over to rest the other one.

∞

A few days previously, Daisy had noticed two women in her tea room whispering to each other in a secretive manner that involved nods and eyebrows raised, their hats so close that they were almost touching.

It was the manner in which these customers were conversing that alerted Daisy's interest, causing her to edge a little closer to them. She made a show of folding freshly laundered linen napkins as she tried to eavesdrop. The little she heard, piqued her interest.

What they were saying seemed to be connected with the local river that exited into the North Sea close to Crumford. The women didn't spell it all out exactly, but

Daisy was left with the distinct impression that what was going on was official and hush-hush.

She was used to not paying much attention to her customers' gossiping as mostly it was pretty dull, but the thought now of what might be so important to these two women snared her imagination, and from then on she began to listen with more attention to her patrons.

It didn't take Daisy more than several days to work out that a secret port was going to be constructed at the Cut, where the river was tidal. A ferry service was going to be added to send munitions to France and Flanders. A lot of horses were going to be transported across the Channel as aside from the cavalry horses, others had been requisitioned for moving supplies, equipment, guns and ammunition. There would also be a camp built beside the Cut where thousands of soldiers would mass before heading across to Dunkirk and Calais.

The chosen spot was close to a noted Roman fortress, and there would be a new railway constructed that would branch to the port from the main line. The river mouth was going to be dredged to create the deeper water required for the port of embarkation.

Daisy knew she shouldn't be so nosy, but once she'd started, she couldn't stop.

Indeed, she was astounded at how indiscreet people were being in their idle chatter as, although Daisy was no expert on what would comprise secret information, one didn't have to be a genius to understand the bulk of this 'intel', as she knew Asa would describe it, had to be highly confidential to the British war effort.

Quite indignantly, as she couldn't help but think that the lives of soldiers such as Asa and Clem might be at risk if everyone didn't keep schtum, but without the wherewithal to acknowledge in any critical sense her listening in, Daisy said as much to Olive one evening.

She was watching her cousin carefully pack her belongings into a sturdy portmanteau, as Olive would be on the train for London the following morning.

Basil Brewer had told Holly to say to Olive that he was very happy to drive her and her portmanteau to Crumford train station, and Olive had accepted his offer as the portmanteau was awkward to lug far. Not for the first time Daisy wished the Grahams had their own car – ideally one she could drive! – as it would make life so much easier, and they wouldn't need to be beholden to others.

'Daisy Graham, you minx, you!' cried Olive, after her cousin had had her say about what she'd overheard in the tea room. 'Or should that be Infiltrator A? I didn't know you had it in you to eavesdrop in this scurrilous way.'

'Well, I wouldn't ordinarily. You know that! But, in this case, I'm sure you'd have done the same and allowed your ears to flap just as mine did.'

'I'm not so sure,' replied Olive a trifle prissily, which made Daisy look at her sternly with her head tilted in a manner designed to make Olive laugh.

Her cousin, used to Daisy's techniques, responded by pointing out that very likely this gossip was being aired within her hearing because as far as the speakers were concerned, as regulars at the tea room, Daisy blended in and they saw her as very much part of the furniture, indistinguishable from the backdrop of the tea room unless they went out of the way to notice her.

And so, Olive suggested, while these people would never have spoken so freely in front of a stranger, because they had known Daisy and her family for years, then naturally their guard was down.

'Charmed, I'm sure,' replied Daisy. 'I've always wanted to be thought of as background scenery. I'm sure the War Office would share that opinion too.'

'Sarcasm will get you nowhere,' Olive joked.

'I'm going to miss you, Olive. Nobody else here makes me laugh as you do,' said Daisy a little later. Then she added in the type of voice to show she was trying to keep Olive smiling, 'Only a little bit, but I will miss you all the same. When I'm not too busy masquerading as a table and chairs, that is.'

'Give over,' replied Olive.

They chuckled, and Daisy then added, 'Actually I *am* going to miss you, Olive, as you and I are quite alike. Who is going to keep me on my toes once you are off irrigating wounds and doing interesting things with bandages and dressings?'

'I know it, Daisy! I'll miss you more than you'll be hankering after me, I promise, but just think – you'll get our bedroom all to yourself,' said Olive, 'and first dibs very likely in all those men working at the Cut, should you not hold back for Ren.'

'Only if I make sure to let it be known far and wide that Violet, Holly and myself are all single as those men won't be encouraged to make themselves known in Crumford,' said Daisy.

'Best not do that,' Olive replied, 'there'll be a stampede!'

Daisy put her arm around her cousin's shoulder and kissed her on the cheek, before saying with a cheeky glint in her eye, 'Now isn't that a thought that would really put poor Mother into a complete spin?'

~

The following morning there was a cheerful peep of a car's horn outside, and Daisy looked out of her bedroom window to see Basil Brewer pulling up in the Rolls, still so new that it looked showroom shiny and with the glass of the headlamp now replaced.

Jared and Cynthia had already said their goodbyes to Olive, as they had had to go to Canterbury on business.

Daisy suspected this business appointment both her parents were so keen to attend was more tactical and face-saving, rather than strictly necessary, as it meant that the visual evidence of Olive getting her way despite Cynthia's objections could be kept at an arm's distance, neatly contained within a non-contentious farewell.

Both aunt and uncle had been warm in their good-byes to Olive though, Daisy had been delighted to see, and so it seemed as if her cousin was pretty much forgiven, as long as the argument could be glossed over.

While Holly raced to open the back of Basil's car, Violet, Olive and Daisy manhandled the portmanteau between them down the stairs and out into the yard.

Basil lifted it into its space in the boot, trying to make it seem as if the portmanteau were as light as a feather. But Daisy had seen just how much Olive had squirrelled away inside it and Basil's wheeze of effort and slight totter illustrated this. Daisy didn't dare look towards the others as she didn't want to risk making anyone laugh when Basil was being so kind, going out of his way to help Olive like this.

Holly jumped into the back seat of the automobile to help with securing the leather strap around the portmanteau, and then Basil held out a hand to Olive, helping her in. Both Violet and Daisy took a step towards the passenger seat beside the driver's, although Violet then moved back, saying, 'You go, Daisy – somebody needs to be here, as otherwise we'll leave Old Creaky empty, and Father will be upset with us when he and Mother return.'

Daisy said thank you to Violet – she would have been very sorry not to have accompanied Olive to the station to say goodbye.

❧

This time the little group of four were almost the only people at the station waving off a passenger, although the platform opposite where people disembarked had several men in khaki uniform lounging about. It was a huge contrast to the noise and bustle of the last time they had all been there, with its promise of fortitude in the air and the new soldiers proud and eager to be off so soon after they had volunteered to fight for their country.

Basil's collar was starched and his hair freshly pomaded, and he looked a whole lot more cheerful than he had been that last time on the platform.

Daisy realised however that in contrast she actually felt sadder this time around, as in many ways she was closer to Olive than to her blood sisters, Violet and Holly, or brothers, Asa and Clem. She and Olive had shared a bedroom every night for fifteen years, and Daisy knew she would hanker after their chats late at night when the rest of the mill house was in darkness.

'You take care of yourself, Olive, and remember you can always come home again if you don't like it. There'd be no shame in that, and there'll be lots of other things to do for women of character as you are if nursing doesn't suit. You only have the one life, so don't waste it,' said Holly, sounding very like Cynthia.

'Don't you dare not like nursing, Olive!' Daisy chipped in quickly after Holly's comments, and at the same time Olive said as she looked at Daisy, their words merging, 'I certainly won't be back for a while.'

Basil got a porter to heft the portmanteau on board the train, tipping him handsomely, probably because he knew exactly how heavy it was.

And after she had given Basil's hand a single firm pump downwards, and kissed Holly on the cheek before clasping Daisy in a lightning quick bear-hug, with no further ceremony, Olive climbed up into the carriage.

Olive looked happy, thought Daisy, as through the open window in the door she placed into Olive's hand a small gift of a hanky on one corner of which Daisy had embroidered with red silk thread 'Nurse Leyman'.

Leyman was Olive's surname, and although Daisy's skills with a needle were poor, as Olive stared at the gift her eyes became uncharacteristically sparkly.

'I hadn't expected you to need a hanky quite so soon,' said Daisy, who felt a bit teary herself.

For an instant it looked as if Olive might be about to bawl outright, but then with a manful effort she got herself under control.

Before Daisy and Olive could say anything else to each other, the station guard blew a loud whistle painfully close to Daisy's ear, which made her jump back quickly, and instantly the puffing billy began to chug slowly out of Crumford station.

Daisy's last sight of her cousin was Olive standing tall and forthright, every inch of her six-foot-plus height seeming destined for great things in the nursing world.

Daisy sighed. She realised she was envious – her cousin was off on an adventure, while Daisy felt that all she had to look forward to was serving huge quantities of tea and bread and butter, interspersed with the occasional earwigging of teashop chatter.

Feeling in need of a little time alone, she told Basil she'd make her own way back to Old Creaky, and as she readjusted the buttons on her gloves, she watched the posh green car putter away as it bore Basil and Holly to the brewery offices.

Deep in thought, Daisy wandered around a few shops in Crumford, although she didn't buy anything, and then she watched a middle-aged man pasting up a poster with a giant heading that screamed 'BEWARE OF SPIES!', and a top line immediately below that instructed 'DON'T TALK. THE ENEMY HAS EARS EVERYWHERE', followed by a further nine points to do with the general public unintentionally passing information to spies.

Daisy noticed that beside the poster man's glue pot at his feet was a canvas bag containing other rolled posters that looked to be the same as the one he was sticking to the wall.

She had an idea.

'Excuse me, sir,' she said.

He turned towards her in a tetchy sort of way, but once face to face with Daisy, who was making sure to smile her most winsome smile, his expression became less bristly and more interested.

Daisy didn't recognise him and so didn't think he came from Crumford. It wasn't a large town and she liked to think that she knew most of those who lived there, even if only by sight rather than by name.

'How can I oblige you, miss?'

He spoke with a distinct Geordie accent, which confirmed he wasn't local.

'Well, I have a tea room just down the road, sir, connected to that mill you can see—' she turned and pointed behind her towards Old Creaky standing proud in their direct eyeline '—and I have a lot of customers who come in for tea and to sit a while. They are nearly all regulars, but I think your poster would be a very sensible thing to paste up in the tea room, just to remind everyone not to talk out of turn while they chat to their friends.'

'Well, I don't know about that, young lady. These posters cost money and aren't—' he began, but he stopped speaking when Daisy flashed another smile at him.

'Of course, I understand, sir,' she agreed in an extremely polite and understanding way. 'You'll be very busy, and all your expensive posters must be earmarked already, and I quite appreciate you're not supposed to deal with individual requests. And in any case you probably haven't got time to stop for a cup of tea, or even two, and a freshly made sandwich. On the house . . .'

He blinked in a slightly owl-like way and waggled his moustache from side to side.

Daisy thought he looked to be fighting an epic battle within himself. Either he'd succumb to her offer of a lunch he didn't have to pay for, or he'd tell Daisy that she should go and take a running jump for suggesting his services could be bought.

It looked to be a close-run thing, and so Daisy channelled every bit of her own inner Cynthia, as her mother was usually very good at getting her way – just not when it came to Olive's nursing career.

Daisy looked downwards to make herself appear more innocent, even scuffing the toe of her boot in a quarter-circle in the dirt of the unmade road, as she added as casually as she could, 'I'm sorry to speak out of turn, sir. It was just that when I noticed how very efficiently you were pasting up the poster, I thought that I have a large number of regulars at my tea room who would be a captive audience, and looking at your poster for much longer than they would if they were walking by it. And of course we are right on the coast here, with France in our direct sight, which brings the war very close to home, and this means we are *very* keen to do all that we can to beat the Hun.' Daisy paused. 'Anyway,

I am sorry to waste *your* time, although before I go, I wonder if you could direct me to the exact person I need to speak to about getting a poster?'

'Oh, I don't think you need to do that, miss. At the mill yonder, your tea room, you say?'

'Yes, that's right. I'm just heading back to pop some scones into the oven, scones with lovely plump raisins.'

'I'll see you when I'm done here.'

'Perfect. There'll be either cheese or pork brawn sandwiches today. With fresh butter from the dairy of course. And home-made pickle.'

He looked a little weak.

Satisfied that now she and the man completely understood each other, Daisy walked smartly back to Old Creaky, slightly concerned – but only slightly, for if Violet were a stick of rock, she would have the word 'capable' running down through every inch of her – that she might have left Violet for too long on her own at the mill.

CRON

It was only later as Daisy was admiring her two 'Beware of Spies' posters, one now pasted on the outside of the door that led into her tea room and another adorning its wall inside, in a prime spot right beside a huge and eye-catching dresser where all of Cynthia's goods were displayed – and knowing that a third had also been pasted to the outside wall right next to where the carts pulled up beside the granary to drop off their sacks of grain (with the promise of different posters next time the man was in Crumford), that a thought struck her.

It was Holly who was different at the moment, although she was working very hard at trying to seem as if she wasn't.

But now Daisy ran a finger over the poster positioned next to a notice announcing a charity children's drawing competition at the tea room with proceeds going to the war effort, it was hard for her not to conclude that Holly had a bit of a glow about her. She seemed confident, and sure of herself. And while it wasn't that Holly hadn't had these qualities previously, they were in clear evidence now if one knew what to look for.

Daisy frowned for a few seconds as she wondered what it meant.

Chapter Nine

The papers reported the allied French and British troops' victory at the Battle of the Marne in September.

Just after Marne it had seemed as if 'our lads' – or Kitchener's Army as many people called the armed forces because of the way Herbert Kitchener, Secretary of State for War, had found the hundreds of thousands of volunteers eager to fight – would soon be wiping the floor with the Boche.

This coincided with growing anti-German feeling among the general public and, even for staunch royalists, an increasing sensitivity to do with the British royal family and their German ties. After all, Kaiser Wilhelm II of Germany was a grandson of Queen Victoria exactly as Britain's King George V was, and therefore that made Kaiser Wilhelm King George's cousin, while in addition King George's wife was once a German princess, Mary of Teck. The surname of the royal family was the Germanic sounding Saxe-Coburg-Gotha, something King George was trying not to draw attention to.

Daisy overheard variations of this discussion several times in the tea room.

She realised it was impossible for those at home to tell from the press quite what was occurring across the Channel, or what was happening to troops still undergoing training on British turf, nor indeed what the government's strategy was generally.

Jared said as much as they buttered jacket potatoes around the kitchen table one supper-time, adding that while it was good to be as optimistic as possible, it would be prudent to remember that the official line would place as positive a slant as possible on proceedings, no matter how dire things might really be, and in reality few people would be party to the *real* state of affairs until well after hostilities had ended.

Cynthia gasped and clutched a hand to her chest, even though he had in no way hinted anything unfortunate had happened already to Asa or Clem, but this was clearly her immediate interpretation of Jared's words.

Immediately, Jared tried to backtrack and lighten the bleak mood that drenched the room. But no matter what he said, it was too little, too late, and he had to watch his family around the table dip their heads in silence as they grappled with thoughts about the possible fates of Asa and Clem, and Olive too.

'I don't want to upset anyone.' Jared broke the silence. 'But let's take heart from the fact that knowledge is a good thing, and we mustn't hide our heads in the sand as that won't help anyone – it never has and it never will. Right now, the press is making it all sound very easy for us yonder in France, and maybe it is. But we must accept the possibility of it being more complicated than Whitehall is letting on, as it might save us some upset further down the line.'

❦

While Daisy was downcast by what her father had said, she was pleased the charity children's drawing competition had got off to a rip-roaring start.

She charged a sixpence entry fee, and already there were so many entries that she had to divide the competition into under-sixes, seven-to-elevens and twelve-and-overs. The prizes would be a florin to each winning child, and Cynthia making the winners a special birthday cake for their next birthday. Daisy had agreed with the *Mercury* that the winners would be announced in its pages.

What Daisy hadn't expected was the amount of extra custom that this competition would bring to the tea room.

Daisy had put up a card in the newsagent's window, and mothers would come with their children's drawings, and then nearly always they stayed for a cup of tea, which Daisy provided free of charge, as she pinned up the picture(s). Very often the women would return with friends, and soon Daisy realised she had a growing clientele among Crumford residents, and Holly pointed out to Daisy the upturn in tea room takings.

One day, a deputation of ladies from various churches came to discuss fund-raising ideas for the war effort. And as they enjoyed some tea, Holly joined in and proved extremely imaginative, making Daisy feel proud of her younger sister, if also slightly jealous she couldn't come up with ideas as rapidly as Holly's off-the-cuff. These included a sponsored Christmas-card making event for local children, raffling a goose a week at the tea room in December, and using the tea room as a kindergarten one Sunday a month so that harried parents could pay to have someone else look after their children for a day off.

The ladies nodded in approval and then bustled away to visit the next business on their list.

As the tea room was almost empty of customers it being well after lunchtime, Daisy took the opportunity to say to Holly, 'More tea? And a teacake perhaps? You were very impressive with your ideas. I'm envious.'

It was a long time since she and Holly had had a companionable chat, just the two of them.

'I'd love another cup,' said Holly.

When Daisy had brought over a fresh teapot and two toasted teacakes, Holly surprised her by saying, 'So, you and Ren – are you keen?'

'Hmm, yes.'

'What is it that you like about him?'

Daisy saw that Holly was staring at her in a penetrating manner that made her seem much older and more worldly than she actually was.

'He's, um, handsome, I suppose,' said Daisy. 'And I think we're a good match. He's, er, very pleasant to talk to too.'

Daisy realised that she was struggling a little to describe why she liked Ren.

'Goodness, it's sounding more that you like the *idea* of him at least as much as you like Ren himself,' Holly pointed out.

Daisy realised Holly had hit the nail on the head.

She was drawn to the notion of Ren, certainly, although maybe not quite as much as back in June. But as for Ren in the flesh, well, Daisy hardly knew him, and so she wasn't certain what she thought. She had liked the look he had given her that day he and Asa and Clem were waved off at Crumford station, definitely, but that wasn't enough to be able to say to Holly anything other than he was very nice.

To divert Holly's attention as Daisy was feeling a little uncomfortable, she said, 'Holly, you've been very quiet about Rosen Brewer, and so I'm assuming there isn't anything there?'

Holly spoke with a clear-eyed confidence that Daisy envied when she answered, 'Oh, Rosen's fine, but he's just a boy. My primary interest is learning about business as I like the way money obeys rules – and the consequences of this seem to talk a language to me.

Of course that's not to say I'm not open to a romantic entanglement.'

Romantic entanglement.

Daisy thought those words enticing – who didn't want romance or a welcome entanglement? 'Holly, dear, I quite agree about the romantic bit, but I promise you that you're the only person I shall ever meet who finds excitement in boring old ledgers and account books!'

Holly laughed, adding, 'You don't know what you're missing, Daisy!'

Chapter Ten

Everyone seemed stunned when the first casualties of war were listed in the local *Mercury*.

They all knew it would be coming as an inevitable result of Britain being at war, but seeing it there in black and white was awful.

In fact, it quite undid Daisy.

The first Crumford soldier named as dead was William Evans.

Daisy felt a real gut punch at the sight of his name, as she read the paragraph announcing his death one afternoon in the tea room just after the lunchtime rush was finishing.

For it was William who had given Daisy her first kiss.

They had been playing kiss-chase after school, a lively game where the girls would hare after the boys, tugging on their jackets or shirts as they tried to plant a kiss, and then the boys would reciprocate by giving as good as they'd got, chasing the girls back so they could land a smacker on the slowest runners.

Daisy remembered that she'd been rather taken with William at the time, and so she had run just fast enough that even though she put up a good show of wanting to escape his clutches, he could still catch her. He'd pounded along behind her, panting heavily, his boots drumming on the ground, the sound of which made Daisy squeal happily with her plaits bouncing merrily on her shoulders with every stride, until she slowed just enough that he could place a hand on her arm.

William's kiss was innocent and left her cheek a bit slobbery, but Daisy had been extremely proud of having had a kiss all the same.

Violet had been involved in this game of kiss-chase too but was scandalised by Daisy's wanton behaviour to the extent that Daisy had to bribe Violet to keep quiet about her and William back at Old Creaky by promising her the last two gobstoppers from Daisy's recent birthday haul.

Despite this, once she had the prized gobstoppers firmly in her grasp, Violet teased her older sister mercilessly in front of Cynthia by repeatedly saying 'Mother!' in a way that made Daisy think that Violet was about to spill the beans, although each time Violet would then follow up the pause after her 'Mother!' by asking an innocent question such as 'what's for tea?', in spite of knowing perfectly well that they always had bread and butter and jam at teatime.

Cynthia had stared back at Violet with an increasingly quizzical expression over each question, eventually asking,

'Violet, have you had a bump on the head?' Daisy thought this was hilarious because of course it meant that the joke certainly wasn't on her any longer.

The whole episode was one of her fondest childhood memories. Daisy and William had been all of ten years old at the time.

Now Daisy stared at William's name in the *Mercury* and her eyes filled unexpectedly with a rush of tears. She had to drop the tea towel she'd been holding – it landed on the floor, where it lay unnoticed – before she raced to stand at the open door to the tea room with her back turned impolitely towards her customers. She blinked furiously as she gazed up at the scudding clouds and swiped at her cheeks with her cuffs if any tears overspilled.

Daisy had been to William's wedding two summers previously, and just the week before his death announcement she had laughed along with William's wife Peggy when they bumped into each other, when buying stamps in Crumford, over how chubby William's baby son Teddy was, and how very like his father he looked.

Daisy felt incredibly sad at the news, but what on earth would Peggy be feeling, she wondered.

William had come from a family proud of its military heritage and he must have been sent abroad ahead of the others because of this, Daisy assumed.

But out of anyone she knew who had volunteered, William had always seemed to her to be the least likely to die as Daisy had expected that words of battle know-how and instructions on how to keep as safe as possible when under fire would have been passed on to him by his father and uncles – all soldiers when they were young – before he left.

His family had been bursting with pride that day at the station, Daisy remembered.

But what drove the sense of William's loss home especially strongly to Daisy was that he and Peggy, and young Teddy too naturally, had been guests at the summer party at Old Creaky. In fact, it was he who had led the shanty singing as he banged the trestle table with his empty tankard to keep the beat, and soon nearly all of the men present had joined in alongside William's fine voice to belt out these traditional favourites. He had looked so content and vigorous as he beamed around at his friends and his wife and son, everyone totally oblivious to what was happening in another part of the world concerning Archduke Ferdinand and his wife.

Suddenly, Daisy needed some time to herself away from Old Creaky so that she could get used to the dreadful news.

She darted across the grass to Old Creaky and shouted up to Cynthia, her voice loud above the noise of the machinery connected to the mill's sails that was turning the millstones.

Daisy asked her mother if she would mind the tea room for a bit, and when she explained why, immediately Cynthia folded Daisy into a tight hug, not liking the look of her daughter's glassy eyes or the pulse that was clearly beating a tattoo at her temple.

Then Daisy's mother undid the hessian pinny she wore when helping Jared, and wrenched from Daisy's grasp a clean white linen apron that Daisy had clutched in her hand but seemed unable to pass to Cynthia.

Feeling almost a little drunk but not having consumed any alcohol since the night of the party, Daisy stumbled her way down to the tidal flats where many varieties of birds had their home, always noisily going about their daily lives.

The lovely view and the fine weather seemed to be in almost unbearable contrast to the bleak news of what had happened to William.

As she felt the breeze caress her face and neck from the direction of the land across the Channel, Daisy allowed herself to give in to a raft of shuddering, gasping tears.

Sea water pooled around the soles of her boots from her stationary weight on the briny sod as Daisy cried for William's loss. It seemed so unnecessary.

She was also sobbing too for all the upset everyone was facing, and all the young men who were yet to die, be they Germans or Brits.

If she were honest, Daisy was crying a little for herself too, and all the other young women who had spent the summer daydreaming but who were now facing some harsh truths.

Try as she might, Daisy couldn't find the sense in any of it, no matter how long she stood that afternoon, pulling a shawl close around her arms as the breeze picked up and the shadows began to lengthen as she stared at the glint of the sun on the sea or the grey shadow beyond the water that was the indistinct outline of France.

She must have appeared upset still when finally she returned home, as the moment Cynthia saw her, she insisted Daisy go and lie down.

Daisy smiled wan thanks at her mother and headed to her bedroom, where she fell on top of her counterpane, suddenly too exhausted to even unlace her boots or remove her hat and shawl.

She slept for fourteen hours straight in the deepest slumber during which she hardly moved.

Cynthia tried to wake her for supper, but when Daisy, ordinarily a light sleeper, didn't stir, she let her be. Gently, Cynthia unlaced Daisy's boots and took them off, and then she removed her hat, which was very crumpled by now. The last thing Cynthia did was fetch the patchwork quilt from her and Jared's bed and carefully lay it over her daughter, and then, quiet as a mouse, she tiptoed from the room.

The next day Daisy felt a little recovered, although her patience was tested when several older male customers complained when their wives sent them to pick up some bread, seemingly in a collective bad mood as the beer in the local public houses was starting to be watered down and – worse! – pubs were having to shut at the ridiculously early time of ten o'clock. Indeed, they hoped Violet's loaves wouldn't be affected in any similar way, they said, even though poor quality seemed to be a trend that was catching on amongst Crumford business people, and so it was likely it would happen in Violet's bakery and Daisy's establishment.

'Sssh!' whispered a horrified Daisy, a finger to her lips when one elderly gent was being particularly vociferous on the topic. 'Don't let Violet hear you say anything about her loaves. She's such a stickler for her baking and she is only next door, you know. She'd be very hurt. I know Father and Mother wouldn't allow any of our own produce to be other than the very best quality. This is the way that damaging rumours start, and that's really not fair on Violet. Or myself, come to that.'

The old man peered crossly at Daisy after she'd finished her uncharacteristic outburst.

'You can climb down off your high horse right now, young lady,' he said chippily, his nose clearly out of joint, 'there's no need for a flibbertigibbet like you to go all hoity-toity. The younger generation has no respect these days for their elders and betters . . .'

Holly was standing beside Daisy at the time, and as Holly touched Daisy on the back in support, she interrupted in a much more abrasive tone than Daisy had used, 'Come off it, sir! You know how honest our father is, and it's no wonder Daisy is cross. As for myself, I certainly don't think you'll have been drinking Crumford Ale, as Basil Brewer wouldn't allow watering down; any Crumford publicans found diluting Crumford Ale beer would be for the high jump, I'm sure.'

The man looked incredulously at Holly.

'In that case, do feel you can take your business elsewhere,' said Holly spikily. 'These are difficult times, and we don't want your sort in here spreading rumour and discontent. It's you who should be ashamed, when we should all be pulling together.'

The man snatched up his loaf and hurried out of the tea room. Daisy felt herself wilt.

She sighed with frustration and it was all she could do not to stamp her foot in temper, because as the man let the door slam behind him, she realised he'd left without paying, although she had no inclination to run after him.

'He didn't pay, did he?' said Holly.

'No.'

'Charlatan!'

Holly's voice in manner and timbre sounded so like Cynthia's that Daisy was convinced that if she had had her eyes closed, she would have thought it was their mother coming to her defence.

Then, the sisters caught each other's eye in a way that made them both laugh out loud despite still feeling cross, and several of their customers applauded them or raised their teacups in salute.

Chapter Eleven

One morning, a day or two later, Daisy was just shutting the five-barred gate from the mill to the road after she had manhandled Asa and Joy's baby Rose through it in a perambulator that was a hand-me-down from when Tansy and Senna were tiny.

Daisy was looking after Rose for an hour or two in order that Joy, who herself looked very peaky and washed out these days, could catch up on some much-needed sleep. It was the first time Daisy had been in charge of Rose, or in fact any baby, on her own.

Until early the previous year the Grahams hadn't had a gate positioned at the property's junction with the road. This had altered after the calm of a spring day had been rudely shattered when out of the blue a frolicking herd of cattle came onto the mill property. The cattle had been made heady with escaping from their nearby field, feeling the wind under their tails, and they bucked and jumped in elation at their freedom, their split hooves slapping pell-mell upon the cindery flints of the hard standing and their huge udders with gigantic teats swaying dangerously from side to side.

The cows lolloped as one onto the mill property, happily kicking their way through Cynthia's lovingly planted vegetables and fruits that were just showing the first signs of growth after the winter, and then they made merry with two bulging sacks of grain they found, which Jared had propped outside of the mill wall so as to be on hand for the next milling. In no time at all the cattle had had great fun pulling the sacks apart so that they could gorge on what was inside.

It had been comical at first to watch them, and to hear Cynthia telling the bovine rascals off to no avail.

But the humour didn't last as Clem had taken a nasty kick to the thigh from one of the cows when he had tried to shoo them back to their field. It had left a bruise that made him limp for over a week, and the doctor said he'd been within a gnat's breath of having had a broken femur. And then the farmer's sheepdog had barked aggressively at Tansy and Senna and scared the girls when the farmer arrived with a sour look on his face and a big stick to drive his beasts back to where they belonged.

To stop a repeat of such events, especially as the farmer had been reluctant to pay for the two sacks of grain, even though the whole calamity was his fault, Jared had installed a sturdy gate with a huge metal spring latch that could be opened from horseback or by leaning over from a cart, although care had to be taken not to get reins or stirrups caught on the latch when passing through.

On the gate there was displayed proudly a huge painted sign that said 'Shut the Gate' in large black letters on a white background, its blunt instruction softened by the pictures of cows that Tansy and Senna, only five at the time, had been allowed to daub in blue and purple beneath the words, the cows' happy expressions and tombstone teeth making Daisy grin every time she noticed them.

Rose remained blissfully asleep as Daisy manoeuvred her over the rutty dried mud and through the gate, and she didn't stir when the latch sprang back into place with its distinct metallic clang once the gate shut.

Daisy was going to push Rose over to the general stores in Crumford as the Grahams were running low on tooth powder and coal-tar soap – Cynthia's firm instructions ringing in Daisy's ears to 'make sure you get Wrights; the other soaps just aren't worth it', a request that had been quickly followed by a 'and make sure you pick up some fresh cream for Joy to have on her morning porridge'. Cynthia always swore this thick cream, maybe even made from the milk of the very cows that had gambolled so joyously around Old Creaky that day, would be a good pick-me-up while Joy was breast-feeding. Then Cynthia added that if Daisy could find some Mackeson Milk Stout too (which came from nearby Hythe), then so much the better as this would be good for the new mother's milk production.

Daisy had had to set off quickly so that the shopping list didn't get any longer.

She double-checked the gate was firmly closed now she and Rose were in the road and was about to turn towards the pram once more when there was the tinkle of a metal bicycle bell.

She stopped rearranging Rose's crocheted blanket that previously she'd not had time to tuck in securely, and straightened up to see Big Tom coming her way on his tricycle.

A tiny man – his nickname was a joke that he'd had to put up with since he was a lad – Big Tom had retired years ago from his job of postman, but the war meant he had been persuaded back into work, even though he was a bit doddery these days, and looked smaller and frailer than ever.

Big Tom braked squeakily as he back-pedalled his contraption to a standstill so that he could pass Daisy an envelope from a canvas satchel that was slung over a bony shoulder, with a 'How do, miss' before he wobbled away on his trike.

When she saw her own name on the envelope in a copy-book-standard cursive script she didn't recognise, Daisy's heart gave a flip. She hardly ever got any post.

And her heart went a second time when she looked at the back of the envelope to discover that Ren had finally written back to her.

As Rose snoozed on and certainly didn't appear as if a delay to their walk would make her peevish, Daisy immediately ripped the envelope open and quickly scanned what Ren had to say.

To her delight he proved to be rather a decent correspondent, certainly streets ahead of her brothers, and Daisy admired his practised, even hand – his copperplate penmanship putting hers to shame.

But what she liked especially was how his words seemed to flow off the page, making it very easy for her imagine that he was actually speaking them out loud to her.

My dearest Daisy

Thank you for your letter, which I very much enjoyed reading.

It was so good to receive one from Crumford that did not want to talk about the price of beer, as yours avoided doing, as it did too the question of how many barrels of ale Crumford Brewery has in the storehouse, and how lazy the current batch of hop-picker casuals have been this past month, and, extraordinarily, you also managed to avoid mentioning anything to do with tax and war coffers. That cannot have been easy at all to judge by how my other post is reading these days, and so hats off to you! And there was no wondering either about how one of Father's draught horses is lame with a nasty abscess that needs daily poulticing, nor how another of the horses has somehow got herself in foal! Well, I suppose that we can all guess <u>how</u> the mare got in foal — but the comedy lies in the fact that Father does not have a stallion at the brewery, and so I guess the mystery of who the stud is will only be solved once the foal is born, and only then if it takes after its father.

I am sorry not to have written back to you sooner, as I do feel very bad about it, especially when you were so kind to think of me in the first place. The truth of it is I have been homesick, much more than I expected, and so I tried not to dwell too much on everyone at home in Crumford, and when I did, I found it difficult to write. I do apologise for being so tardy and hope you understand.

I have spent a lot of time with your brothers and my two brothers though, which has cheered me up no end, even though they are all rascals, and so we have made up a very jolly gang of five, and I can't pretend that we have not laughed a lot, often over the most silly of things. We have even taken bets on which local stallion is the father of the foal! If it turns out to be that noisy donkey over at the Convent, which is Clem's bet, then Father will be so put out, albeit more on the mare's behalf than his own, I fear. If that does indeed turn out to be the case, I won't be able to resist yelling 'Heehaw!' as loud as I can at him – I mean at your Clem, and not Father. If I were to try shouting it at Father I think I would only be able to get the 'Hee' out, before he came down on the 'Haw' like a ton of bricks.

That was an excellent idea of yours about me and Alder and Rosen having our photographs taken, by the way. Father was very pleased with his photographs, so much so that I told Clem that he and Asa must have theirs taken too as I'm sure Mr and Mrs Graham would appreciate the gesture, and Clem agreed. I made sure to go along and supervise, so it actually did happen. I thought they both looked very handsome when they had their pictures taken, and so I wonder if you have seen the photographs yet?

To be honest I am not sure if Alder and Rosen will send their pictures to your sisters. I told them they should, but they said neither Violet nor Holly had written to them, and they feel too embarrassed to make the first move in this respect, especially as they have now been gone such a long time and I suppose they feel the moment has passed. I can tell you however that they are not writing to any other young ladies and don't seem to have any intention of doing so, and therefore if Violet and Holly did feel able to correspond, I think the response would be positive from both my brothers.

Meanwhile, I enclose a photograph of me; thank you for sending the one of you – yours is small enough for my wallet and I do treasure it as it is such a reminder of the last day when all of us could be happy and without a care in the world. That makes it feel special. You look very fine indeed in the picture.

Of course I would appreciate it if you cared to write back to me. I can't promise to be a very regular or a particularly quick responder, but do please know I will be thinking of you all the same.

We are not supposed to tell those at home where we are exactly or what our experiences have been. I guess you know this, but I mention it in case not – it is so hard to suppose what people at home know and what they have no idea about.

Suffice to say that that pleasant summer afternoon at the party at your mill seems in complete contrast to all that has happened since. I very much enjoyed our walk close to sunset, and I hope you have fond memories of it too.

And I have a good memory as well of seeing you and everyone else wave us off from the train station, with the Union Jacks waving in the breeze and the band playing. It was a special moment, was not it?

Thank you again for writing, and I remain your obedient servant.

Yours truly, Ren Brewer Esq.

Her heart gave a little double-thump now that she could see it in blue ink – Ren did indeed want her to write to him.

He must think there was something between them, surely?

Then Daisy studied carefully the photograph Ren had included in the envelope.

It was small, being at the most about three inches by two. The image showed Ren's body angled towards the photographer with an elbow on one thigh and a hand on his other, as he sat stiffly and rather awkwardly on a wooden crate in front of a painted backdrop of what appeared to be a bucolic scene in the tradition of an old master. There was a prop of an ancient wooden plough in the corner of the picture behind him for no reason that Daisy could fathom.

It had clearly been taken in a photographic studio, or else the photographer had come to the depot where the lads were billeted with camera and backdrop and props. There was probably good business to be had with troops who wanted to send photographs home to loved ones.

Daisy wasn't at all sure about the photograph of Ren, if she were honest. It looked posed and old-fashioned, and completely lacking in vigour.

Ren appeared handsome enough, she supposed, but also as if he were rather a dull man, the sort who would love a hobby such as stamp collecting, and who would be overly fond of routines and would always love clotted cream before jam on scones, and never think to try it the other way around, not even once. The sepia tones of the picture made Ren's puttees look too obvious and as if his lower legs were in better focus than the rest of him, whilst what seemed to be a blank expression on his face because the image had become so light-sodden during the exposure of the plates that Ren's face seemed washed out, didn't make him look particularly recognisable either.

In fact, Daisy wasn't certain she would have said it *was* Ren, should there not have been inked 'Ren Brewer, 1914, age 21' on the reverse of the image.

There was nothing in what she saw in the photograph, try as Daisy did to see otherwise, that suggested Ren's friendly personality or how lively he was, no sense of him either being continually in movement, or that he had just smiled or was about to, all of which were the attributes that Daisy thought stood out most about Ren Brewer.

Somehow the photograph and her memory of him just didn't seem to match, a feeling added to as she knew he was really twenty-two years old, and not twenty-one, although Daisy supposed the age would be easy for the photographer to get wrong if he was photographing a lot of young men on the same day.

However, the photograph Daisy had sent to Ren of herself hadn't been particularly wonderful either – Ren had been exaggerating massively in his assertion she looked 'very fine indeed'.

A pre-war Daisy might have tried to convince herself the adage 'love is blind' was true in regard to Ren's comment, but now she was realistic and concluded he was just being polite.

Anyway, staring at the photograph he'd included in the letter, Daisy wondered if perhaps what she was looking at was pretty much par for the course in its shoddiness of a professional photographer taking pictures of young soldiers. She didn't have anything to compare it with as Asa and Clem's photographs were yet to arrive at Old Creaky.

Still, the picture that she had sent to Ren had the advantage that its image was unmistakeably that of Daisy, albeit a much more harum-scarum version of herself than how she liked to think she presented herself to the world.

There was a reason for this.

Every Yuletide Cynthia had a local photographer come out to the mill several days before Christmas to take pictures of the whole family, which were then lovingly added to the family photograph album that was Cynthia's pride and joy, and then everyone would laugh at these annual photographs and how they had or hadn't changed as time had passed.

But the Christmas of 1913, the photographer was already quite sozzled by the time he arrived at the mill house, as his previous client had been unnecessarily generous with the porter.

And when Jared wouldn't be dissuaded from giving him a large tot of rum for festive cheer, despite all of Cynthia's vociferous advice to the contrary, the quality of the subsequent portraits had taken a distinct downturn. Jared had had to take quite an earful from his wife once the photographs were ready for collection.

Daisy's photograph was the worst, although Cynthia's had run hers close. Daisy had been the last one to pose, and by that point there was definitely a lack of focus to the image itself, as well as a rather cross look about her eyes as she had grown impatient with the fiasco of the situation, an impression mirrored by her hair looking quite a bit more untamed than it had when she had brushed and pinned it up upon the photographer's arrival.

The photographer who visited Old Creaky when three sheets to the wind that December day had volunteered at the same time as Asa and Clem, and Daisy had seen him clamber onto the same train that day at the station.

She wondered if the war really would be over by Christmas, as some people still claimed (Daisy herself increasingly dubious of this fact), and whether the photographer would be back with them in a couple of months eager to take this year's photographs for Cynthia's album. If so, they'd better make sure the kettle was on for a pot of tea, and that they had hidden the rum from Jared, just in case he had forgotten the previous year's fiasco.

Rose gave a snuffle, and with a small start as she had completely forgotten about being in charge of the baby, Daisy remembered what she was supposed to be doing, which was taking Rose for a walk in the autumn sunshine.

She slipped the photograph and letter back into their envelope, and stuffed the envelope deep down into her reticule. And then she began to push the pram in the direction of the shops in Crumford, the springs to the wheels giving Rose quite a bouncy ride on the unmade road.

Daisy purchased the items Cynthia had requested, and stacked them in the pram at the end nearest its push-handle as Rose's little toes were nowhere close yet to reaching down to that bit of the pram.

But then instead of turning towards home, and even though she knew Holly had asked her to make sure she was back as soon as possible to relieve her in the tea room, Daisy dawdled around the pretty streets of red-brick houses, many of which were centuries old.

Crumford looked enviably picturesque as what might be one of the last blasts of golden autumn sunshine that year was bringing out all the lovely russet tones of the deep-red brickwork of the shops and houses she passed.

As she strolled along, Daisy thought how rarely she allowed herself to really look and appreciate living right next to such a pretty town.

As she listened to the soothing sound of the turn of the pram's wheels, Daisy found Rose's presence oddly companionable too, and she realised that she was enjoying herself, and that this was the first time she had actively felt content since the night she and Ren had kissed.

She looked down at Rose's face, and decided that at the moment the baby girl didn't really take after either of her parents, with none of Asa's wild eyebrows or Joy's steely jawline.

Rose was perfect though, with the sweetest small hands, a rosebud mouth and long eyelashes fluttering upon her cheeks as she slept.

Up until this point Daisy hadn't really paid Rose much attention since she had been born. There'd been other things to think about, and Daisy had told herself that she didn't seem to respond to babies with quite the same cooing eagerness that Violet and Holly did. Should Joy give either of them the slightest come on, they were always ready to dandle Rose on their laps and play peekaboo, even though Rose was far too young to give any sort of response.

Her own lack of likewise inclination had made Daisy suspect she wasn't really cut out for motherhood, and this had made her wonder now whether this meant she might not really be cut out for marriage either. She didn't feel horrified by these thoughts, she discovered, at least in the way she might have been on the day of the twins' birthday party.

She supposed it was because Olive leaving to train as a nurse seemed to have driven it home that not all women need these days be content to marry and have children.

In fact, she was somewhat surprised now by her assumption of just a few months back that a marriage and a family were necessary for all young ladies. Instead, to have one's own offspring seemed these days to Daisy to be a huge additional responsibility that one was wise to be very wary of, especially having seen the dark shadows under Joy's eyes when she'd collected Rose earlier.

As she walked, Daisy realised it was nice to play hooky from her usual routine for just a while.

Daisy was pushing the pram along a twisty narrow street, when the light was such that she caught sight of herself in a shop window, her reflection thrown into sharp relief by the angle of the sunshine and the shadows falling across the street. It was as if she were staring right into a gloriously huge mirror.

Daisy couldn't pull her eyes away from the image of herself with the pram, growing larger in her sightline step by step, even though she told herself off for being so vain.

She had always prided herself on not being conceited in the slightest about her looks, although when she had once mentioned this to Violet, her sister quite literally howled with laughter as she declared Daisy must be suffering from delusions as she was one of the vainest people Violet knew.

But there wasn't a full-length mirror at the mill house, and so this was a rare opportunity for Daisy to see what she looked like from head to toe.

She was more impressed than she should be, she knew, thinking her figure not bad at all, while her clothes, admittedly not quite London fashionable, were certainly fashionable in terms of Crumford.

And she rather liked the sight of herself becoming larger as she got closer to the glass of the window as there was something jaunty about the way she walked, and she smiled, enjoying the way in which window-Daisy smiled right back.

Then Daisy's attention was caught by the shop itself. It was one she didn't recognise or, more exactly, it looked as if it were undergoing a refurbishment, although for the life of her Daisy couldn't recall what had been sold previously on the premises, even though this was a street she knew well.

Suddenly Daisy moved into a patch of shade that meant she could see right into the window beyond her reflection.

And there quite high up a stepladder was an unkempt-looking man in his shirtsleeves, with his cuffs rolled up to reveal hairy forearms. He was looking right at her with the sort of scrutiny that told Daisy she had been well and truly caught out in the act of admiring herself.

How extremely awkward.

The man held her eye further, not paying any attention to either the paintbrush or the small pot of paint that he was holding. Daisy didn't recognise him, and felt sure she had never seen him before.

There was no hint of a smile or welcome. Indeed, Daisy fancied he was frowning at her, perhaps even admonishing her for her vanity.

To moor herself, as she felt oddly at sea under the scrutiny of such an unflinching gaze, Daisy glanced up towards the signage above the shop window as if knowing what the shop was for would be a comfort, but it was blank, being obviously newly painted over and now awaiting the lettering to advertise whatever it was that the shop would be selling.

Daisy nodded at the man in acknowledgement of them having caught each other's eye as she wasn't sure what else to do. But he didn't respond or do anything other than very slightly tilt his head to one side as he stared back at her.

And then abruptly he turned his back on Daisy, as he dipped his paintbrush back into the pot of paint he had in his other hand, and continued with what he had been doing, which was painting in a neutral colour the backdrop of what presumably would become the window display.

For a second Daisy felt as if the sun had suddenly gone behind a cloud.

Uncomfortable as the man's look had been, it had felt a very powerful spotlight of the sort Daisy had never experienced before.

In fact, if she'd been asked to describe what she was feeling, she'd have said it was like a bolt of lightning had hit the ground right beside her, close enough to make her stir, but not a direct hit.

For an instant Daisy wanted to tap on the window to get the man's attention again, but then she told herself not to be so stupid as what on earth could she say to him that wouldn't show her in a worse light than she already had?

Trying not to think about his quite long dark hair or the red neckerchief loosely tied around his neck, inside the open collar of his shirt, the neckerchief's two pointed ends suggesting they were indicating the path towards something male and forbidden below, Daisy slunk away.

Feeling thwarted by his complete lack of friendliness but oddly excited at the same time, she risked a glance back at the window to check if he was still turned from her, but the windowpane was now showing her reflection again and not the man behind the glass.

Rose let out a bleating sound.

'Quite right, poppet,' Daisy said in the tone that adults often use when talking to very small children, 'we don't need rude men like that in Crumford, do we, you clever girl, Rosie?'

Rose stared up at her aunt with her lower lip protruding.

Daisy pulled a silly face and Rose responded with a hiccough that even the inexperienced Daisy could work out meant that Rose was peckish now and that the staring man was of no consequence. Rose's unwavering blue eyes told Daisy she had better look to her laurels and get them home as soon as possible, as while Rose didn't want to cry and make a fuss, she would do so soon if her lunch wasn't imminent.

Daisy marched them back to Old Creaky as quickly as she could, her long strides gradually calming the rising feelings within her.

∽

That evening, Daisy wrote to Ren as she sat up in bed before turning her lamp off, and she found it a soothing way of passing a few minutes.

Dear Ren

Only a short letter from me today. But I wanted to say thank you for <u>your</u> letter, and the photograph – both are very nice to have and arrived safely this morning.

Holly is helping with the books at the brewery. I am going to ask her to keep me informed once that mare foals – the hussy!

Meanwhile not much news here, other than William Evans has died in action, which you may already know about. I think that even if you can't recall him from when we were all younger, you might remember him from the night of the party. It was William who led the singing of the shanties. I have felt sad since I read the news of his loss.

Please take care of yourself, and make sure that my daft brothers look after themselves too, and your brothers also. We need you all to come back to us safe and sound.

One thing I wanted to ask you is if there is anything you need? In the church hall, local women are gathering to knit scarves and socks, and while I expect these will be welcome, I'm not going to volunteer for this as nobody is going to want anything that I knit! I am simply dreadful at any practical skills like this, and Mother has even advised me against volunteering to sew sandbags (apparently lots are needed in the defence of the Kent coast; there's a huge operation going on in the grounds of Canterbury Cathedral, so I hear).

But if you need anything like notepaper or envelopes, or laces, or books, or anything else at all, do please know that I would do my very best to get them for you. And the same goes for my brothers or your brothers — we all want, us left at home, to look after you all as best we can.

Very kind regards, Daisy Graham

P.S. If you could give Asa and Clem a nudge to send us their photographs, then we could actually see them. I checked with both Joy and Marguerite and neither have had them, and nor has Mother. Mother is not best pleased!

In comparison with the man from earlier, the Ren she conjured up as she thought what to say to him seemed a solid and reassuring presence in Daisy's mind, one that felt sensible and safe, a haven in a storm.

The next day, Daisy took her letter into the tea room, where she propped it behind the wooden box into which she placed her takings after each customer had paid.

She intended to ask one of her more reliable customers to post it for her in Crumford, as it was a busy day for her as she was more or less on her own.

This was because, aside from Jared being hard at work in the mill with Cynthia at his side, Violet and Holly had left for a day in Canterbury. Daisy just had to take Violet's loaves out of the oven to cool on wire racks once they were ready.

They had left quite early in Basil Brewer's shiny green car, Holly because she needed some boots and gloves, and Violet because she wanted to visit the very splendid cathedral for some quiet contemplation.

A little later, Daisy was getting the orders ready for the loaves of bread that Marguerite delivered daily to the elderly residents in Crumford.

Although it would change once her baby was born, Marguerite was, at the moment, despite her pregnancy tummy having popped out, happy to ride Clem's delivery bicycle with its two large panniers, dropping off the loaves as he had done in recent years.

Daisy thought a lot of pregnant wives would be reluctant to ride the bike in her condition. It was ancient, heavy and hard to steer, and had totally inadequate brakes no matter what Jared did to them to try to make them better. But every time Daisy told Marguerite she shouldn't feel she had to make the deliveries, Marguerite always replied that she was happy to do her bit in this way as it made her feel close to Clem when she was pedalling away.

Daisy was just finishing her list of who was having what on Marguerite's round, after double-checking that the various loaves were correct in the panniers, when she looked up at the sound of heavy, uneven footsteps she didn't recognise. Daisy prided herself on knowing the sound of most of her customers as they walked, but these footsteps stumped her.

When she glanced up, Daisy's mouth almost fell open in surprise.

For before her were not one but two men, both looking exactly like the surly man she had seen the day before in the shop window in Crumford.

They glowered at her, and then noisily pulled out two chairs and sat down, promptly placing their elbows on the table, which was something Cynthia was insistent that no Graham ever did, seeing as it was 'common'.

These men didn't look as if they gave two hoots about what was common, and what wasn't.

Daisy suddenly found herself feeling clumsy and hot.

To give herself a chance to compose herself she spent a little longer than she ordinarily would have checking the list, which she then gave to Marguerite so she could get on her way.

Marguerite meanwhile was signalling to Daisy that these two men were new to the area, and were mighty fine, to judge by her lifted eyebrows.

'Watch it,' whispered Daisy, 'else I'll tell Clem on you.'

Marguerite rubbed the mound of her pregnant belly in a rather significant way.

'Outrageous!' said Daisy, making sure she didn't laugh at her sister-in-law's cheekiness.

'You bet,' said Marguerite.

And then Daisy made sure she spent some more time adjusting the hot plate beneath her kettle to get it ready for a pot of tea for these two new customers, should they want it, before she went over to the table the men were sitting at.

'Good morning,' she said to them, her heart still beating fast. 'And what may I get you?'

Chapter Twelve

Afterwards, Daisy wondered what she'd got herself into a tizzy over.

The two men, twins obviously, were perfectly well behaved, a little elbow impoliteness aside.

They had asked for tea and a slice of buttered toast each of which they consumed quietly, and they had left a decent tip and had also bought a large white loaf, some tea cakes and a jar of Cynthia's jam to take away with them. They'd known when to say please and thank you, and they left the tea room without letting the door slam. All in all, they were perfect customers.

Daisy had no idea which twin she had seen in the shop window staring at her so bluntly, and so she didn't say anything about that, and neither did they.

Maybe whichever one it was hadn't recognised her.

This would be unusual in Daisy's experience although not *totally* inconceivable.

She did think at first that they stared at her very intently. But then so did a lot of other people when they first met Daisy, often saying to her later it was her energetic way of doing things that had caught their eye, or how her hair was an unusual shade of brown and her eyes almost violet in a certain light.

And actually after a while she came to think the twins might not have been looking at her in an intense way, after all. It perhaps was something about how their faces were put together that gave the impression that they were looking hard at whatever their eyes were turned towards.

She pondered why it might be that neither had gone to fight, but when she looked at their faces, she noticed quite deep wrinkles etched around their eyes.

These folds in the skin weren't so deep as Basil Brewer's or Jared's, but definitely more obvious than those of men around Daisy's own age or a few years older, even for those that worked outside all day long, when they would be grimacing against bright sunlight, or heavy wind or rain.

She thought that perhaps these twins might feel themselves too old to volunteer.

They were a striking pair though, and once they had gone Daisy found herself thinking about them for longer than she felt they merited.

∞

Violet was much better at keeping in touch with old school friends than Daisy, and she had volunteered for the scarf- and sock-knitting session over at the church hall that evening. Daisy decided to ask Violet to find out quietly who the men were.

'Only if you come with me,' said Violet.

'I can't do that! They'll try and rope me in,' Daisy said.

'Exactly!'

Daisy tried silence as a way to stop this discussion, but Violet was on to her, joking, 'Don't you dare for a moment think that you not saying anything means that you're not coming with me, Daisy. It's not happening without you there!'

Actually, even though Daisy thought in principle that she would hate sitting with the Crumford women-folk, she found she really enjoyed it. After, as she had told Ren would happen, her test pieces of stitching and knitting were received with hoots of merriment by the committee, and subsequently rejected for reasons of 'quality control', Daisy was put to packaging things up, and making some posters asking for donated wool.

The ladies were so welcoming to her and nice about rejecting her pitiful attempts at sewing and knitting that Daisy found herself warming to them and subsequently the whole group, and she could see completely see why Violet enjoyed spending evenings with these women.

There was something heart-warming about the com-panionability and the sense that they were all there for a worthwhile reason: making the British men abroad more comfortable.

And who could argue with that?

Nobody, Daisy decided, and then felt churlish for her previous reluctance to get involved.

Worming out the information that Daisy wanted to know about the twin brothers didn't take Violet long.

In fact, Daisy found herself impressed with her sister's interrogation skills, cloaked as they were in her seeming as if she were merely chatting about this and that at the same time as she steered the conversation, slipping in her pertinent questions most unobtrusively.

'Oh, you mean the triplets who have moved into old Mrs Cant's haberdashery in Market Street?' a nicely dressed woman said to Violet.

'*Triplets!*' interrupted Daisy, with her voice screechy and no mind given to the fact that she had clearly been eavesdropping. As, oh my, that was unexpected and downright exciting news to hear.

It was as if the room had been lit up. Voices rose, and in the blink of an eye everybody seemed to have an opinion on these new Crumford residents, sometimes distinctly on the bawdy side.

'Ladies, ladies, do keep it down,' called the vicar's wife, 'remember to be nice.'

Nobody really took any notice.

And so a further much merrier hour was passed in this congenial way.

⁓

Once the sisters were home and had made cocoa for themselves and Cynthia, who hadn't yet gone to bed,

162

they were still excited, to judge by the firm shush that their mother gave them for being too noisy as they sat down with her in the parlour.

'Sorry, Mother,' said Violet, even though she hadn't been the one making the noise.

'Yes, yes,' said Daisy, ignoring her mother and quite unable to keep the impatience from her voice. 'Go on, Violet, tell Mother what we've found out from Mrs Lang.' Mrs Lang was the well-dressed woman Daisy had noticed earlier.

'Well,' said Violet, 'according to Mrs Lang at the coal higglers, the haberdashery has gone to share premises with the ironmonger, and the old haberdasher's shop has been rented to three brothers. Triplets! One is an artist, one a photographer, and the other is crippled and has to sit down a lot. The artist and the photographer are both working officially for the War Office, or was it the newspapers – sorry, I can't remember, but it is something important anyway. And the one with the gammy legs is going to take studio photographic portraits once the shop has been properly converted.'

'Their poor mother, having triplets. One has got to feel for her,' said Cynthia, wincing at the thought of the logistics of three newborns at the same time. She'd found Senna and Tansy difficult enough, and they were just twins. 'Imagine what changing those babies must have been like, and the feeding, and the putting them down for naps. How on earth did she cope with feeding if all three were crying, or getting them to sleep when just one is restless, or at bath—'

'Mother, please!' hissed Daisy, firmly enough to stop Cynthia's train of thought.

And then before Cynthia could reprimand her again for risking waking up the twins, Daisy dropped her voice to say to Violet, 'I didn't hear whether any of them was married, did you? I'm just curious, you see.'

'Curious? Downright nosy, I'd say. Can't think why you'd be interested,' teased Violet, adding after she had made Daisy wait, 'According to the fount of all triplet knowledge, Mrs Lang, there's not been any sign of that, although apparently there's been lots of interest locally about them. What she can say is that they're not regulars at any of the public houses, and they seem to keep themselves to themselves. Mrs Lang thinks they're used to living together and taking care of themselves, as she stopped one of them in the street and offered to find them someone to come in and do a bit of cleaning, and she was quite put out when he said no, they didn't need it.'

'Sounds like Mrs Lang has set up camp outside their home!' laughed Daisy.

And a heartbeat later, Cynthia added, 'Of course Betty Lang is the sort of woman prone to imagining that she knows better than anybody how somebody else should be doing things, so she wouldn't like that. I expect she was trying to get inside their lodgings for a bit of a snoop. Are these men identical?'

'The two I have seen are, and so I suppose the third is too,' said Daisy. 'I wonder why the third one is so poorly. Did Mrs Lang have a view on that?'

'No, she didn't, but she is very keen to find out,' said Violet, 'although possibly she's even keener to find out their names. And now I'm off to bed as I am tired, and I have to be up at four thirty which is—' she glanced at the clock '—less than six hours from now.'

'Before you go, I might write to Ren again tomorrow, Vi, to tell him about the triplets as their arrival might make him laugh. If I do, shall I say that you will be contacting Alder, as I mentioned already to you?' said Daisy.

'Yes, of course she'll write to Alder,' said Cynthia very quickly, before Violet had a chance to reply. 'And you can say too, Daisy, that Holly will be writing to Rosen.'

Violet looked from her sister to her mother, and rolled her eyes dramatically as she said, 'Lord, give me strength.' She looked at them in mock fierceness, and added after she'd rolled her eyes a second time, 'And that one's on behalf of Holly. I don't think either of us will be writing those letters.'

To judge by Holly's recent glow, Daisy knew she wouldn't be suggesting that Holly would write to Rosen. Such a thing seemed a long way from Holly's agenda at the moment, her sister couldn't help thinking. It was glaringly obvious too that Violet wasn't going to be writing to Alder either, in spite of their mother's entreaties.

Daisy didn't feel Alder or Rosen would be at all upset, to judge by what Ren had told her.

And after Violet had closed the door behind her on her way to bed, Cynthia dug Daisy rather hard in the ribs with her elbow, wondering at Daisy's obvious interest in these new arrivals in Crumford.

The World Turns

Chapter Thirteen

Daisy had a shock the next morning as she picked her way across the first frosty grass of the autumn to the tea room. For when she went to unlock the door at just gone seven, it was to find Violet and one of the Crumford triplets chatting companionably outside.

He was absolutely the last person Daisy expected to see, and was perched on the armrest to a wooden bench that Daisy had had placed there, looking very much like he belonged, while Violet was smiling broadly as she was talking, wiping her floury hands on her pinny.

'Look who's here, Daisy!' called Violet chirpily. 'I was just putting the last loaves in, and I saw a shadow go past the window, and when I went to see who it was, I found, er—' Violet looked at the man, who gave a little nod as if in encouragement '—um, Mr Grover, who is waiting to see *you*.'

Daisy felt discombobulated. And she certainly didn't totally trust the insistent twinkle in Violet's eye, indicating that Violet was joking with Daisy somehow. But it was very early in the day for joshing, even though Violet was known amongst the Grahams for having an overdeveloped funny bone.

Suspicious, Daisy looked down quickly to make sure that her skirt was hanging tidily. She raised a hand to her hair to make sure it hadn't already sprung from its softly swirled pompadour style – the Gibson Girl she'd spend months perfecting even though her hair was a bit too springy. Although, having had a tussle with it only ten minutes previously, she doubted it would already be escaping its pins.

And she hadn't touched the coal scuttle that morning and so was unlikely to have a dirty face. Everything seemed as Daisy hoped it would be, at least looks-wise, which was a relief.

Violet had to be amused over something else, Daisy reasoned, and possibly therefore Mr Grover had just made her laugh.

'Good morning, Mr Grover,' said Daisy, unable to keep a note of caution from her voice as a quickly flicked glance in her sister's direction showed that Violet still seemed a bit peculiar.

Daisy added, 'What a surprise. How may I help you?'

She was slightly taken aback that he wasn't scowling, as she'd assumed that was how he always appeared.

Instead, he seemed quite cheerful, and this made Daisy curious, although not necessarily in a way she wanted exposed in front of Violet.

Daisy shot Violet a stern look to tell her to get back to her loaves.

Her sister responded with a smile that let Daisy know she had every intention of staying put.

Mr Grover didn't say anything, but instead sprang up and then walked to the side of Daisy and looked at her, and then he repeated the same action on her other side.

What an unexpected and confusing man he was!

He was taller than Daisy remembered, and strong-looking.

A confused Daisy watched him, convinced she had seen a similar expression on farmers at the local market, when saltmarsh lambs were being sized up for the amount of meat on their haunches.

Her own haunches were quite well fleshed, she knew, but Daisy liked to believe that her skirts disguised this.

Violet was still standing nearby, obviously keen to get some gossip so that she could get one up on Mrs Lang at the next ladies knitting session.

'I need to open up the tea room,' said Daisy, determined to outmanoeuvre her sister so that she could hear in private whatever he had to say to her, 'and so you had better come inside for a cup of tea, Mr Grover. I know you've had one recently, Violet, as I saw your cup and saucer out in the kitchen at the mill house and the kettle still had steam coming from its spout.' Daisy's smile in the direction of her sister was sickly sweet.

Violet looked a tad deflated, and Daisy congratulated herself.

Daisy unlocked the door to the tea room, although as she led the way inside, she thought she could feel Mr Grover's eyes studying her rear view.

'All the same, I'll come and get some tea in a little while,' chirruped a not-yet-quite-defeated Violet, her head poked around the open door to the tea room.

Putting aside her feelings of fluster at Mr Grover's gaze, Daisy replied as a final parry,

'Don't worry, Violet, I'll bring you some in.'

She turned to Mr Grover, and said, 'Why don't you sit at the table nearest the wall here? Violet's ovens on the other side of the bricks keep it warm, and it's parky outside.'

'Won't you sit down too?' he asked.

There was a gravelly timbre to his voice, as if he'd smoked a lot of tobacco.

It must have been his brother who'd done the talking on their previous visit to the tea room as she hadn't noticed anything unusual about his voice that day.

It was very different to the way Ren talked; the way he spoke was softer, with something of a Kentish burr to it.

'All right, but only for five minutes as otherwise it will put me out for the whole day,' Daisy said. 'Let's not beat around the bush – what is it you want to speak to me about?'

'I am Silas Grover, and although I am now working as an official photographer for the Ministry of War . . .'

Daisy didn't hear the next bit of what he was saying as she found herself distracted by wondering what he was photographing locally. A job like this sounded exotic almost, definitely something rare in her experience. And for her to be in such close proximity to someone who seemed to promise excitement made Daisy realise anew how narrow her life had been to date.

But then Mr Grover was a man, of course, Daisy reminded herself, and so there were more opportunities for what he could do.

Her thoughts broadened. With Kent and Sussex having what could well be the bulk of Britain's troops and supplies setting sail from their shores for France and Flanders, there must be a good chance Mr Grover was photographing what was happening in this respect as presumably the government wanted a visual record of what was happening.

She knew better than to ask exactly what his work entailed, of course, although Daisy couldn't help speculating whether Silas – she had always liked the name since reading *Silas Marner* – was itching to get to Europe to be more actively involved in cataloguing what was going on there on the front line.

'. . . And so I hope you might forgive my impertinence, as I wonder whether that might that be something you would be interested in?' Silas asked. 'You would be paid of course, Miss Graham.' He was looking at her with unwavering concentration.

Daisy had no idea what she was being asked about.

This wasn't good, as her lack of attention was going to make her seem an utter ignoramus, and she felt bad for not concentrating on what Silas Grover had been saying to her.

And there was something about the man before her than made her reluctant to seem a silly young girl, although Daisy wasn't sure why.

In spite of the knowledge of what Cynthia would have to say on the matter, as her mother had long been pointing out to Daisy that she should ask people outside of the immediate Graham family to be less informal when addressing her, and that they should call her Miss Graham or, if Daisy knew them quite well, Miss Daisy, Daisy wanted to divert his attention.

So, to buy herself a little time to collect herself, she said, 'Oh, do please call me Daisy. Everybody else does. My mother can be a stickler, and would love for people to use Miss Graham for me, Violet and Holly, until we marry. But I'm happier with Daisy; it's informal but it does the job, I find.'

Goodness. Now she was prattling inconsequentially. What on earth was the matter with her? Daisy gave what she hoped remained an inward grimace.

'And you must call me Silas, otherwise you are going to get very confused with the two other Mr Grovers, especially with us all looking very similar,' Silas replied as if Daisy was indeed saying something sensible.

'What are their names? Tell me about them.'

'Roscoe was the first to be born of the three of us, and he is an artist and will be leaving Kent soon as the War Office have sanctioned him an official war artist; he came with me when we visited your tea room a few days back. Then I was born, and finally Briar is the youngest of us but only by a few minutes, and he is a photographer too, although studio-based. I expect you have heard about Briar and the sticks he uses – he suffers from cerebral palsy and can't walk far, and he doesn't care to stand for long. To be more accurate, the doctors think it happened during birth, but they can't say for certain. It doesn't hold Briar back though, and he is definitely a better photographer than me,' said Silas.

Daisy wasn't sure what to say but she knew her 'Oh' was on the feeble side.

Then she said, 'I wasn't expecting quite as much detail.'

Silas shrugged a trifle self-consciously at her honesty.

Now it felt as if they were talking properly as they sat on either side of the table, and Daisy found it hard to believe that previously she had ever thought he looked grumpy. Certainly he didn't look cantankerous in the slightest at the moment. Silas just had one of those faces that was very expressive, she decided.

His shaggy hair and unbuttoned waistcoat gave him a slightly reckless air that was unusual among the men of Crumford.

Daisy found it distinctly eye-catching.

Silas interrupted Daisy's train of thought by smiling as he said, 'Probably not, but to explain everything properly is a calculated move on my part, as then you'll be able to put right all the customers who talk about us here. And I'm sure that once you have filled in one or two people, the bush telegraph will see to the rest, and you'll save the three of us a lot of bother. I daresay some locals have had their interest piqued by our arrival. We find that us being triplets does arouse a lot of curiosity.'

'In that case,' said Daisy, 'you forgot the three most important things that people will be wondering about, if I'm to sound as if I know what I'm talking about, which are: do you have money? How old are each of you? And are you married?'

Daisy liked the way Silas's eyes had a distinct twinkle in them.

He said, 'Well, I'm thirty-four.'

Daisy waited for him to tell her how old Roscoe and Briar were. And then when he laughed at her, although not in a mean way, she felt incredibly stupid at his teasing, as the thing about triplets was that they would all be the same age.

'Ah!' she replied heavily.

Heavens to Betsy! Silas was going to believe her a total nincompoop.

Silas drew a veil over this, continuing, 'Briar and myself are unmarried, but Roscoe has a wife in London, and they have two children. All three of us have cars and are solvent, if not yet rich. Briar and me jointly own a house in Ashford, but for work reasons it looks as if all three of us will be sharing the premises in Crumford for a while – we don't know when Roscoe will be sent abroad, and then it will be down to Briar and me, and then just Briar. Although of course there's always the possibility that Briar will marry a local lass by the time we get back.' Daisy must have looked a bit shocked at his forwardness, as Silas added, 'I'm joking! Although, for the rumour mill, Briar is keener than me to find a wife, but this is another area he's better in than me. I've always followed my work, rather than my work following me, and work for me comes before anything else. And so Briar is used to fending for himself, and dealing with advances from the ladies.'

Silas spoke naturally, as if Briar was obviously husband material, and Daisy felt herself pinken as if caught out.

She had never had contact with anyone young who walked with sticks before, and she realised by her surprise at Silas's words that she had had an unformed assumption that a disability from birth would naturally preclude such a sufferer from both a career and a married life.

But Silas's attitude did not comply with either of these two notions in the slightest, Daisy could tell, even in such a few words spoken on the matter.

She felt thoroughly ashamed; what a dreadful conjecture for her to make. Clearly, there was no reason that obvious weakness in moving about should prevent anyone being thought of as husband material or impaired in a way that they couldn't do a good job in their chosen profession.

Just when she was feeling more grown up generally, life always seemed to have a knack of showing how very little one knew, Daisy thought.

To date, her existence at Old Creaky had been restricted and sheltered, but there was clearly a whole big world away from what she knew that was simply bursting with different attitudes and opinions.

It wasn't that Cynthia and Jared had done anything wrong in how they had brought up their children – indeed they were excellent parents – but more that there was a prevailing conservative attitude to all things in Crumford, something Daisy had been oblivious to until fairly recently. Olive and Holly had seemed to intuit this before her, Daisy felt, and she didn't like it that this hinted that her own attitudes had been previously stuck-in-the-mud, old-fashioned ones.

Silas was watching her intently, and although Daisy didn't feel brave enough to admit to everything that she had just been thinking, she thought she'd better fess up at this point to her inattention earlier.

'Silas,' she began and his expression changed to one that made her spring up with her chair squeaking in complaint as she hurriedly pushed it back to head for her kettle, even though it hadn't yet come to the boil and wasn't yet quite hot enough for tea.

But she needed something to do, as that look he'd given her rattled Daisy, and so she reached for a teapot and clattered some cups and saucers about.

'Silas,' Daisy began again, 'you and Briar might need to get the local young ladies in an orderly queue when it becomes known that you both are unattached. That aside, I have a confession to make. I was thinking of something else as you were speaking just now, and so I have absolutely no idea what you were asking me.'

Silas frowned in puzzlement.

'You know, that thing I might get paid for,' Daisy had to prompt. 'I don't know what it is.'

The noise that Silas made was best described as a snort. If anyone else had made that noise Daisy wouldn't have been impressed, but in the case of Silas she didn't feel that way.

'Oh dear,' he said, 'this is my fault for arriving so early and then springing it on you before you'd had time to collect your thoughts for the day. But I have to be in

179

Canterbury at half past eight, and so I took a gamble on coming to you first.'

'I wish I could agree with you, Silas, about it being the early hour that is making me dense, but I fear whatever time you came here, the result would very probably have been the same,' admitted Daisy, as she placed a cup of tea in front of him.

'Thank you, and I'll begin again.' He took a sip from a cup dwarfed by the size of his hands. 'In normal times I do a lot of photography for magazines and newspapers, often in the realm of ladies' fashion. I have just one last commission to fulfil in that respect, which is to photograph a young mother in the clothes of a London fashion house, but in a more homely setting and with their baby. I am thinking of a series of outside shots and Crumford is the perfect location, I think, as it is so old as to feel comforting; the client will like the impression that many generations of mothers and babies have walked these streets, I'm sure. A beautiful young woman in the latest clothes and with her baby in a new pram, well, it certainly gives both the impression of a wife waiting for her soldier husband to come back home safely to her, and that the war is for this new generation, and thus be the sort of woman that a magazine's readers could aspire to. I could bring a model down from London, of course, but I'm not sure I'll get what I want if I do that. Even though we're at war, the fashion house I have been commissioned by still wants this one last advertisement to run as a way of encouraging young ladies to keep up morale at home by making sure they always look as nice as possible.'

Out of all the things Daisy might have guessed Silas would say, it wasn't this.

'Oh, I see. Right, I'll see if I can think of anybody suitable who has a small baby,' she said. 'There would be Joy, of course—'

'I'll stop you there, Daisy. It's *you* I was thinking of! I saw you pushing your baby towards the shop and all I could think of was that image would make an excellent series of photographs, but with you dressed in the new clothes of course. I brought Roscoe with me to your tea room as I wanted a second opinion, and he thought you were perfect.' Silas looked a bit uncomfortable, and then he put a finger inside his collar as if it were a bit tight, before he added hastily, 'Perfect for the commission, I mean.'

And this was Daisy's second shock of the morning.

While she knew that some other young ladies – she was thinking of Holly – might be flattered at such attention from presumably a successful photographer, and being thought of as an ideal clothes horse, instead Daisy felt as if her humiliation was complete.

Aside from already that morning having made herself looked unbearably stupid as well as unable to follow a simple conversation, now clearly Silas thought her a mother who hadn't married her baby's father.

And then another thought struck Daisy.

'Did you tell Violet what you were going to ask me earlier?' she asked.

'I did! And she said she thought you would be made up with the idea.'

'I see,' said Daisy.

She was going to have words with Violet, very firm words, as now her sister's ribbing from earlier made complete sense.

'And so by your unenthusiastic response, I'm supposing that you and your lovely baby are not interested in my proposition? Even though it will be well paid? Maybe as much as five pounds for a couple of hours.'

Daisy gulped. That *was* a lot of money. She would have to work many hours in the tea room to earn the equivalent amount.

'Maybe I should have checked with your father and mother first . . .'

'Silas, it's not that. I'm afraid Violet played a little game with you, and I am sorry. That baby you saw me pushing along wasn't mine. Rose belongs to my brother Asa and his wife Joy. And Violet was very naughty not to set you straight. But I can speak to Joy about it to see if she's interested if you want?' Daisy said.

Silas looked deep in thought.

Then he said, 'It's you I want to take the picture of, Daisy. I don't think I can get what I want with another woman. Do you think Joy might allow you to do this with Rose? She is a very handsome baby.'

'I'm not sure little girl babies are ever handsome – it seems the wrong word to me,' said Daisy. 'I will ask Joy, but the five pounds would have to go to her of course.'

'I understand.'

He drank his tea.

Then Silas added, 'If you do this this for me, Daisy, then do know that I shall owe you a favour.'

'Let's not get ahead of ourselves – Joy may hate the idea,' Daisy pointed out.

'She won't.' Silas sounded very confident. 'In my experience five pounds is enough to make nearly anyone agree to a proposal such as you will make, and especially when she wouldn't need to lift a finger to earn it.'

Daisy suspected Silas was correct. If the boot were on the other foot and a photographer were offering Daisy five pounds to hand her own baby over for a couple of hours to be photographed for a respectable fashion magazine, then she'd be shaking off the hand of the photographer.

'You can say too to your sister-in-law that Briar will take some studio shots of Rose for free that she can keep,' Silas added. 'He's got a real knack, and the pictures will be good.'

'And my brother Clem's baby too when he or she arrives in a couple of months? I know his wife Marguerite will be very jealous if nice photographs are done of Rose, and not her baby.'

'You drive a hard bargain.' Silas grinned.

'You may not have seen anything yet regarding my bargaining power,' said Daisy. 'Remember that I haven't quite decided what the favour is that you need to repay me with.'

'I'd better go now, else I'll be late to Canterbury,' said Silas. 'When you speak to Joy, you'd better tell her it might be at short notice, as I'll need a sunny day. We won't require her pram as they will send down a new one, and clothes for Rose to wear. I must be off – I don't want to risk spoiling my day if you request something impossible.'

'Best go quickly then,' Daisy pointed out. 'Although – and this is not part of my favour, mind – I would think Joy would like to keep the new clothes for Rose.'

Silas shook his head ruefully, before he said, 'Agreed.'

But it took Silas a while to stand up as they found themselves chatting companionably about other things, and he only did when Violet came in looking for her cup of tea.

'Sorry, Violet, Silas drank the teapot dry,' said Daisy, even though this was blatantly untrue. 'He was so shocked about me being an unmarried mother, you see, that it took a lot to revive him.'

Violet appraised Silas with a slow look up and down, before she said, 'Mr Grover looks to me like a man very used to looking after himself, and as if nothing much shocks him, least of all somebody being an unmarried mother.'

'Where your sister is concerned, I'm not so sure that she doesn't have the power to shock me, Miss Graham. Good day, ladies,' said Silas. He stopped in the doorway and looked at Violet. 'But you are right that a young mother without a ring on her finger isn't something I'd get worked up about.'

Violet laughed, while Daisy felt a little weak.

Daisy glanced at the clock hanging on the wall.

It was only twenty-five minutes past seven, but she felt as if she had had a very busy morning already.

And she couldn't work out if Silas had been complimenting her, or not.

Violet, naturally, proved to be of very little use in helping her work out the sort of man Silas was.

Chapter Fourteen

Later that morning, and with Holly in the tea room looking after things, Daisy went to see Joy in her and Asa's small cottage across on the other side of the mill.

She took with her a loaf, a pot of jam and some shortbread that Cynthia had made that morning, and she made sure to take the same for Marguerite, who lived in the adjoining cottage, as Daisy didn't want either of her brothers' wives to feel they were being singled out for special treatment.

Joy was looking much perkier, and had Marguerite sitting with her, as Joy was showing her how to put a nappy on little Rose. Both women seemed to be enjoying themselves.

'You look cheerful,' said Daisy, as she put the food she had brought on the table.

'We've had letters this morning, and photos, from Asa and Clem,' said Marguerite, who passed the photograph of Clem across to Daisy.

It was the same backdrop that Ren had been pictured in front of, and again the light saturation made Clem look washed out. He was posed similarly to how Ren had been, sitting on the crate with his arms in the same position.

Asa's photograph was much better. He was standing with his shoulders back, and had his foot on the crate and a hand on his hip, with a smile on his face. He had grown a moustache since leaving Old Creaky. This time the photographer had got the exposure better, and Daisy thought Asa looked virile and dashing in his uniform, his moustache adding a pleasing jauntiness.

'How nice for both of you,' Daisy said. 'I hope they've also sent photographs to Mother and Father, otherwise there'll be hell to pay. Did they write much?'

'I think they are enjoying themselves,' said Marguerite. 'From what I can gather they seem to be larking around.'

Joy said, 'Asa feels they'll be posted soon, so I suppose they are making the most of their time still in this county. It will be very different once they are on the other side of the Channel, he says.'

Both of her brothers' wives looked pensive at this thought.

'Yes, it will be different,' said Daisy, 'but how nice to have the photographs. And I'm sure Asa and Clem will look after each other – they are very likely to be kept together, and so they'll have the other's back.'

Rose lifted the mood of the room by laughing.

'Goodness, she is growing up,' said Daisy. 'What a sweetie.'

'She's just been fed, bathed and changed, so it's no wonder she's in a good mood,' said Joy. 'I don't want to put either of you off, but having a baby takes all of my energy, and I've no idea how Cynthia found it in herself to have *seven* children.'

Marguerite looked down at her rapidly expanding stomach and said, 'Well, it's a bit late in the day for me to be put off, isn't it?'

'Mother says women forget all about the birth and how tired babies make them after quite a short while; it's nature's way of making sure the human race survives, according to her,' said Daisy.

Both Joy and Marguerite looked sceptical.

'But I'm here with a proposition, Joy. I don't know if you are aware but three brothers have moved into the shop that used to be the haberdasher's. One of them – Silas Grover – came to me this morning with a proposition that you might be interested in,' said Daisy.

Joy looked at her questioningly.

'When I took Rose in her pram to Crumford the other day, Silas saw me pushing her along. He is a photographer by trade, and has lots of experience photographing young ladies in new clothes that fashion houses are promoting, and these photographs appear in magazines. He's going to be a full-time war photographer for the government, but he still has one last commission to complete. It's from a fashion house that wants to advertise their clothes in a magazine and this particular advertisement needs a young mother and a baby in a spanking new pram.'

Joy sat up straighter.

Daisy definitely had her full attention now.

'Silas has asked me to play the role of the young mother. And he wondered if Rose could be the baby . . .'

Joy looked out of the window.

Daisy thought her sister-in-law might be wondering why she'd not been asked to be the mother, but then Joy surprised her by saying, 'Well, I see the reason he wanted you. But I'm not sure Asa would like Rose to do this – I'll have to write to him to ask permission.'

'I'm not sure there'll be time for that,' explained Daisy, 'as the photograph will have to be taken on a sunny day, and there might not be too many of those to come now.'

'In that case I can't say yes, I'm afraid.' Joy's face was resolute.

'You can keep the clothes Rose will wear.'

Daisy allowed that to sink in.

'And Silas promised that his brother Briar will do a professional session photographing Rose in his studio.'

She turned to look at Marguerite. 'And if we go ahead with the photographic session with Rose, then Briar will photograph your little one too in the studio, after he or she arrives.'

Marguerite obviously liked the idea of this to judge by the speed in which she turned to stare meaningfully at Joy.

'What a nice memento to show Rose when she grows up,' said Marguerite, 'so you might be very regretful if you don't do this, Joy.'

Joy sniffed in a very unjoyful manner, and pointedly looked at Rose.

All the same, Daisy imagined she could see a slight softening in Joy's face.

It was time for the trump card.

'I almost forgot – you would be paid a whole five pounds in addition to everything else.'

Joy gasped.

'I know!' said Daisy. 'And what is really special about it is that it will only take an hour or two. All you have to do is make sure that Rose is fed and presentable, and we'll do the rest.'

Joy was thoughtful.

Then she said, 'If they throw in the new pram too, then yes, Rose can do it.'

Marguerite beamed as she understood that this would mean that she could have Joy's current pram. Right now the plan had been that she and Joy would share it, but if they both had prams it would be much easier to take the babies out together.

Daisy admired Joy's negotiating skills, previously unsuspected, and she felt a new respect for her sister-in-law.

'Of course, I can't make any promises about the pram as I don't know what the rules are for this sort of thing,' said Daisy. 'But I can certainly ask.'

She was rather pleased to have an unexpected opportunity to go to see Silas with this request. She almost hoped he wouldn't agree as that would mean she could deliver that news back to Joy and then return to Silas once more with Joy's response.

Daisy didn't for a moment think that Joy wouldn't agree to Rose appearing in the fashion photograph should the new pram not be forthcoming.

She wished she'd asked Silas what time he would be back from Canterbury.

Chapter Fifteen

Daisy gave it until about two o'clock, and then she closed the tea room early.

She headed for the photography studio in Crumford, but wasn't able to go inside as an ancient man was balanced precariously up a ladder directly in front of the door, painting the sign above the shop window in black script on a cream background.

'Grover Bros. Photograp' was as far as he had got.

But the signwriter was helpful. He told her that Silas was back from Canterbury and was down near the sea, where lots of birds nested, to watch local wildlife and try and work out how he might photograph it.

Daisy looked around, just in case Mrs Lang really was keeping watch from somewhere nearby, but she couldn't see her or anything else suspicious.

Then Daisy headed seawards promptly, taking a short cut that she remembered from when she was little. She wandered about, remembering when she had cried for William's death, as now she scanned the horizon back and forth trying to pick out Silas's outline.

The chalk fen looked desolate and empty, and Daisy pulled her coat close as the breeze was sharp in the lengthening shadows.

She'd never been particularly interested in the waders and the wildfowl that Asa had told her were abundant in this area, and for a moment she thought how much her eldest brother would love to be standing beside her as she surveyed the scene.

It was a lonely sight before her. Few people wandered these parts, and especially now that nobody had time for birdwatching. There was the odd metallic clanging noise drifting across the flats which Daisy thought would be to do with the new secret jetty system that was being built for the ferries. But Daisy couldn't see any evidence of this from where she was standing.

She wasn't exactly surprised that the view before her felt so uninhabited, but she had expected to see Silas before now, if he were on the flats as she'd been told.

It was at that moment that she almost trod on him.

He was well camouflaged upwind of Daisy, obviously having taken care to conceal himself as best he could. He was lying down propped up on his elbows upon a waxed canvas tarpaulin as he stared out to sea through binoculars.

'Ahoy, Silas,' she said cheerfully. 'I bear news.'

He gave a massive start and dropped the binoculars in fright, so Daisy guessed he hadn't heard her coming up behind him.

'For God's sake, Daisy, keep your voice down! You'll be the death of me,' he snapped at her out of the side of his mouth.

His face had the annoyed expression that Daisy had seen previously, and her heart sank a little as she'd hoped they'd moved beyond that stage now.

But obviously not.

'And stop standing up, woman. You're advertising the fact we're here.'

He reached up to yank her hand, and the next thing Daisy knew was that she was kneeling on the tarpaulin right beside Silas.

She began to protest as his behaviour, but he gave a firm 'Sssssh!' as he placed a finger on her lips. And then he turned back to stare seawards once more as he fiddled with the binoculars.

Daisy felt breathless.

The brief second when Silas's finger had rested gently on her lips felt like the most intimate experience of her life.

She didn't understand it as she didn't like him much, but it was an intense feeling all the same.

There was a good foot of space between them, and Daisy realised she felt excited just by being so close to him. She knew she wouldn't be feeling like this at being in such close proximity to any other man.

She thrilled further when Silas pulled her hand again to signal that her outline was still too obvious with her kneeling up and that instead she should lie down on the tarpaulin.

As she nestled down beside him, in Daisy's mind's eye she could imagine Cynthia's scandalised face if she could see her eldest daughter at this very minute. Daisy couldn't stop a smile at the thought.

Then Silas passed her the binoculars, and he put his lips close to her nearest ear to whisper, as he gazed intently towards where he was pointing a finger, 'You need to keep as flat as possible, and as quiet as you can. Look over there, Daisy. It's a mother and baby seal. Have you ever seen anything so perfect?'

Daisy hadn't seen anything at all, as her eyes were closed. The sensation of his breath and his lips so close to her ear felt almost too much for her.

She must collect herself.

As quietly as she could, she wriggled herself up on to her elbows to mimic how Silas was lying, and stared intently in the direction he was pointing, and then she tried to position the binoculars. She had never looked through a pair before and it took her a while to find what she was searching for.

Just now and again her shoulder closest to Silas nudged his with the smallest of bumps, although Silas gave no indication he noticed this.

When she did find them, the mother and baby seal certainly looked adorable together.

'And look over there, Daisy. And there.'

And the more Daisy stared towards the different parts of the flats to where Silas was indicating, the more she seemed to see. It was as if there was a town of animal, insect and bird inhabitants busily living their lives all around her.

She thought her heart would explode then as he shuffled his body over to lie on one side so that he could face her, as he leaned his head on the hand of the arm now supporting his weight, the upper arm flat to the ground.

Daisy couldn't prevent a shiver.

Silas reached behind him and groped in a bag, his hand coming back with a blanket that he flung out quietly so that it unfolded, and then with an unexpected gentleness he placed it over Daisy, with a solicitous 'You're cold – I always have a blanket with me when birdwatching, as it can get very chilly.'

Daisy's blood was racing, and she felt the least cold that she ever had in her life, but she didn't disabuse Silas.

She felt that it was very possible he'd allowed his hand to linger for almost a second longer than was necessary close to her hip bone, although above the blanket, and then she saw that he was staring unblinkingly at her face.

It was as if he were seeing her with the intensity that he had looked upon her that first time.

His eyes were dark and his expression sombre; he no longer seemed to be thinking about the seal and her pup, or the birds.

The strength of his gaze almost made Daisy's ears hurt. It felt as if all her senses were ridiculously amplified, with the sound of the wildlife and the sea nearby only interrupted by the rasp of her quickened breath.

It was as if Silas were looking deep into her very soul, and then Daisy felt that she was gazing right back into his too.

Tentatively, she moved her own hand to his hip, and then they stared at each other for what felt a lifetime, and then he replaced his own hand above the blanket where he had touched her before.

There definitely seemed to be a conversation going on between them, one that didn't require words.

Then his fingers tightened almost imperceptibly on Daisy's hip bone, and Daisy trembled as she felt as if she could pass out at this gentle pressure.

Throwing caution to the wind, she moved her head towards his and she kissed him. It was very much her that took the lead. She hadn't planned it, but in the moment it seemed unavoidable, and Daisy knew that if Silas didn't pull away, then it was pretty certain it wasn't going to end with just a kiss. And that was fine with her.

This was very different from the time she had taken the lead and kissed Ren.

It was because there was something magnetic about Silas, something that called to her.

Quite simply, Daisy felt that whatever was about to happen between them was inevitable.

She didn't care it was daylight and they were out in the open. And she certainly had no intention of halting what they were doing.

She had come across Silas without too much trouble, and so although Daisy knew that this probably meant that anyone out on the flats could find them too, she didn't give a jot.

And right then she didn't give two hoots either what Cynthia or anyone else she knew might think.

It didn't stop at kissing. And Daisy didn't want it to.

Silas took it almost unbearably slowly, asking Daisy's permission with his eyes as he progressed further and further as he loosened her clothes, each time her nodding very earnestly back.

It took a little time for her confidence to grow enough to reach for the buttons on his clothes, but after a while this seemed to Daisy what she had to do.

And what went on to happen then was the best thing Daisy had ever experienced.

Her body felt fresh and new, and capable of things she hadn't known it could do.

And afterwards, as they rearranged their clothes, none of which had been removed as it was too cold, Silas gave a laugh and it was only when he said a simple 'Daisy' that she realised that they hadn't spoken a word to each other all the time they had been entwined.

Daisy felt she was smiling secretly deep down inside.

'That wasn't quite why I came to find you,' she said, breaking a companionable silence after she'd snuggled close to him, and he'd arranged the blanket over both of them as their breathing returned to normal.

'I assumed not,' he said.

Then he lifted her face so that she was looking at him. 'I want you to know this doesn't have to mean anything more or less than you want it to. I am older than you, and you probably have a young man. He need never know . . .'

Daisy felt herself stiffen for a moment.

She didn't want to remember Ren now.

All Daisy wanted to do at that moment was to lie in Silas's arms for a bit longer and ignore the rest of the world.

'I know all that,' she said. 'Let's not talk about it. I just want to be here for a bit longer, listening to the birds. With you, Silas, like this.'

Silas didn't say anything, but he pulled her close to him in a way that made Daisy wish she could lie in his arms for ever.

～∞～

It was only when she was home, and Violet was picking a broken sprig of sedge out of her hair with raised eyebrows, Daisy remembered that she hadn't said to Silas why she had been looking for him, and he hadn't thought to ask her.

Holly's slightly accusing eyes seemed to intimate that she knew exactly what Daisy had been up to.

Fortunately, Jared chose that very moment to call them to set the table for supper, and Daisy was able to avoid a difficult moment with her younger sisters.

Chapter Sixteen

The next day Silas wandered into the tea room, ostensibly for a loaf of bread.

Daisy coloured deeply.

He'd seen into the very centre of her, and now she felt exposed in a way that she'd never experienced before.

But Silas gave no clue to any watchers about the previous afternoon, and instead he asked her if she had spoken to Joy.

'I have,' replied Daisy, 'and she is agreeable to Rose being photographed . . .'

Silas smiled.

'Not so hasty,' she said. 'Joy wants to have the new pram thrown into the deal too on top of everything else, otherwise Rose can't be photographed.'

Silas scratched his eyebrow as if he thought that Joy was swinging the lead now, but also that he didn't want to upset Daisy.

'I don't think Joy's being greedy as such,' said Daisy. 'Well, perhaps she is, just a bit. But I think it's more that if she has a new pram, it means the one she is using right now can go to Marguerite, and then when Marguerite's baby is born, they can all go out together.'

Silas looked at Daisy. He looked half amused and half not.

'The plan right now is that Joy and Marguerite will share the old pram you saw me with for both babies,' Daisy added, in case he hadn't quite got the point.

A deep groan rumbled from Silas.

'Go on then, you've worn me down,' he sighed. 'My reputation will be mud at the magazine after this. I'm known there as a hard man, and this is really going to damage that. I'll forever be known as being an easy pushover.'

Daisy laughed. 'Well, you'll just have to make sure the photographs are extra-special then, and your client will feel them worth every penny. And how lucky you're going to be working for the War Office, and so won't have to worry what the magazine thinks.'

He put his hands up in supplication and picked up the loaf, as if to go.

'Just one more thing, Silas.'

He looked at Daisy with a deliberately put-upon expression that very much said, *what now?*

'I've thought about how you can repay me over me not charging you for the photograph.'

'I'm not sure I can bear to hear this.' Silas's smile showed he wasn't being serious.

'Actually, I've got two things to ask you.'

He closed his eyes, which reminded Daisy of when they were sharing the tarpaulin. She swallowed.

'Go on, Daisy.'

'Father needs some help in the mill, and I was going to get on to this, and weeks have passed and I haven't done a thing . . . So when you are out and about, would it be possible for you and your brothers to keep an ear to the ground for any man, or two men, who might be able to help my father do some milling? They'd get paid of course, and even if they could only do a couple of hours here and there, it would be a huge help as Father is wearing his fingers to the bone.'

'Granted,' said Silas.

'Thank you. This sort of thing comes better from a man, I've found. I did mention to several people when I first thought of it, but I think because I'm a woman I've not yet been able to persuade anyone, and in any case a high proportion of my regulars just aren't up to the lifting required.'

Dramatically, Silas lifted his eyebrows to suggest there was maybe one man not one hundred miles from where Daisy was standing whom she had been able to persuade without too much trouble.

But his voice was even when he asked, 'And request number two, Daisy?'

'That you take me birdwatching another afternoon.'

Silas nearly dropped the loaf.

She'd shocked him she could see. When would she ever learn not to say the first thing that came into her head?

But then his gravelly voice was higher than normal when he replied, 'I expect that can be arranged.'

⌘

Later that day Daisy suddenly had mixed feelings over what she had done with Silas, and she was embarrassed about how flagrant her quip about the birdwatching had been, although very possibly not enough to void her intention of doing it again, if at all possible.

What did this all say about her?

She had no idea.

Daisy knew she was by nature impulsive – her schoolteachers and her family had always told her so – but she'd never really thought about it much.

But maybe innocent impulses became dangerously reckless once they crossed the point of no return.

All the same, somehow Daisy felt innocent still, deep down. Granted, she'd not been sensible or well behaved, but what she and Silas had done hadn't in the moment felt bad.

But possibly she had been badly behaved.

While Daisy couldn't feel as if she had been, not really, she knew that others would think differently.

Cynthia and Jared had done their level best to bring up all their children with solid morals and a good sense of right and wrong. And this was how Daisy chose to repay them. It made her feel she'd betrayed them somehow, and she felt sorry for letting them down.

And once she allowed this guilt into her heart, it swept through every inch of her.

She didn't know why the wave of guilt arrived with the ferocity with which it did.

Perhaps it was the strict manner in which society expected all young ladies to behave, Daisy pondered. Or that transgressing the lines of the straight and narrow could well have implications – as her parents had always intimated – that could lead to far-reaching consequences.

But what she couldn't deny was what she had done had changed her, and it was as if a river lying deep within her had been breached that previous afternoon, and there was no way of ever restoring herself to what she had been. This left Daisy agitated and possibly in quite a precarious situation.

Actually, this wasn't to deny that there was a large bit of Daisy that didn't regret a thing.

It had been special with Silas, and wonderful, and it made her feel lucky to have had such a lovely first time.

Instead, her negative feelings centred around her family and her position in Crumford, and then herself and Ren.

While a lot of local girls weren't virgins on their wedding day – the lure of the casual workers in the area each summer putting paid to that – Daisy was now a terrible example to all her younger sisters, she felt.

And Cynthia and Jared would be simply livid, if they ever found out.

Silas simply wasn't the sort of man that her parents would pick for her, Daisy knew, and on paper he wasn't what she would pick for herself either. They would feel him to be sly and much too old for her, too experienced and selfish, and they would definitely believe he wasn't 'husband material'. His work was too irregular and he had shown no interest in meeting them or showing himself as presentable or polite, and they definitely wouldn't find any of this reassuring in the slightest.

Daisy had to agree with all of this.

Even in her wildest imaginings she couldn't convince herself that Silas was likely to remain around Crumford for long, war or no war. If his war work didn't take him away, then she suspected the call of the bright lights in London and the models he worked with would lure him that way at some point.

Her instinct told her that Silas just wasn't the 'walking out with a girl' type, and very probably wasn't a one-girl type either as he seemed too bohemian for that. He certainly didn't seem the sort who was eager to marry.

And despite what Silas had said in the tea room when she'd blatantly suggested they do it again, Daisy knew she mustn't assume that would necessarily be the

case as she had heard from school friends more experienced than she that men routinely ignored anyone
they had had a sexual interlude with, once they had
got their way.

Cynthia and Jared would think Daisy criminally
imprudent with a man she barely knew, and they would
blame Silas for what had occurred, when in fact Daisy
knew that in nearly all ways, she had been the one in
charge. If she hadn't reached for him, it would never
have progressed as it did.

There were wider implications too as to what had
happened.

Daisy suspected that her liaison with Silas had
ruined her chances of ever finding a local man who
ignited such passion in her, and this seemed a crying
shame.

Twenty seemed too young to very possibly have
had one's best sexual experience ever, she thought,
and Daisy felt her shoulders slump when this occurred
to her.

Every lad she could think of who had grown up in
Crumford seemed downright parochial and dull in comparison to Silas. And Ren was no exception to this, sadly.

Silas represented an exciting world that felt a long
way from Crumford.

And Daisy suspected that the safe and innocent
ways of Crumford, and how she was very much a
product of those as she would seem so straightforward

and innocent compared to the much worldlier women he would have known previously, were very likely precisely the attributes that made her attractive to Silas, qualities that by their definition could not last.

Daisy recognised that deep down in her heart she wasn't as innocent as all that, despite her inexperience in dealing with men. Otherwise, how could she explain what she had done? Or that she recognised something reckless about Silas that had her feeling equally reckless too? She was wise enough to know that wonderful as it had all felt in the moment, it wasn't necessarily a trait likely to make either her or Silas happy should things between them continue from here.

And the fact that she had consummated whatever it was that she had with Silas meant also that inevitably she had made herself less marriageable, as respectable Crumford lads would expect her to be a virgin on her wedding day. Ren was very likely to fall into this category. Even if the couple jumped the brush before marriage, it would be on the condition that Daisy had only ever had sex with her intended.

Perhaps nobody need ever know about what had happened that afternoon, but Daisy was of the opinion that secrets like this rarely stayed secrets for eternity, and so she had inserted a blasting cap into her life that could surface and explode with the least warning, causing who knows what damage.

In the cold light of day, Daisy found it hard to believe that she had thrown herself at Silas with the abandonment she had, and on such little evidence that he was interested in her.

She didn't feel ashamed – something that good couldn't be wrong in the big scheme of things, surely – but she did feel peculiar about the discovery that there was this sensuous Daisy inside herself, a woman who was much closer to the surface than prim, tea-room, older-sister Daisy realised, and who had been very insistent on being released at that particular moment, no matter what.

Daisy couldn't get around the fact that those two kisses she had shared with Ren seemed like mere flutters in comparison, almost nothing to the tumultuous sensations experienced with Silas.

If the mildness of those kisses on the day of the party were what she and Ren would have to put up with throughout their lives together, should they go on to marry, then Daisy didn't think she could face such a future as she would know what she was missing. Nice and presentable and kind and marriageable as Ren undoubtedly was, and no matter how high on the social scale such a union would elevate herself and the other Grahams in the eyes of Crumford society.

Daisy didn't feel she could write to Ren about any of this, saying she felt differently about many areas of her life since he had left, including the two of them.

She didn't think for a moment that he'd be heartbroken if she told him that on reflection it didn't feel right between them, but she didn't want to risk distracting him in even the smallest way when death could strike in a second if a soldier didn't keep their wits about them.

She didn't want to embarrass Ren either, especially not now that some of Daisy's customers had made comments after the party that suggested more than a few assumptions were being made by Crumford inhabitants that she and Ren were more deeply involved with each other than they actually were.

And Daisy recognised still that in theory she and Ren *were* a good match. She hadn't been a fool those months ago when she had been planning Tansy and Senna's birthday party. Both she and Ren could do a lot worse than each other, and she knew that many young women of her age would merely chalk what had happened with Silas up to experience, and decide to settle with Ren or, if he didn't want her, the next best Crumford-born young man.

Did Daisy feel bad for letting Silas run his hands over her body?

Not in the slightest.

But it had added an unexpected complication to her life that an inexperienced Daisy just didn't know how to deal with, and it wasn't exactly anything she could discuss with her sisters or Olive or – horror! – Cynthia.

Still, Daisy wanted Silas, and even if that went against all the good sense in the world, she couldn't deny it.

How might it play out?

Probably with her getting her feelings trampled on, Daisy acknowledged. But if that was the price asked, then she would be very happy to pay it.

Chapter Seventeen

Daisy and Cynthia decided to have an unplanned outing to Canterbury.

This came about when a visiting journeyman, who was at the mill to fine-tune some of the turning mechanism, needed to go to Canterbury in order to pick up a particular sort of tool that he needed, and he offered Cynthia a lift over and back in his automobile.

Cynthia chose Daisy to accompany her on the jaunt as she was looking – in Cynthia's words – 'a little peaky' and as if she could 'do with a break'.

Daisy felt a fraud as she knew exactly why she was looking a little wide-eyed and harum-scarum, but what could she say in the wake of her mother's concern?

A quick glance out of the window told Daisy the pewter-grey clouds were set in for the day, so she knew that Silas wouldn't want to take the photographs for the magazine.

Suddenly she was filled with an overwhelming desire to escape the confines of Crumford for a few hours, and so she said, 'How lovely,' to Cynthia, and her mother smiled back at her happily.

Once they'd been dropped off in Canterbury and the journeyman had chugged away in his motor car, Daisy found that she'd forgotten what good company her mother could be when in the right mood, which Cynthia clearly was today.

Daisy found it very companionable to stroll through the ancient streets with her mother, their arms linked at the elbow as they wandered around, enjoying the fact that for once they didn't have a set agenda to follow, or anything particular that they needed to do, or even a time they needed to be back at Old Creaky.

It was so rare for either of them not to have a list of tasks that they must complete before the evening, that it felt very strange to them not to have the sense of a clock ticking away in their heads and a list of things that had to be ticked off, and consequently mother and daughter agreed that they would make the most of this unexpected opportunity.

And so Cynthia and Daisy diverted themselves by discussing inconsequential matters such as the merits of a change being as good as a rest, what Olive might be up to and if Daisy had any idea whether either or both of her sisters were seriously interested in any of the young men still left in Crumford, now that things seemed to have stuttered to a halt before they began between them and Alder and Rosen.

As they walked, both women remarked that there were quite a lot of military personnel wandering about, all in uniform, and some nurses too. Canterbury seemed the busiest that Daisy could remember the town being.

It looked different to how it had pre-war, which Daisy put down to the uniforms of the soldiers and nurses, more large flags about, and to St George's Hall being converted into a YMCA meeting place for troops that provided refreshments and writing materials.

'Let's go and visit an eatery,' said Cynthia, after they had spent some time wandering about and picking up some leaflets to leave in the tea room about volunteers the Canterbury and District War Work Depot needed. They had already put some coppers into a Blue Cross tin that was collecting funds to help look after the horses at the front, and then spent a while leaning on the balustrade of the bridge over the River Stour as they watched a few ducks going about their business. 'We might even be able to pick up some new ideas for ours,' Cynthia added, still talking about going to a tea room.

'Maybe.' Daisy sounded vaguer than usual, and she noticed her mother looking at her with a slightly too penetrating gaze.

She added quickly, 'Of course I meant, yes, let's have some tea, Mother. How nice, Mother. My "maybe" was only me wondering about the standard of our tea room and whether it could compete in a larger place like Canterbury, and not whether I was peckish. You know me – I'm a gannet. But however excellent where we go is, I doubt anyone's preserves will hold a candle to yours.'

Cynthia simpered quite girlishly and then looked down coquettishly at her kid gloves.

Daisy was surprisingly touched at how obviously pleased her mother was to be told something nice about herself. She thought then that Jared and Cynthia weren't the sort of couple to be complimenting each other frequently, which Daisy decided was a shame, as when Cynthia had smiled at Daisy's praise, she'd looked at least ten years younger. It really hadn't taken very much at all to make Cynthia so happy.

The tea room they chose was quite close to the cathedral. This meant the waitresses were kept very busy as since war had been declared many people had made pilgrimages to the cathedral as its Archbishop, Randall Davidson, was the leader of the Church of England. Daisy couldn't help wondering how many of the devout would have their faith tested should the war last a long time or things turn bad for Britain.

They ordered sandwiches and scones, and Daisy was gratified to discover that those she doled out to her own customers were just as good, if not superior to what they were now tucking into.

Cynthia agreed as she looked around at the brisk trade. 'Daisy, after the war, maybe we should consider opening a tea room here in Canterbury – you'd wipe the floor with the competition. And Holly could run the one at Old Creaky. Or Violet could if Holly takes over the bakery.'

'I can't see either Holly or Violet being terribly keen on that, can you?' said Daisy. 'And I suppose long term you and Father will have to decide whether to keep the tea room and bakery going with outside help once us girls get married off. It could be we find ourselves living somewhere else, a bit like the way in which Joy and Marguerite came to us.'

'Well, yes,' said Cynthia, 'what you say is true. Don't say anything to anyone, but your father and I have asked each other if down the line possibly Joy and Marguerite might want to be involved. When their kiddies are a bit older, of course.'

'Um, that could work, I suppose. But Violet might have to be dragged away from her ovens kicking and scream—'

Daisy's words died on her lips as her attention was snagged by a familiar figure across the road.

Speak of the devil!

For as she spoke of Violet, who could Daisy see out of the window of the tea room but her sister Violet.

She was on the opposite side of the street, just turning into a side road.

Daisy blinked, in case her eyes were deceiving her.

But when she peered across the road again, it was most definitely her sister.

Violet wasn't supposed to be there, Daisy knew, as she had definitely said over breakfast that she'd be spending most of the day baking extra loaves to go to a bakery shop she had not supplied previously; apparently some local women wanted to put on a tea in a church hall for servicemen and had made a special order for Violet's bread.

Right now the Violet in front of Daisy didn't look in the slightest as if she were thinking about baking.

Aside from the fact that she had led her family to believe that she would be fourteen miles away back in Crumford, to Daisy's eyes Violet was behaving furtively, and it was this uncharacteristically shifty attitude that had snagged Daisy's attention in the first place, she realised.

Violet was strangely dressed up, wearing a very fashionable green coat and a heather-coloured hat and light gloves, none of which Daisy had seen before, and which put the much dowdier ones that she was wearing to shame.

In fact, Daisy had never seen her sister so smart, or looking so confident.

As Cynthia tapped a waitress on the arm as she went by to ask if their teapot could be refreshed, apparently not having noticed Daisy's lapse of concentration, Daisy watched Violet stop in front of a narrow house, just down the side street. She took out something from her pocket – it was a cigarette that she proceeded to light! – and then Violet had a quick look around her.

Seemingly satisfied that she couldn't see anyone she knew, in a trice she knocked on a front door, which opened almost immediately, and she stepped inside, the door closing behind her.

Even though Daisy had craned her neck, she couldn't see who had let Violet in, or whether it had been a man or a woman. And what a gesture of independence that cigarette – which Violet looked practised in lighting – was!

The whole thing was over in a matter of seconds, leaving Daisy almost doubting what she had seen.

'Where would you like to go when we are done here?' asked Cynthia, oblivious still to what had been occurring behind her.

'Let's dawdle up the High Street,' said Daisy, reluctantly turning her attention towards her mother.

She knew she mustn't alert Cynthia to what she had just noticed as this might lead to all hell breaking loose, and Daisy wanted to be very sure of what was going on before risking dropping her sister in it.

Violet must have a good reason for being at that house, even if it were a clandestine one, Daisy reasoned.

And with Holly being coy about what she was up to these days, and her own behaviour recently, Daisy wondered if the outbreak of war had unleashed something tempestuous inside all of the Graham sisters, which was leading to all these secrets.

Cynthia smiled a 'thank you' to the waitress meanwhile as the refreshed teapot was placed back on their table, adding her familiar gag of, 'Shall I be mother?' as she went to fill up Daisy's cup once more.

Daisy looked out of the window again. There was nothing obviously suspicious about the house that Violet had gone into that Daisy could see.

Fortuitously, it was directly on the route that she and Cynthia needed to take to the High Street.

Daisy considered whether it would be too obvious if she dropped her gloves outside the house, so that she could linger over a closer look at the property. It seemed too good an opportunity to miss.

Ten minutes later, Daisy did indeed do just that.

Cynthia called her a clumsy ninny as Daisy slowly leaned down to pick the gloves up, making sure to eke out a bit of extra time by pretending she needed to adjust her laces.

Daisy needn't have bothered.

The house was totally quiet, and very ordinary, with elaborate lace curtains over the windows to prevent any nosy parkers looking in.

It was very frustrating.

Chapter Eighteen

'Hello, everyone,' trilled a familiar voice later that evening as the Graham family congregated in the parlour after supper. 'Cooee!'

The family wasn't expecting anyone to bustle in and disturb their evening and so they looked at one another in surprise at the interruption.

They had been helping Tansy and Senna run through their lines for the nativity play that would be performed in the church come Christmas the next month.

The twins were both going to be donkeys in the stable where baby Jesus would be born, and after everyone had had to listen to Jared's impression of a donkey, there had been a discussion over what they would wear. Daisy's suggestion of hessian sacks shaped and stuffed with other bits of old sacking was shouted down in favour of Violet saying to keep costs and everyone's time down, why didn't all the children involved wear simple masks of the animals and angels that could be painted onto cardboard, with holes cut out for the eyes and mouth.

Holly added that the Sunday school should think about getting the real-life donkey over to Crumford that was rumoured to have sired the forthcoming offspring of Basil Brewer's carthorse, as then Mary would have a real mount to ride.

Daisy knew without a doubt that should this happen, the donkey would make a mess in the church.

Unfortunately, it was Marguerite who had penned the play for the Sunday school, and Daisy had had to try very hard not to laugh when she read what the twins were expected to say. Although well intentioned about the true meaning of Christmas, when Marguerite's words were said out loud they were inappropriately preachy for seven-year-olds to utter.

Daisy knew that although Marguerite would be sitting right at the minute just across the grass in her own snug parlour, Daisy must be seen to be treating the play with the utmost seriousness, as it would be hurtful if either Senna or Tansy said to their sister-in-law that Daisy had found anything about it amusing.

Violet seemed to know what Daisy was thinking as behind the backs of the twins she lifted her top lip up to expose her upper teeth as if she were a donkey, and then pinched her nose as if there were a bad smell.

In short, it was a typical family evening for the Grahams, although while they had been eating earlier, Daisy spent a bit of time carefully watching Violet, although she took care that Violet didn't notice this.

Even though Daisy gave Violet a couple of opportunities to come clean about what she had been up to, and even raised the issue of women smoking cigarettes, her sister made no mention that she had been in Canterbury earlier that day, or that she looked to be a seasoned secret smoker.

Thwarted, Daisy turned her attention to Holly for a while, deciding it still looked as if her younger sister was nursing her own secret as she just seemed to have a coy mood about her these days.

'Olive!' Daisy cried now in response to the 'cooee' as she leaped up out of her seat. 'What a welcome diversion you are! You're just in time to help us with some *wonderful* nativity lines.'

Olive came in, bundled up in a thick coat and scarf, and she and Daisy hugged.

'You should have let us know that you were coming, Olive,' said Cynthia. 'Are you hungry?'

'Starving!' said Olive. 'I didn't know I had some time until a couple of hours ago. I've two days' exeat, and so of course I wanted to be here and see you all.'

Adding as she clasped the twins to her, with a wink towards Daisy, 'And there's nothing I like more than listening to nativity lines, Senna and Tansy, especially *wonderful* ones.'

∞

Olive and Daisy stayed up late chatting in their bedroom, although Daisy didn't mention Silas, other than

222

to tell Olive that she and Rose were going to have their photograph taken by him for a magazine, and the fact that he and his brothers arriving in Crumford had caused a bit of a stir.

And she didn't mention Violet or Holly seeming to have their own secrets either.

Instead, Daisy opted for asking Olive all about everything that had happened to her since she had left Crumford.

Olive spoke of her first impressions upon arriving in London, and how big and noisy it was, and the sheer number of shops. But that it was filthy dirty, and how thick fogs were common.

'They call it smog as the smoke from everyone's fires mixes with the fog. It really catches in the back of your throat, and it can make your eyes sting and water unbearably, and for some people it makes it very difficult to breathe,' said Olive. 'And the hustle and bustle of the place has to been seen to be believed. The roads are really busy, with horse-drawn carriages and carts squeezing each other for space, alongside automobiles and omnibuses. I've travelled upstairs on an omnibus to sight-see, and even been on an underground train – it's so loud that it makes your ears ring, and the mice run along the tracks when you are waiting at the station for the train to come.'

Daisy had never been to London, and she couldn't really imagine any of it.

Olive's descriptions made her envious though, as the furthest places Daisy had ever visited were Canterbury, Margate and Dover.

'Have you been to a music hall, or to a play?' she asked.

'I have. I went with some other nurses and we stood in the gods, and they made a collection at the end for our servicemen,' said Olive. 'And I've been to the cinema too, for the latest instalments of *The Perils of Pauline* – I'm very glad not to be Pauline.'

'I am so jealous, Olive. You are seeing the world, and I'm stuck here,' said Daisy. Even to her ears, she sounded dowdy. 'It all sounds so intoxicating, and so glamorous for you. Much more so than my cups of tea and Mother's shortbread.'

'Those are the highlights. Don't get me wrong, for most of my time, it's been endless bedpans and draining abscesses, or holding a bowl for a patient to vomit into,' laughed Olive.

'Are you enjoying it? Please say you are.'

'I am, very much indeed.'

'Even the bedpans and the vomit?'

'Even those.'

∞

The next day dawned sunny, and Silas sent a message over that he needed Daisy and Rose at the studio for nine o'clock, to make sure that when the low winter sun hit the street, as it had before when Daisy had pushed Rose in the perambulator, Daisy would have had time to get ready and rehearse what was to happen.

Daisy tried to persuade Olive to cover for her in the tea room, but Olive said firmly, 'Not on your Nelly Duff, missus. I wouldn't miss this for the world.'

Marguerite, clearly thinking of easing the way to the pram she would get, said she would look after things for Daisy, and Daisy agreed even though she knew Marguerite's sandwiches were more of the door-stop variety than the daintier versions Daisy liked to serve, while Marguerite's tea was always distinctly wishy-washy.

But it meant that Daisy, Olive, Rose and Joy could arrive at the Grovers' studio just as the church bell was chiming for nine o'clock. Joy had to come in case Rose got grizzly or hungry, or needed a new napkin.

They hadn't been there more than five minutes before Olive whispered to Daisy from the side of her mouth, 'So that's how it is then!'

'I've no idea what you mean.'

'The heck you don't, Daisy,' murmured Olive, with a pointed look toward Silas, who had his back to them and a range of baby attire in his hands that he was show-ing to Joy. 'Pinocchio!'

Daisy was saved the bother of trying to think of a witty comeback to her cousin for at that moment Briar wheeled himself into the room to introduce himself.

Previously, Daisy had always been sceptical about the concept of love at first sight, despite what Chaucer and countless others had had to say on the subject.

But that evening she swore to Holly and Violet that the very moment Olive and Briar clapped eyes on each other, there was a crackle of electricity in the room, and for the rest of that morning they could barely peel their eyes away, with Olive asking him about his medical condition and Briar encouraging her to tell him all about her nursing.

It wasn't long before Silas noticed too, and raised his eyebrows at Daisy, who lifted hers back in acknowledgement.

Neither of them made a comment out loud in front of the pair, but just after Daisy had done her first practice walk with the new pram, which was much lighter and easy to manoeuvre than Joy's current one, Silas said, 'That was unexpected, your cousin and Briar.'

'I've never known Olive take the slightest interest in any man before,' admitted Daisy. 'But I literally can't pull her away from him. Goodness knows how I'm going to get her to do my hair as she promised.'

'Us Grovers are hard men to resist.'

'Ain't that the truth!' laughed Daisy.

Now she was with Silas, her guilt and negativity had drifted away, and she felt light-hearted, bursting with energy and determined to enjoy the day.

'I'd better get changed now,' she added.

'They sent three outfits, each in three different sizes, so make sure you have the best fit, and there's footwear, hats and gloves – they've sent a list of what goes with what. I want two photos with the pram in the street and one of you with Rose in the studio. The headline is going to be "The Military Touch in Winter Fashion", and so you'll notice some different detailing in the clothes to what you will have seen before,' Silas explained. There was a pause, and then he added, 'If you need help with any buttons, you know where I am.'

Daisy felt a surge of desire at his flirting and she knew she'd turned quite pink, although more through excitement than any sense of embarrassment.

Making sure not to catch his eye again, she went through to the screened-off area in the studio that Briar had indicated previously, and slipped out of her clothes.

What Silas hadn't said was that the magazine had also sent underwear, stockings and garters, and even dusting powder and rouge for her face, and pictures of hairstyles, including several that were short.

Daisy and Olive had never worn any makeup and neither of them had any idea how to apply it. It didn't seem like the moment to experiment and so Daisy thought she'd only attempt to put some on if Silas insisted.

The clothes she was expected to wear were beautifully made and very obviously luxuriously expensive, and Daisy noted that the hemlines were higher than anything yet seen in Crumford, showing her leg for several inches above her ankle bone, so a couple of inches shorter than she was routinely wearing.

She suddenly began to dither over if she was doing the right thing by putting on these clothes. She couldn't decide whether to wear these posh items was patriotic or not. On the one hand, it seemed to encourage profligate spending when everyone should be pulling their belts in, but on the other many soldiers at the front probably wanted their wives to be well dressed, if they could afford it, in order to show the Hun that life would go on as normal in Blighty.

Daisy heard Joy say something, and this reminded her of why she was going to have these photographs taken – there was a new pram and a whole five pounds at stake for Joy and Rose, and Asa would be horrified if she didn't help them out in this way. Either to go ahead, or not to go ahead, seemed verging on the immoral, but Daisy decided to override these concerns and give Silas everything she had in the photographic sense.

Cynthia was very likely going to have something stern to say about this, but Daisy didn't care what her mother's opinion would be.

In fact, just an hour previously, Cynthia had made it known that she wasn't at all keen on Daisy and Rose being photographed.

But for the unexpected five pounds plus all the other various perks Joy would get, Daisy had seen Cynthia bite back anything further she wanted to say when a week or two earlier Daisy had told her what was going to happen, presumably because she knew the photographing was going to go ahead anyway, whether she, Cynthia, wanted it to, and so she might as well save her breath.

At last it was declared time for Joy to gently rouse a snoozing Rose and dress her in the first outfit.

Soon 'mother' and baby were posed with Daisy standing in front of a plain backdrop rolled down from a large bar hanging from the ceiling in the studio. Under Silas's supervision to make sure both of their outfits were shown to the best advantage, Briar took several photographs using a Lancaster Plate camera with a concertinaed bellows from on top of a large tripod.

Olive stood behind Briar waving a fluffy rabbit to get Rose to look their way, and when Rose got bored with the rabbit, Olive had to blow a tiny trumpet. Rose looked wide-eyed with shock at this strange sound. Daisy laughed, and both Silas and Briar agreed after Briar had quickly clicked the camera, 'That's the shot,' exactly as Daisy said to Rose, 'If you think that sounds odd, just you wait until you see your Auntie Marguerite out with her Salvation Army pals.'

Next it was a change of outfit for both Rose and Daisy. This was going to be the picture with the most expensive clothes, and Rose, dressed in lemon yellow, would be propped up on a bank of contrasting dark coloured silk pillows in the pram so that she could clearly be seen in the black-and-white photograph.

This was to be the first outdoor shot and Silas used a different camera this time, a Goerz Anschütz, with him and the camera tripod atop a sturdy wooden table in the street, in order to give them about the same height as when Silas had been standing on the stepladder when he'd first spied Daisy.

Daisy had to wait at the turn of the road, which Roscoe had just rinsed clean of horse droppings from the carts, and then come forward on Silas's call when he was happy with the sunlight. Joy's job was to jump up and down calling to Rose.

Roscoe had to hold any carts and pedestrians back so that the street was empty; luckily, it was a street that wasn't a main thoroughfare and so there wasn't too much difficulty in this.

Briar made them all laugh as they were waiting when he recounted a set of pictures that Silas had taken on Oxford Street in London that had required the help of the police to secure the road, when there had been a lot of catcalls and bad language from both shopkeepers who were miffed about missing trade and people who wanted to get through.

And then Briar told Daisy and Olive about a man Silas had found who had agreed to help Jared out occasionally at the mill, although this discussion got cut short by Silas's yell of 'Daisy!'

The third outfit had Daisy posed in a patch of sunlight with the pram sideways on, with Rose in her arms as if Daisy were just about to put her into it. This stationary shot took the longest as Silas kept wanting to try it in different ways, with Daisy and Rose in slightly altered positions.

Rose brought the posing for that picture to an end with a hungry grizzle, and Silas said after he and Roscoe had had a quiet word, 'Why don't you feed Rose, Joy? The kitchen will be private, and Briar can show you the way. I'd like to try something else but only if Daisy is amenable.'

Daisy and Olive looked at each other, but shrugged their shoulders as neither knew what this would mean.

Back in the studio, Roscoe spread some newspaper on the floor, and Silas bade Daisy to sit down, which she did rather cautiously, glancing towards Olive for moral support.

Bold as brass, Silas removed Daisy's hat and took out her many hairpins, allowing her hair to tumble free from its pompadour and down onto her shoulders.

He crunched her hair in his hands, and then said, 'Pomade,' to Roscoe, who went out of the studio to return a few seconds later with a jar. Silas rubbed some of the contents of the jar on his fingers and then clutched locks of Daisy's hair in his closed fingers, and when he held up a mirror to show Daisy what he had done at the back of her head, she was surprised to see the extent of her hair's natural wave.

'Do you trust me enough to allow me to cut it, Daisy? To here.' Silas indicated his jawline. He picked up a photograph the magazine had sent. 'So it would look like this.'

Olive peered at the picture, and then she lifted Daisy's hair up so that Daisy could get a very rough idea of what it might be like.

'You'd look stunning,' said Olive as she admired Daisy's reflection in the mirror.

Daisy felt that to cut her hair as Silas suggested would be very bold, and it would definitely be another thing that Cynthia would have a lot to say about.

But the image staring back at her from the mirror looked modern and carefree, and Daisy wanted to be a woman exactly like that.

'Do it,' she said to Silas, her heart beating fast.

'Are you sure?'

'Yes,' Daisy told him. 'Quite sure.'

Years later, when Daisy had become familiar with the word 'erotic', she described having Silas remove the mirror from in front of her and then wrap a sheet around her, and then stand so close to her that his legs were touching hers, as he wielded the scissors for the first snip, as the most sexually charged moment of her life.

Quickly, as if in a hurry to finish before Daisy changed her mind, Silas pulled bunches of her locks straight down towards the floor and then cut them off several inches below her jawline, so that her hair hung in a straight line all the way around her head. He asked for a bowl of water and he dipped his hands in and then dampened and pomaded various sections of Daisy's hair as he encouraged it to spring up and be as wild as it wanted. He further defined some curls with the pomade, and finally he trimmed the strands of hair framing her face slightly shorter.

Roscoe moved the mirror back, but Daisy couldn't see herself yet as Silas was before her, quite painfully pinching her cheeks for colour. Daisy told him about the rouge but he said that this would be better.

'Bite your lips hard,' he said, and Daisy did as she was told.

'Perfect,' said Briar, and Olive breathed in an awed voice, 'Oh my, Daisy, you look ravishing!'

Silas stepped back and removed the sheet with a flourish.

Daisy hardly recognised herself.

She looked chic and completely different. She looked as if she was the sort of London-born woman who only dressed in the latest fashion, the type of person who was decisive and knew exactly what she wanted in life and who was pretty likely to get it.

'Daisy, Joy, outside now with that baby,' commanded Silas, but not before he twisted a couple of buttons of her blouse at her neckline and her cuffs undone. 'No hat, no coat, no gloves, Daisy.'

This time Silas had Daisy do a walk with an exaggerated sway down the street with Rose in her arms, with Silas trotting beside her as he took pictures using a Kodak Vest Pocket camera that he simply held to his eye. It was a tiny camera in comparison to the ones on the large tripods that he and Briar had used earlier.

Then Silas halted and called to Daisy from just a little behind her, 'Stop and don't turn fully to me. But hold Rose so she can see me, and now look back at me yourself. Over your shoulder. This is the last one.'

Daisy couldn't help laughing as she did as he wanted. Silas looked so serious as she turned back to face into the low winter sunlight, and she could see Roscoe making silly faces as he played peekaboo and waved his arms at Rose from just behind Silas so that she would look directly at the camera.

When Silas came up to Daisy after Joy had relieved her of Rose, she was surprised to see tears ready to spill from his eyelashes.

He took out two five-pound notes from his waistcoat pocket, and wordlessly pressed one of the large black-and-white notes into Joy's hands and then one on Daisy.

'But—' said Daisy, intending to say to Silas that there hadn't been an agreement between them that she'd be paid.

But Silas had already gone, striding back to the studio without a backward look as he wiped his cheeks.

'You get off now,' said Roscoe, as if Silas's abrupt departure were perfectly normal. 'Do feel free to take all the gubbins with you, even the things you didn't wear and those pillows too. They won't be expected back at the magazine, I promise. You've all been amazing, and that baby is a total wonder.'

Joy was grinning happily as Daisy thought it terribly profligate of the magazine not to care whether any of the clothes or makeup made it back to London. But obediently she and Olive piled all the outfits, the makeup and her own clothes she'd worn over to the studio any old how into the pram destined for Marguerite, while Joy popped Rose back into the new pram.

'I'm staying here for a bit,' said Olive then, and Daisy nodded at her.

Olive hadn't needed to explain that this was so she could spend time with Briar.

Daisy knew that just a few months earlier Olive would have been living at Old Creaky and that she would have been content to let Briar make the running; but now it seemed that time felt short to everyone, and women like Olive weren't as ready nowadays to take a back seat.

Women wanted more agency over their own lives, and suddenly Daisy realised that after the war, people like herself and Olive and Holly and Violet were all going to expect much more from life in general than Cynthia's generation had.

Those of her mother's age, and probably the majority, if not all, men wouldn't like it most likely, but Daisy could not see how she and others like her would be happy to be put back in the boxes that traditional society expected to keep them in.

As she and Joy drew close to Old Creaky, Daisy felt dazed and weary now that she was no longer concentrating on Silas and what she had to do in front of the camera lens.

It was as if she couldn't focus on anything Joy was saying to her about where on earth was she, Joy, going to be able to change the five pounds into smaller denominations, as she doubted any of the Crumford shops would be willing to give her change on this, the whole experience of Daisy's morning having been so intense.

Then Rose began to bawl and bawl as if to say she had had quite enough of being a star baby.

And as Daisy touched a cheek exactly where Silas had pinched it to ignite the colour he'd wanted, she had never been so happy to hear a baby cry as it meant that while Joy was taken up with placating Rose, for a few minutes Daisy could be alone with her thoughts.

Chapter Nineteen

When Olive arrived back at Old Creaky close to midnight, she lit a nub of candle that was on the small table between their beds, and then with a 'move over', slipped into Daisy's bed so that they could have a whispered conversation without any danger of being overheard.

'What a day,' declared Olive.

'It was a *day*, that's for certain,' said Daisy.

'Was Cynthia furious about your hair?'

'She was incensed, and told me that Basil Brewer and Ren would hate it, and what was I thinking of, making myself look an outright *floozy*!'

Olive laughed.

'And that I've made myself into the laughing stock of Crumford,' said Daisy. 'Then Holly told Mother not to be so fuddy-duddy, and that everyone would be looking like me before too long. Mother caught sight then of the short length of my dress, as I hadn't had time to change, and she went so red as she shouted "scandalous" that I thought she was going to pass out. But then it all calmed down when Father announced that my hair is very fetching, and that it would be much more practical for all women to wear skirts well above the ankle as it would save on a lot of cleaning, and that surely was a good thing. And then I quickly gave Mother those two silk pillows that we'd used in the new pram, and the five pound I'd not been expecting, saying that she and Father deserved a bit of luxury in their bed, after which Mother spent quite a bit of time stroking the pillows and saying they were very fine.'

'Thank heaven for Jared,' said Olive.

'Goodness, yes, Father totally saved the day,' said Daisy. 'I think Mother would still be furious with me if he hadn't been there. But that's enough about me.'

Olive smiled in a self-satisfied way.

'You're looking very pleased with yourself,' Daisy encouraged, 'and so you like Briar, I take it?'

'I do! He's very, um, I don't know, but it's hard to ignore . . .' said Olive.

'Yes, those Grover men seem to share that quality,' agreed Daisy.

'Anyway, I'm going to look into getting transferred to a hospital closer to here. I know they will need nurses locally,' said Olive.

'Are you sure? That's such a statement to everyone, and you've only just met him.'

Olive sniffed in a cross way at Daisy's comment, and Daisy realised that she knew almost exactly what Olive was feeling. If it were Silas, and she had been training in London, then whatever anyone else might say to the contrary, Daisy would be thinking of coming back to be close to him.

Daisy thought too about how she had pretty much thrown herself at Silas, and she remembered the proverb 'Those in glass houses shouldn't throw stones.'

'I'm sorry, Olive. I wasn't thinking,' Daisy said. 'You are the only person who knows exactly how you feel, of course. And that's what is important.'

'It is,' agreed Olive. Then she proceeded to list all the things she liked about Briar, finishing with how easily he made her laugh, and how she couldn't see any sign of his disability holding him back.

'Did he kiss you?'

'Does a lady ever tell?'

'Lucky you're not a lady then, eh, Olive!'

Olive sniggered and then proceeded to give Daisy chapter and verse, finishing with, 'Now that's enough about me. It's time for you to spill the beans.'

Daisy was quiet for a while, forcing Olive to give her a rather painful nudge under the covers.

'I don't really know where to begin, Olive. I've acted in a manner I didn't think I was capable of,' said Daisy.

'At the beginning maybe,' Olive prompted.

'Well, I saw Silas for the first time by chance when I took Rose to Crumford to give Joy a rest – and he scowled in a very rough way as if he really didn't like the look of me. And then a day or so later he and Roscoe came into the tea room and I thought they both looked extremely rude and bad tempered, although actually they were very polite. Then Silas was waiting for me outside the tea room first thing the next morning. Encouraged by Violet, I may say, who allowed him to go on thinking I was an unmarried mother when she could easily have put him right, as he'd seen me pushing the pram and he'd assumed Rose was my baby, and it turned out he wanted us both for the magazine pictures. We got it sorted out that Rose wasn't mine, and I suggested that he photograph Joy, but he wanted me—'

'I bet he did,' interrupted Olive.

Daisy laughed, and went on, '— and the thought of that made me feel tingly. And when I got it all arranged with Joy, I went to find Silas, but he was down near the shore watching the seals, and then before I knew it, I was kneeling down beside him as he made me be quiet so as not to scare the birds, and then he made me lie beside him so that I could see through his binoculars a seal mother and pup. And then after a while, well, you can guess what happened then,' said Daisy. 'It was totally unplanned and very unexpected as I didn't think Silas had noticed me at all in *that* way. It wasn't him that made the running, either, I confess.'

'This risks sounding like something out of a Thomas Hardy novel!' cried Olive.

'I know! Let's just hope it doesn't have that sort of tragic ending.'

'Did you go all the way?'

Daisy gave a bashful nod in the candlelight.

'Daisy Graham! I knew it!'

'Ssssh! Stop it,' said Daisy as Olive's exclamation had been too loud. 'Let's not wake up the household.'

'I knew there was something different about you – something so grown up and *experienced* that I guessed as much the very moment I saw you,' Olive insisted.

'Well, I hope Mother and Father aren't of the same notion.'

'I don't think they are; they see you all the time, so they probably don't *look* at you much. Indeed, I don't suspect anyone is, as it seems as if both Violet and Holly are busy with other things. While the war is grisly and all that, it's giving you the perfect cover, as everybody else has got far too much to think about aside from what Daisy Graham might have been up to while "birdwatching".'

'And you can tell all of that from just the few hours you've spent in everyone's company since you've been back?'

'Yes, surely.'

'You are a white witch!'

'Stuff that,' said Olive. 'I want to hear all about how it was with you and Silas.'

Daisy told her, and Olive spent a long time questioning her, sometimes with quite medical sounding queries, and then she gave some detailed explanation over exactly how babies are made, quite a lot of which was news to Daisy.

In fact, a rather embarrassed Daisy admitted to Olive that she hadn't even worried for a moment whether she could get pregnant or not.

'I see,' said Olive. 'Let me explain some more, so that you can look after yourself.'

Olive spoke for a while, and then she asked in a contemplative tone, 'I take it you want to do it again with Silas?'

'I very much do. But I know he might not think like that, not now he has had his way.'

'And where does this all leave you with Ren?'

'Ah. Ren. That's difficult. I really don't know where it leaves us,' admitted Daisy. 'I don't want to string him along unfairly, and I can't even decide at the moment if writing to him is part of that, as my head is so tipped upside down by Silas. But I can't pretend that me and Silas can go any sort of distance long term. I don't know Briar, but I thought earlier that he seems much more stable than Silas. And if Silas were out of the picture, then I could do a lot worse than Ren. But I have no idea what he feels about me as we certainly made no declarations towards each other before he went. Would I tell him about this, or not? I just don't know.' Daisy's voice was getting quieter and quieter.

'You may be right about Silas and Briar,' said Olive. 'But it could be that Ren won't be a problem either.'

A soft snore from the other side of the bed told Olive that Daisy had fallen asleep as she was talking.

Olive smiled to herself, and then turned her thoughts back to those of herself and Briar.

∽

The next day Olive was with Daisy in the tea room discussing the man Silas had found to help Jared in Old Creaky. He was a Quaker and consequently a 'conchie' – a conscientious objector – or at least he would be if conscription ever came in, but even so, a lot of people whose loved ones had volunteered generally had no time for those who expressed conchie beliefs.

Their discussion was interrupted when they heard the sound of postie Big Tom's tricycle bell, and Olive ran to the gate so that he didn't have the bother of climbing down and bringing the letters in.

There was one for Daisy, and it was from Ren.

'You read it,' said Olive. 'I'll hold the fort for a few minutes.'

Daisy sat at an empty table in the corner with her back to the customers, and opened the envelope. Inside were two small photographs, along with a note.

Dearest Daisy,

I hope you are well, and your family too. We all are tip-top, and have finally been posted and are still together. Any scarves or gloves appreciated, and so I am thanking you in advance. Cigarettes too please if you can manage it, as we use them to gamble with when we

243

play cards, and as Clem says a bit too often, clearly I am no card sharp and so am in dire need of a lot of what passes for currency around here.

I have not got long to spend writing to you today, but I wanted to send you these photographs. I took them myself! Father sent me and my brothers each a Kodak Vest Pocket camera, and I thought you might like the pictures I took of the horses tethered in a long line to a rope while they were waiting for their nosebags – it was on my very first roll of film. There were literally hundreds of horses there, and if one neighs the others answer him and so it can be very noisy.

No news I can say otherwise, except we are playing a <u>lot</u> of cards.

Do please write to tell me everything you have been doing.

With kind regards,
Your obedient servant, Ren Brewer, Esq.

Wordlessly Daisy passed the note across to Olive, who glanced at it and then said, 'Awkward. On many levels.'

'Bother,' replied Daisy. 'Now what am I to do?'

'Distract with a scarf and cigarettes. A mountain of ciggies,' said Olive. 'I think that will do the trick. Until you properly know what you want to say to Ren, that is.'

There was a silence as Daisy stared at the two photographs. The images were grainy and not very well chosen, but she was surprised at the number of horses.

'Who'd have thought Ren and his brothers would also have a Kodak Vest Pocket?' mused Daisy miserably. 'I'm pretty certain that was the camera Silas used for that last picture yesterday.'

'Well, don't they always say that art imitates life? Except in your case, it seems the other way around,' said Olive.

'Technically, Ren would have had his camera first, maybe? Certainly before the picture yesterday, so maybe Silas was really more the art bit imitating my life,' mused Daisy.

'Please!' said Olive. 'I haven't got the wherewithal for you going all philosophical on me. I'd better go now to see Briar before you get too deep for me.'

'I am the least deep person in the world,' announced Daisy.

Olive's grin told Daisy that on this at least, the cousins were agreed.

Chapter Twenty

The next day Olive went back to London, and the conscientious objector arrived for his first day helping Jared.

Daisy was sorry to see Olive leave as it had been quite like old times with their late-night chats, but she was delighted that Jared had some help at long last as although a sleep-deprived Cynthia never complained, she had become quite short-tempered through helping in the mill, and then doing her fancy baking and preserve making for the tea room after the twins had gone to bed.

The conscientious objector was called Perry – short for Peregrine – and he was also a part-time ambulance driver, although should there be an invasion, he was only at Old Creaky on the condition that he would move to doing the ambulance driving full-time either on home soil or at the front across the Channel.

Daisy had never seen a conscientious objector before, and she was slightly taken aback to see that he looked perfectly ordinary, and actually quite diminutive, if she had had to come up with a word to describe him.

Senna and Tansy were calling each other 'conchie' in jest by teatime that day, but Violet came down hard on them, saying they mustn't use that word, and absolutely not about Perry. He was a man of principles and deserved respect for that, Violet added, and he would be getting a lot of abuse for his beliefs so he didn't need two small girls adding to this.

'But why doesn't he want to fight?' said Tansy.

'Is it because he's scared?' Senna asked.

'I don't know for certain, and maybe one day you will know him well enough to ask him,' said Violet. 'But for many people, it's because they believe their lives are to be lived differently.'

'I think Silas said that Perry is a Quaker, and so that would mean that Perry believes in pacifism, and that violence and wars are wrong,' said Daisy to the twins.

'And that all humans are equal to one another,' said Violet, and there was a note in the tone in which she spoke that Daisy couldn't stop thinking about afterwards.

∽

Daisy decided to head for the photographic studio in the hope that Silas would be there. He had been suspiciously absent since the photographic session.

Only Briar was at home, however, with the other two not yet returned from work assignments, but he invited Daisy to come in for a cup of tea.

247

She sat in the kitchen and watched Briar expertly make them both a cup of tea as he leaned on a walking stick to keep his balance.

'Olive was sad to leave this morning,' said Daisy cautiously.

'I was sorry to see her go,' Briar said, placing the drink in front of Daisy without a single sloshed drop of tea in the saucer. 'Your Olive really is a remarkable woman.'

'Isn't she? I respect her no end.'

Neither said anything for a little while, and then they both spoke at once, with 'Did she say anything about me?' from Briar, and 'I think she is very taken by you, even on such short acquaintance,' from Daisy.

They laughed, and then Briar spoke in a very natural way about Olive, although he ended by saying, 'I'm not sure though what she'd see in someone who's an old crock like me.'

'I don't think you should think that for a minute, Briar, as it is to do yourself down unfairly,' said Daisy, being mindful that she mustn't fall into the trap of her previous thinking about Briar's disability. 'Olive and I have shared a bedroom and all our secrets since we were five years old, and in all that time Olive has never so much as mentioned any man to me, nor shown any romantic inclinations at all. She spoke to me of you however after she had got home on the day of the photographs, and so I knew she'd changed through your meeting. She's a strong woman who knows her mind, and if she doesn't see a problem with your health, then my advice to you would be to take her at her word. But only if you are interested in her too, of course.'

'I am interested. Very. Did she say to you that she might come back to East Kent to finish her training?'

'As a matter of fact, she did. Would you like that?'

'Do kittens chase a piece of string? Of course I would,' said Briar.

'Then good luck to you both,' said Daisy.

They fell to talking about the technicalities of taking photographs, after which Briar showed Daisy their darkroom and explained that Silas was waiting for a delivery of a De Vry cine camera so that he could begin to shoot moving images.

Briar was very patient in explaining the intricacies of photography in a non-stuffy way that often made Daisy laugh.

She realised Briar was good company, and that she thought him and Olive were a good match.

And just then the front door opened and Silas walked into the kitchen where she and Briar were now enjoying a second cup of tea.

'Hello,' he said in a reserved way.

'Hello,' mumbled Daisy, holding back just as much.

Silas grunted.

'Briar was giving me an introduction to the technicalities of moving photography,' Daisy said in a stilted fashion.

'I'm just going to go and tidy the studio,' said Briar.

Neither noticed him make himself scarce.

'The weather looks to be closing in, so let me escort you home.'

'Thank you, Silas.'

⌒∞⌒

They were walking through the fields close to Old Creaky talking about the most inane of subjects, when Daisy laid a gentle hand on Silas's arm to stop him.

She turned to face him, and said simply, 'Silas.'

He looked at her, and in a shaft of light suddenly showing through the quickly moving clouds of the inky silk of the night sky, Daisy could see the reflection of the gibbous moon shimmering on each of his irises.

Silas stepped to her and their lips gently brushed.

And then he led her to the lee of a hayrick near the edge of the field they were standing by, so that they were out of the wind.

They kissed more deeply, and every time Silas ran his hand through Daisy's short hair, he gave a murmur of appreciation.

Then, without them lying down, he lifted her skirt as he pressed her back firmly against the rick.

This time was very different from the day on the flats near the sea with the marsh birds calling, but Daisy found it more passionate – she wouldn't have thought it possible, should anyone have asked her about it that morning, but it was indeed the case – in part as she could feel Silas's breaths and sighs close to her ear as he moved inside her, with her mouth answering those cries as near to his ear as she could possibly get.

As the turning sails of Old Creaky chequered her sight, there was no doubt in Daisy's mind that it was just as profound an experience for Silas as it was for her. And after they had finished they stayed holding each other close, and not very long afterwards they did it again, this time each barely moving, the sensations so intense.

Daisy felt that she could have gone all through the night in this way, but there was an unpleasant splatter of rain that led to Daisy wrenching her skirt back down. They ran down the road and then Silas watched from a patch of shadow as Daisy scuttled through the gate to Old Creaky and across the grass to the mill house, where, pausing for a moment outside, she checked that all her clothes were arranged properly, and that she had brushed all the wisps of hay from her hair and clothes.

And then with a cheeky wave in the direction of where she thought Silas was – it was too dark to make out quite where he might be – she slipped inside.

❦

The tea room the next morning was incredibly quiet, possibly because the weather had grown squally and miserable overnight.

As if in reflection of these bleak conditions, Daisy couldn't help but dwell on the latest reports from the front in the newspapers, which were slowly becoming grimmer than anybody would like.

Over the past few weeks Daisy had noticed too a growing mood of discontent amongst her clientele.

In her opinion there was more talk amongst her customers about the danger of spies, while others moaned impatiently about rising prices in the shops. And Daisy knew that because of shocking shortages of many ingredients, Cynthia had had to eke out sugar in the cakes and shortbread she baked to be sold in the tea room. This meant that nowadays they were barely sweet at all, and so Daisy suspected too that there had been possibly the odd whispered comment about this, not that anyone had dared to say anything directly to her face, although this would only be a matter of time, no doubt.

Maybe, Daisy mused, everyone was starting to share a general sense of battening down the hatches, and perhaps it was this as much as the overcast skies outside that were deterring Crumford folk from being out and about this morning.

Certainly the optimism she had felt when waving off Asa and Clem from the station on that sunny day in August felt like a very long time ago now; it had seemed back then such a pure and simple surge of patriotism and belief that going to war was quite the right thing to do, a feeling that was shared by all.

But since William Evans's death had been announced in the *Mercury*'s Roll of Honour, as far as Daisy was concerned everything to do with the war had become tinged with complexity and ambiguity.

Still, after giving a drenched and shivering Old Tom, who had just come into the tea room, a cup of tea that Daisy made clear was on the house and putting him by the warm bit of the wall next to Violet's ovens, with his oilskins hung on the back of a chair nearby so that they could at least be warm when he had to put them on again, Daisy could see she had an opportunity.

While she'd never relish a slow day for her business, it meant that she could nip next door to have a word with Violet and they would be unlikely to be disturbed.

Daisy poured a cup of strong tea for them both, and made some buttered toast, which she took into the bakery on a tray under cover of a tea towel to keep the rain off, after she'd also popped a slice in front of a grateful Old Tom.

'Ahoy, Violet!' she said a moment later.

Violet put down the newspaper she'd been reading while waiting for something to come out of the oven, and smiled up at Daisy.

'Grim old day outside, Daze,' Violet said, using the nickname she used to call her sister by, 'so you are a sight for sore eyes.'

'You're only saying that because I've come with food,' said Daisy.

'True,' Violet agreed through a mouthful of toast.

They talked a little about the photographs Silas had taken of Daisy.

Violet didn't ask Daisy any questions about her romantic feelings for Silas, which relieved Daisy as she didn't want to discuss it with her sister.

But although Violet didn't seem particularly interested either way in Daisy and Silas, this could also have been because Daisy had made sure to gift some of the items of clothing that had been sent down from London for the photography session to her. As a diversion, Daisy didn't wait for long to ask whether Violet was pleased with them, which she was.

Actually, after keeping the clothes she had actually worn and setting aside two of the coats for Cynthia, and of course the silk-covered pillows, Daisy had scrupulously divided everything else equally between Holly, Violet, Joy and Marguerite. Holly was also given the makeup, which she seemed happier about than the clothes or shoes.

'Violet, dear, may I ask you something?' asked Daisy when she felt the time was right.

Her sister looked at her rather coolly, and then said, 'Hmm, I'm not sure I like the sound of this overmuch, but I suppose so.'

'Oh, you don't have anything to worry about. Unless, that is, you have a secret that you're keen to keep to yourself . . .' Daisy paused, and a feeling of significance began to swell in the bakery.

Violet tried to brazen it out, with a snipped, 'I'm sure I have no idea what you mean, Daisy.'

Daisy held her sister's eye, keeping her own eyebrows raised.

Violet took another bite of toast, which she attempted to chew in a nonchalant fashion.

'Perhaps a secret that's something to do with a most striking coat and hat you've not cared to show any of us?' said Daisy, undeterred. 'And a visit to Canterbury a little while ago, when you shouldn't have been there but indisputably were seen, by me I should say, sneaking – there's no other word for it – into a strange house within a stone's throw of the cathedral? When you paused to light a cigarette outside in a most familiar fashion. Ring any bells?'

Violet paused for a moment, stock-still, and then she capitulated.

'Damn and blast you, Daisy. I hadn't wanted to say anything to the family for a while.'

Daisy must have looked a bit upset at being lumped with the rest of the family in this abrupt manner, as Violet added as she shook her head, 'To be honest, Daisy, I especially didn't want you to know yet as you're so conservative, and you're such a blabber-mouth. Holly said I should tell you, but I was worried you'd say something to Mother and she'd stick her oar in and cause problems. But I think we're far enough along now that it probably doesn't matter.'

Hearing Holly had been taken into Violet's confidence and she hadn't, and that Violet had made a definite choice not to include her, gave Daisy a real pang of jealousy that clenched at her insides in an almost physical way, and suddenly she felt as if she might cry.

She always tried to do the right thing by everyone, and it was painful when she wasn't treated likewise back.

'Oh,' was all she could manage to say as she fought the wobble in her lower lip.

And then Daisy added in a small voice, 'I'd never say anything to Mother.'

'Don't be like that, Daisy. In part, I didn't want to put you in a difficult position, in case you did feel you had to talk to Mother,' said Violet. 'And Holly was already in, you know.'

'But I wouldn't have said a thing about whatever it is.'

Violet didn't say anything.

'So it was fine for you to confide in Holly, and not me,' cried Daisy then, feeling a renewed stab of jealousy now Violet's preferential treatment of Holly was sinking in. 'What's Holly got that I haven't?'

'This is exactly why I didn't tell you. If you want to know, Holly just has a much more independent mind than you. She also seems to know more people who can give me a lift to Canterbury than you do.'

'Poppycock. The hell she has a more independent mind than me!'

'Look, this isn't about you, or Holly, come to that. That's your problem, Daisy – you always think that everything is about *you.*'

'Give me strength, Violet. You're telling me, you're not thinking about yourself right now?' Daisy's voice was loud, and if she were another type of person, Daisy felt as if she could give Violet a real push or a thump just at this minute. 'Honestly, for two pins, I could get Mother right now, and tell her to worm it out of you!'

'I rest my case,' said Violet, looking inordinately pleased with herself.

Daisy realised that she was being silly and immature, and that the threat of running to Cynthia harked back to childish spats between the sisters and, worst of all, it was exactly what Violet had just claimed she'd do and she'd denied it, only to be proved wrong a moment later.

Daisy could have ground her teeth in frustration at herself.

'I'll be jiggered! You do what you want then,' Daisy said grumpily.

Violet crunched on another piece of toast, and Daisy drank some tea.

Violet calmly waited Daisy out.

'Go on then, what are you up to?' Daisy asked in a slightly more conciliatory tone, once she was calmer and curiosity had got the better of her.

'I'm helping start a magazine.'

Daisy stared agog at her sister.

There were many things Daisy could have imagined Violet saying, but this wasn't one of them.

Violet had never shown a particular interest in her schoolwork (which had led Daisy to assume that 'words' weren't high on her sister's agenda), nor since then had Daisy noticed Violet being a big reader of magazines.

And Violet had hardly mentioned or been interested in the photographs that Daisy had had taken that were commissioned by a bona fide magazine.

To hear now Violet claim to be starting a magazine seemed so improbable and implausible as to be ridiculous.

'It's a magazine by suffragettes that's for suffragettes,' announced Violet proudly, unable not to sound downright smug, Daisy thought.

'But you don't believe in women's emancipation or the Women's Social and Political Union. And you don't even like Emmeline Pankhurst!' Daisy stared at her sister in incomprehension.

'How do you know, Daisy? When did you ever talk to me about what I think about any of this, or whether I belong to the WSPU? Just because *you* might hold old-fashioned beliefs, it doesn't automatically mean that I do too. You've always been a know-it-all, so certain you don't miss a trick and assuming everyone is just like you. But let me tell you, you know *nothing* of what is going on around you.'

Daisy thought about this and realised that to a large extent, it was true.

She wasn't at all aware of what Violet, or Holly for that matter, really thought on the subject of women's emancipation, or indeed on much else. Well, she remembered Holly once mentioning something about the choices women could make, but Daisy couldn't quite recall what Holly had actually said.

Actually, if Daisy were honest, she couldn't remember the last time she had asked her sisters' opinions on anything.

She felt ashamed. What did this intimate, both for her as a person generally, and also as the role model for her younger sisters that she liked to think she was? Not very much that was positive, that was for certain, Daisy admitted to herself.

While she'd been growing up and discovering the limitations on life at Old Creaky, of course – although she had never thought it – Violet, and possibly even Holly too, would both have been thinking differently about their own lives, and what they wanted, as they matured into young women.

It wasn't that any of them were unhappy with their lot at Old Creaky, but more that for each of them there seemed to be a bigger life waiting elsewhere, rather than just being content to be the middle-class daughters of a prosperous mill owner.

And suddenly Violet in her secret green coat and purple-toned hat made perfect sense, as these were the colours of the suffrage movement.

It also made Violet's explanation of the beliefs of Quakers – that people should be respectful of others' beliefs – now have a slightly different interpretation than Daisy previously assumed.

Presumably Violet thought herself a woman of emancipated principles who should be respected for her own beliefs. While Daisy didn't disagree with this, rather shamefully she had to admit to herself also that she had never thought terribly deeply on the ins and outs of women's emancipation either, and she was a bit hazy over precisely what they wanted.

Before the war, women chaining themselves to railings in London seemed a long way away, and very far removed from the traditional day-to-day life of Crumford that Daisy was used to.

'But, Violet, you've never said you agreed or sympathised with those women breaking windows and arguing with the police?' said Daisy with a bit of a breathy catch in her voice.

'Those are symptoms and not the cause, and anyway those activities of the suffrage movement have been ceased while we are at war – what's much more important is that I believe with all my heart that women should have the same voting rights as men, and that the world would be a better place if men had to listen to what women had to say on a whole range of topics. And that is what my magazine will be about,' said Violet, her voice ringing with confidence.

'Well, I believe in that too,' cried Daisy.

'Do you?' Violet sounded surprised.

'How could you think I don't?'

'Well . . .' Violet seemed unable to put into words why she had assumed that about her older sister.

The sisters stared at each other in confused realisation that they really didn't know or understand each other at all, with Daisy seeing that Violet thought her the compliant daughter who was always ready to uphold the traditional family values still hanging over from Victorian times that were still so prevalent in Crumford, with Daisy understanding that her previous conjecture that Violet was a much duller person than she, Daisy, was herself, might be extremely wide of the mark.

'So what are you doing at the magazine?' Despite being taken aback by Violet in the last few minutes, Daisy couldn't for the life of her think what she had to offer in setting up something complex like a magazine.

'I'm the publisher and business manager and I shall be organising the printing and distribution, and I'll suggest some writers too. We are thinking of it as a Kent sister version of *The Suffragette*, the emphasis on "sister" and so we might name it *The Sister*, or possibly *The Daughter* to show its descent from *The Suffragette*. Holly is doing our accounts and bringing in funds and sponsorship,' explained Violet.

'But how do *you* know how to manage anything?' said Daisy, still nonplussed. She wasn't being mean, so much as trying to get it all straight in her head. 'And what on earth benefit can Holly bring to raising finance? If you two are the best that are around, then I can't give the magazine long.'

'Just listen to yourself, Daisy,' snapped Violet, incensed. 'You are forgetting what I do every day in my bakery, which takes a damn sight more organisation that swanning about in a tea room, if I may say, as I have to deal with suppliers and plan ahead, and work out new recipes. And as far as the magazine is concerned, Holly and I are learning as we go along, and you know what, we're turning out to be *damned* good! Holly is a star in the making, let me say, although you're too stupid to notice. And the difference between us and you is that we are putting our necks on the line and doing *something*, while you're stuck in a rut, going nowhere fast but thinking you're better than us all the same.'

'I am indeed going to tell Mother,' was the best Daisy could come up with at this point, and immediately she could have bitten her tongue out as it wasn't what she wanted to say at all but merely harked back to her rote response when under pressure during a sibling argument.

And she'd said it through a sudden gale of gulping sobs, which definitely diluted the impact, especially as the last thing she intended was actually bringing Cynthia into this fracas. That wouldn't help anyone.

Daisy had never had a major quarrel with either of her two elder sisters since they had all left school, and she was used to them following her leadership.

Then, Daisy realised with a clang of humiliation, that perhaps neither Violet nor Holly had ever really done what she'd told them to.

She thought back, and she could see that both sisters were good at nodding agreement at what Daisy said, but then they usually went and did what they wanted.

It was clear those days of Daisy feeling sure where she stood in the Graham family dynamic were well and truly over now.

Violet drew herself up tall as if to indicate that she knew exactly what she was about.

'As I said earlier, you behave from here in whatever way you want, Daisy,' Violet drove her victory home. 'I really don't care what you think or how you carry on.'

Biting back more hot words she wanted to fling at her sister, Daisy pushed past Violet and ran back to her tea room, now mercifully empty of Old Tom, who had been her only customer all morning.

Rain started to bucket down even harder, slashing the windows, and as a thoroughly discombobulated Daisy put her head on to her arms and bawled loudly, it was as if the heavens were howling in accompaniment.

Chapter Twenty-one

The next couple of days were tense for Daisy.

Violet totally ignored her. Holly gave her a wide berth too, although that may have been Daisy reading too much into what were possibly quite normal interactions between the pair of them.

It all amounted to the same thing; an unhappy Daisy who felt isolated, even though the mill house at Old Creak was as busy as usual.

Amazingly, Cynthia and Jared seemed totally oblivious to the tensions between the three sisters. Instead they were enthused by an idea that Perry had had, which was taking up all their attention.

For Perry had suggested that they should consider starting to produce hard, unsweetened biscuits to sell to the local supply depot of the army, to be sent in metal tins to soldiers at the front as part of their regular supplies.

The idea had fallen onto fertile soil, and now Jared, Cynthia and Violet were busy experimenting with different flours and recipes on various of Violet's large array of baking sheets and trays, and Holly was involved in working out acceptable profit margins, and whether they should include the metal tins, which they would need to source, in their costings.

Daisy was forced to watch from the sidelines, as she didn't know anything about flour or baking, or metal tins, and it had become abundantly clear to her that nobody at home was terribly interested in what she thought on the matter, or how they might deal with the army supply department when it came to trying to sell the biscuits to them.

Had it always been this way, that she'd never been really listened to by her nearest and dearest? Perhaps so, Daisy had to acknowledge.

Still, it was very irksome for Daisy to watch Violet hamming it up in being so useful to Jared and Cynthia, in an exaggerated way that Daisy was convinced was designed to rub salt into her own wounds.

Violet spoke in avid support of Perry's idea at what felt like every meal, and once, when it got too much, and determined not to be completely outdone, Daisy chipped in with encouragement.

Her parents' surprised faces at her speaking up as she had were a rather embarrassing testament to the fact that Daisy rarely talked much about what other members of her family were up to, and so it was apparently something of a shock to all of them, Daisy included, that she had chosen this particular moment to do so.

Daisy took to spending a lot of time alone in the tea room reorganising the tables and moving things about, as the atrocious weather was set in and she had virtually no customers.

It was too wet to go and see Silas, as for Daisy to venture into Crumford and get completely drenched would have raised too many questions back at the mill house which she wasn't in a mood to answer.

And he didn't come to see her even though it would have been easy for him to do so if he wanted to as he had a car.

All in all, Daisy felt very miserable and sorry for herself.

∞

The weather had to break at some point, and at long last it did, dawning reasonably fair one morning, although it was very chill and the days were getting short now.

Later that afternoon as Daisy was getting ready to close up the tea room, Silas surprised her by walking in with a large, flat package wrapped in brown paper under his arm.

Silas shook his head at Daisy's offer of tea.

Instead, he told her that the package contained the photographs the magazine had chosen to be used in the fashion feature, and he had reproduced copies of those pictures for Daisy to keep.

Daisy felt a shiver of apprehension, as what could she say if the photographs were bad and she looked ugly?

It was as if Silas read her mind, as he smiled at her with a 'Don't worry.'

They sat at one of the larger tables and Silas spread the pictures out. Daisy was astounded – little Rose looked exactly like she did every day, only a bit more adorable with her fluffy hair, clear gaze and the sweet puckering of her lips.

But when Daisy concentrated on her own images, she couldn't actually recognise herself in any of them, as the young woman in the photographs had a glamour and confidence about her that Daisy definitely didn't share at that moment.

Indeed, this woman before her looked intrepid and very much like the sort of friend that Daisy wished she had, and she reminded her of the window-Daisy that first time Silas had seen her, much more than flesh-and-blood Daisy.

When she said as much to Silas, he answered that this was precisely what a good fashion spread should do. It wasn't about selling reality, but a better version of reality.

'Do you like the photographs?' he asked, staring at Daisy with the expression that she had once thought indicated grumpiness but now she knew meant that he was concentrating.

'I'm not sure,' she said.

Silas laughed, adding then, 'Don't beat about the bush with me, Daisy. Say what you mean, why don't you?'

'I mean, you have taken beautiful photographs, but it's not me I see. I feel that the me in everyday life is second best to these images, and anyone who met me having seen these first would immediately be disappointed with the me in real life, and that is a peculiar sensation, as usually it takes a little while, at least a few minutes, before I disappoint new acquaintances,' Daisy explained. 'Your photographs are kind of real and not real at the same time, if you understand me, Silas, and they make me feel a bit dizzy. I think that if I didn't know they were me, I'd probably be more impressed with them.'

'Daisy, nobody is ever going to be disappointed when meeting you, I promise,' he said.

'You're too gallant, Silas. You should have a word with Violet and Holly right now, as they would be ready to disabuse you of any thought that I'm not disappointing.'

Despite Daisy's self-deprecating words, she felt a warm glow in her belly at Silas's compliment.

'To be honest, I've heard professional models say much the same thing on seeing their photographs, but I think they get used to it after a while,' said Silas. 'I probably should have warned you. But you've not seen the best one yet.'

Daisy remembered the last set of photographs, when Silas had just cut her hair and had followed her down the street with the Kodak Vest Pocket.

She'd been so taken aback by the way she looked in the ones Silas had already shown her that she'd quite forgotten about the pictures taken once the official shoot was over.

Silas looked bashful as he slid the picture over to her.

In the photograph she looked a little untidy and windswept, and decidedly casual without her coat and hat, with her newly cut hair and the buttons undone at her neckline and cuffs. She was nowhere near the coiffed image in her other pictures.

But there was something about the light in her and Rose's eyes, and their genuinely happy expressions, as they looked at the camera in what seemed to be a totally unposed way, that cleaved Daisy to this extraordinary picture. It radiated an inexorable sense of life and goodwill.

She'd never seen a photograph quite like this one, and now she had, Daisy was unable to stop looking.

And then she began to sob.

'Oh, Daisy, that's not the reaction I was hoping for,' said Silas gently.

'I don't know why I'm crying,' gulped Daisy, as she dabbed at her face with a hanky. 'It's just that I didn't know I could look like that.'

'The magazine agrees. They are going to use it on their front cover, and so you and Rose will be on newsstands up and down the country,' said Silas.

They were interrupted by the sound of a throat being cleared behind them, and Daisy looked up to see Perry standing there, come to collect the loaf of bread that Daisy gave him for free every three days.

'Silas, can you tidy the pictures away while I sort Perry out?' said Daisy.

She didn't want to share the photographs with anyone else just yet.

Daisy stood up and smiled at Perry, who gave her a gentle smile back. He was a shy and unassuming man who'd been born in Margate. But Jared had said over supper the other night that looks could be deceiving as one of the journeymen had told him that Perry had once very bravely saved a young lad from drowning in the sea.

'Get out of here! I'll bloody sort that conchie out, you see if I don't,' called a male voice from a table nearby, his chair legs scraping on the floor as he lurched to stand up.

The speaker was a man known to everyone in Crumford as Flo Squires – short for Florian – who had shown up at the tea room distinctly tipsy that morning.

But Daisy had allowed him to sit down as this was unusual behaviour for him as he was a church warden, and in the last edition of the *Mercury*, the loss of his son Ainsley, his only child, had been announced in the Roll of Honour.

'Please sit back down, Mr Squires,' requested Daisy.

But Flo Squires lurched over and stood right in front of Perry in an intimidating way, his fists clenched and his wide-legged stance showing that he meant to make something of it.

'You're NBG. NBG, do you hear me? I don't know how you dare to hold your head up,' Flo shouted, small flecks of spittle splattering Perry's face.

Perry didn't flinch or back away.

Daisy had never heard the term 'NBG' before, and she looked at Silas, who mouthed back 'No Bloody Good', and Daisy responded with a quick nod of understanding.

Perry didn't say anything but slowly he drew his hands up so that his palms were held high and were facing towards Flo as an indication that he didn't want any trouble.

Silas moved calmly to Flo's side as if he were going to usher him quietly out of the tea room, but before he could lay hands on him, Flo had punched Perry in the face, the hard blow knocking him clean out.

Perry went down like a ninepin, right on to the table behind him, mercifully free of any customers or hot teapots, but his weight pushing the table back in a way that knocked four chairs to the floor in a crescendo of noise.

Flo lurched around to look drunkenly at Silas, screaming, 'You fucker!' in Silas's face, and he took a swing that Silas had to block with a raised arm.

As Jared and Cynthia and Violet ran in from the bakery, where they had been discussing the latest batch of the hard biscuits, having been alerted by the noise, Flo took a second jab at Silas, who ducked out of the way.

271

Instead it was Daisy that he whacked hard in the face with his elbow, knocking her back several feet and bursting her right eyebrow apart with a spatter of crimson blood spurting out right across the photographs Silas had taken of her.

Incensed at seeing Daisy physically hurt, Silas threw himself at Flo, as did Jared.

Cynthia ran to a very shaken Daisy, who couldn't quite work out what had just happened to her, while hurriedly Violet requested the remaining customers leave, saying that whatever they had had was on the house and they could come back on another day for a second free visit.

Luckily, there weren't many customers as it was so close to the end of business for the day, but those that there were looked on wide-eyed with shock at the sudden turn of events.

Violet then ran back to attend to Perry, who was still unconscious, dragging him out of harm's way.

For now, even with Jared and Silas doing their best to subdue him, Flo was like a man possessed, as he tried to smash tables and chairs around him in a crescendo of agonised grief, and at one point sweeping a whole shelf of crockery from the dresser onto the floor.

It was only when Cynthia yelled at him in her most bossy voice, 'Mr Squires, control yourself!' that Flo's temper abated just as suddenly as it had risen.

He fell to his knees with his head in his hands, his spent body convulsing with huge gulps as he cried, 'I can't bear it that my Ainsley is lying cold and rotting in France, and that fucking conchie is walking around without a care in the world, determined not to do his bit for king and country.'

Daisy opened her mouth to say that he wasn't being fair and that she was sure that Perry would go on to do his bit, just not with guns and a bayonet, but Cynthia put a hand on Daisy's arm to tell her to keep quiet.

Then Perry gave a little moan and tried to sit up.

To avoid further trouble, quickly Silas knelt on the floor beside Flo, making sure that his body was shielding the sight of Perry. He put his arms around the distraught man, pulling Flo close as his harsh words gave way to more tears of extreme grief and he howled wetly into Silas's shoulder.

Without saying anything, Silas flipped his head in the direction of the door, indicating that everyone else should leave.

Daisy tried to stay, but Cynthia put an arm around her shoulder and made her walk outside and into the mill house, and it was only at this point that Daisy realised that she had blood running down her face and dripping on to her bodice.

Violet helped Perry stumble inside too, and Jared ran to Crumford for the doctor as Daisy obviously needed stitching up, while Perry looked to be severely concussed given how often he was saying the same words of 'I am so sorry for your loss.'

Daisy never knew how long Silas held Flo Squires for, but by the time Jared had returned to Old Creaky with the doctor there was no sign of either man, nor the bloodied photographs that Silas had taken of Daisy, although Jared said he was sure that Silas would have made sure that Flo got home safely.

The tea room looked a complete wreck, according to Violet, as she described the carnage left behind to a now very groggy Daisy, but Daisy was too shaken to care.

Then Violet insisted that Daisy mustn't worry about it at all, and should probably go to bed as it must have been a huge shock. In the meantime, Violet and Holly would sort everything out in the tea room once Holly was back from her afternoon stint at the brewery.

Cynthia was kept busy running between the camp bed in the small room the visiting journeymen used when they had to stay over, where Perry was now lying (although in his confusion, he kept trying to get up, muddling the cold fireplace with the door to the room), and the kitchen where Daisy was sitting, her dress quite ruined by the amount of blood she had lost from her split eyebrow.

'That was the damnedest thing,' said Cynthia to Daisy. 'I've never seen a man treat another as Silas Grover did poor Flo Squires. The way he put his arms around him, and held him tight. It was extraordinary, and very much the best thing to do.'

'Poor Mr Squires. It's a hard thing for him to lose Ainsley. I almost didn't let him sit down earlier as he was clearly squiffy, but I know he's a widower and Ainsley was his only son, and I suppose my heart went out to him,' said Daisy.

'Daisy, even though it ended badly, you did the right thing,' said Cynthia kindly. She put an arm around her eldest daughter's shoulder and drew her close for a moment. 'If we can't extend a hand of friendship at a time like this, then what would that mean? It's a crying shame that you and Perry were hurt, but nobody could have anticipated what was going to happen, and Flo Squires will be ashamed of himself once he is sober. But thank heavens Silas Grover was there too, otherwise the end result could have been much, much worse. You and Perry will get better, and we can replace a bit of crockery and repair the furniture in the tea room and give the customers who were there their next visit on the house, but nothing is going to bring poor Ainsley back to Crumford and his father.'

Cynthia went to take Perry a cup of tea, leaving Daisy to muse on how quickly a nice afternoon could take a turn for the worse as the doctor sewed up the cut with some thick catgut thread. And not for the first time in her life, Daisy thought, thank heavens for Silas Grover.

She tried hard not to flinch as the doctor went about his work, suturing her brow, but even though he told her to think of nice things and to pinch her leg if the pain got too much, the needle going in and out of her flesh hurt a lot. Daisy thought to herself that she was going to be more hideous with the stitches than with the open gash through her eyebrow. Meanwhile the doctor told her that she could dab salt water on to it and that he would come back in a week's time to remove the sutures.

There was one good thing that came out of this afternoon, however, which was Violet and Holly ended hostilities with Daisy. And the sisters got on much better afterwards than they had for several years.

However, if this was what it had taken, then Daisy was happy to once again feel a proper part of Old Creaky, firmly back once more in the comforting bosom of the Graham family fold.

Chapter Twenty-two

The next day Daisy had a screamingly painful head and was unable to face the thought of standing up in the tea room all day. Her eye socket especially was fat and swollen, with her bruised skin an array of livid colours, and her eye only half open. She felt shaky and distinctly woozy.

The twins teased Daisy that it looked like she was winking at them, and even Jared said her face suggested she'd gone a couple of rounds with his hero, world-famous heavyweight boxer Bombardier Billy Wells.

Daisy tried to take their chaffing in the good-natured way that they had meant it, but the sutures were throbbing and itchy, and she felt very groggy and confused, and so smiling at their comments felt a big effort.

Cynthia took Daisy's place in the tea room, coming back in the afternoon to give her a new set of the photographs that Silas had dropped off for her, along with a book on basic photography that he'd thought she might like to read and – according to Cynthia – profuse apologies that he couldn't stop as he had somewhere he needed to be.

That teatime the whole family stared in amazement at the photographs Silas had taken of Daisy and Rose, and then in awe at Daisy, who was definitely relieved Silas wasn't seeing the much less glamorous version of herself with a bashed-up face.

Jared said as he indicated the pictures, 'You'll be upping sticks and off to London, then, for more of this.'

'Oh no,' said Daisy in horror. 'Well, not at the moment anyhow. I mean, just look at me!'

Dutifully, the family looked at her injured face and then back at the photos and at Daisy once more.

Holly broke first with a hoot of laughter, and Daisy joined her ruefully, and then the rest of the family plunged in, with Cynthia saying as everyone quietened down, 'Talk about going from the sublime to the ridiculous, Daisy,' which for some reason set everyone off laughing again.

Then Daisy said to Jared, 'I admit I was jealous at first of Olive going to the bright lights of the big city, but I think I'm here for a long while as when things like an injury happen you want to be with your family, or at least I do. You're not going to get rid of me that easily. I'm not sure London would ever have anything to offer me that I can't find in Crumford. Sorry! These photographs aren't real life, are they, and I really don't see myself doing it again.'

'Whatever you decide, Daisy, you're always our daughter, and Old Creaky is always your home,' said Jared seriously.

Daisy gave him a hug, and whispered, 'Thank you, Father, that means a lot,' into his ear, and the pair smiled at each other.

'Silas might have something to say about you not posing for him again,' interrupted Holly, which made the twins go 'woo' in a way that showed they meant to tease Daisy about how taken Silas was with her.

She thought that the fact the twins did this meant that nobody in the family had guessed quite how involved she and Silas were, as if they had, Daisy doubted they'd tease her so obviously.

'He won't care one way or another. This was Silas's last commercial work like this until after the war is over and he only did it because it was already under con-tract when the war broke out,' Daisy explained, hastily pushing away an unbidden image in her mind of exactly how she'd like to pose for Silas, which didn't involve too much clothing. Not that she would ever dare to confess this to anyone, even Silas.

She added, 'And somehow I don't think Silas will be happy to return to this sort of thing—' Daisy nodded in the direction of the photographs '—once everything is back to normal. I'm not sure why, but I think he'll want then to photograph much more important things than clothes and prams.'

'All the same, these are *very* nice pictures to have of yourself,' Holly said enviously. 'I'd love some like that of me. Just think, Daisy, when you're in your dotage, you'll be able to show them off to your grandchildren and say "that was me", and they won't believe you!'

'Yes, they are nice to have, I suppose,' agreed Daisy thoughtfully, as she ran a finger along the bumps of the stitches in her brow.

While she did love the photographs themselves, her feelings were now complicated.

The shock of seeing Flo Squires and his terrible grief over the loss of Ainsley almost immediately after she'd first looked at the pictures had meant the two things had become inextricably linked in her mind, with the result that now the photographs felt immensely trivial and inconsequential in comparison to the loss of Ainsley Squires and all the other men like him.

And that was exactly how it should be, Daisy thought, as she resolved to remember this when she felt better.

⌒⌒⌒

The next morning Daisy still felt under par with a splitting headache, and so again Cynthia was looking after the tea room.

Mid-morning Daisy was sitting in the kitchen with Holly, who had finished her morning stint helping Violet in the bakery, when suddenly there was a terrible keening noise from outside. It sounded like someone was in terrible pain.

Daisy felt a surge of fear that for a moment threatened to engulf her, and she had to grab at the tabletop for a moment to steady herself as it felt as if the world about her was going to physically upend.

Everybody – Cynthia, Jared, Daisy, Holly and Violet, and Perry too – ran out onto the grass between the mill and the mill house to find a distraught Marguerite standing there in Joy's arms. Marguerite was clutching a crumpled telegram as she screamed into Joy's shoulder.

Daisy experienced that terrible sinking sense of terror one gets when it's obvious that bad news is about to be given, and she looked at her family, and their serious faces suggested they were all sharing a similar sense of misgiving.

The noise of the grinding stones in the mill, still going like the clappers, heightened this feeling, almost sounding like a furious underworld was below them all, poised to drag them hook, line and sinker downwards to Hades.

And the shock of this somehow leached all the colour from around Daisy, and as she looked desperately about, suddenly all she could see were tiny but irrefutable signs all over Old Creaky that indicated the tough times they were in.

There were some patches of peeling paint on the smock mill, and weeds in the path from the gate, which ordinarily her mother would never have let happen. And Cynthia's vegetable bed and fruit cages looked sorry for themselves. Nobody had time to do the many small things the family usually took such pride in.

As Marguerite continued to bellow in agony, Daisy wondered how she'd not noticed any of this before. It was as if the mill was physically starting to crumble and buckle, mirroring the way she felt inside.

As Daisy stood there frozen, apart from the trembling in her knees, Cynthia seemed made of sterner stuff. She stepped forward and gently lifted the telegram from Marguerite's hand.

It was from the army, Cynthia told them all in a quiet voice, and it said Clem was missing in action.

Daisy's heart clenched.

Cynthia went on to explain that the telegram was an official pro forma document from the officer in charge of records that had a section in type which was printed as part of the telegram, Clem's details having been written in pen above.

Cynthia then read out loud this section:

The report that he is missing does not necessarily mean that he has been killed, as he may be a prisoner of war or temporarily separated from his regiment.

Official reports that men who are prisoners of war take some time to reach this country and if he has been captured by the enemy it is probable that unofficial news will reach you first. In that case, I am to ask you to forward any letter received at once to the Office, and it will be returned to you as soon as possible.

Should any further official information be received it will be at once communicated to you.

Daisy felt unable to fully take in what was happening.

Joy said needlessly, 'It's just been dropped off by a telegram girl.'

'What does it mean?' asked Holly, looking confused.

'It means that they don't know where Clem is or what has happened to him,' said Jared, obviously shaken to the core but trying very hard to be brave so as not to upset everyone further.

'But this says here that Clem went missing ten days ago,' cried Cynthia then, looking closely at the date that had been added to the telegram, 'and we're only just hearing about it now?'

As Jared tried to tell everyone to look on the bright side as at least they hadn't found a body, Daisy found herself ignoring her father.

To her, it seemed very much as if Clem had died.

She hoped this wasn't the case, but there seemed so many horrible things happening these days, that Daisy found it impossible to see a lighter possibility.

Poor Asa too, she thought, if that was the case – it would be terrible for him to lose his brother in this way when they had sworn to look after each other, and Daisy knew he would feel very guilty.

'Let me get Rose, and then I'll take over in the tea room,' said Joy, who seemed to be coming into her own during these last few days in a way that Daisy wouldn't have thought previously was in her, 'and you all go inside the mill house as you need to talk about

283

this. Violet, do I need to get anything out of the oven for you?'

As Violet gave instructions as to what needed to be done in the bakery, Daisy noticed that Marguerite seemed virtually senseless, although her breathing was now reduced to irregular gasps, as she leaned still against Joy. Marguerite's time for having the baby was quite close, so Perry, who'd seen this too, said he'd go for the doctor, to be on the safe side.

To her horror, Daisy found herself wanting to make a joke that the doctor had better move in to Old Creaky as he was becoming such a regular visitor. She bit the words back, although even with a hand clapped over her mouth, she was unable to claw back a rather hysterical giggle escaping that made everyone look her way.

Marguerite's expression was one that seemed to Daisy to be pure venom, but then Cynthia said in a comforting way to Marguerite that she should pay no mind to Daisy who, they should remember, was still recovering from being hit so hard in the face and clearly wasn't herself yet, and the laugh was most likely due to shock rather than her finding anything to laugh about in the situation.

Daisy nodded furiously to indicate that Cynthia was right, and she hadn't meant any harm. But nobody noticed this.

'Daisy, go and lie down,' instructed Jared quite brusquely, once they were all back in the mill house, 'and we'll let you know if there's any news.'

Daisy didn't want to be parted from the others, but she could see that Jared needed her to be out of the way in case she did something else to upset Marguerite.

And she realised that actually she felt queasy from hearing the news about Clem, and distinctly unsteady, and so reluctantly she stumbled up to her room, although not before she had said to Perry, who was helping Marguerite inside now that Joy had gone to fetch Rose, that after he'd found the doctor, could he possibly go to the post office to send a telegram to Olive with the news, as she would definitely want to be told.

Daisy lay on her bed, but her thoughts felt jumbled and fuzzy, and the bed seemed to be rocking in a way that made her feel quite seasick.

When she eventually fell into a deep but restless sleep, it was plagued with relentless visions of marching enemy soldiers wearing their spiked Pickelhaube helmets, their boots drumming as they made their way towards the British Tommy Atkins. She was awoken by Olive gently giving her a shake, her body highlighted by the open door to the lit corridor outside.

It was pitch-black in the bedroom so Daisy knew that she had been out for the count for hours.

'Olive, it's so good to have you here,' Daisy croaked.

'There's no further news of Clem,' said Olive as she perched on the bed beside her cousin. 'But you look as if you have been in the wars, my dear.'

'I'm afraid I have. I don't feel very well, but it seems churlish to complain right now,' said Daisy.

'Understandable. It sounds a very nasty moment for you, what happened in the tea room, and one that really could have been a lot worse, from what I'm told. You know people can die from injuries to the head, if there's a bleed on the brain,' Olive told her in a very nursey way.

'Thanks, Olive, I really wanted to know that, I don't think.'

'Silly! I expect it would have happened to you already if it were going to,' Olive said briskly, 'so I'm pretty certain you are on the mend, but you have to take it easy for a while. Holly and Violet have shown me the photographs Silas took by the way – you don't need me to tell you how good they are. Anyway, that's enough about you! I have to go back tomorrow afternoon, but I have a very nice matron who said that as I was on earlies, I could come back to Crumford the minute my shift ended today. A fellow trainee at the nurses' home brought the telegram to me at the hospital, and I caught the train down.'

Olive leaned down and undid her boots, which she then kicked off.

'Budge up, Daisy, it's freezing in here,' Olive said, and then she slipped under the covers after Daisy had shuffled over. 'From what I can tell, nearly everyone downstairs is holding up pretty well, and Joy has apparently gone full matron this afternoon, having the time of her life lording it over everyone in the tea room. Cynthia is being very stoic, and refuses to believe that the worst has happened; Jared is more circumspect, but is trying to jolly everyone along. Violet and Holly are saying that we should get letters from Asa and Ren soon, and the twins are, well, the twins. It's Marguerite whom everyone is worried about, and the doctor is too, as he's concerned about the baby. He wanted to admit her to hospital this afternoon, but she wouldn't go, and so he's coming back tomorrow.'

Daisy's queasy feeling hadn't abated, but she realised that it was a symptom of worry more than anything else.

'I'd better get up,' she said. 'I want to make my peace with Marguerite as I let out a terrible laugh when she was so upset. I don't know why I did it. I certainly wasn't finding it funny.'

'It's a symptom of shock, Daisy,' said Olive, 'so don't be too hard on yourself.'

Daisy had a cup of tea downstairs with everyone, but she found she wasn't hungry even though she hadn't had anything to eat since breakfast time, and not very much even then.

Marguerite and Joy were there too, along with baby Rose.

Daisy went to sit by Marguerite. She took Marguerite's hand in hers, and they sat quietly for a while, each comforting the other just by being near. It didn't seem as if they needed to say anything to each other, and Daisy found her racing mind soothed. She hoped Marguerite felt similarly.

∽

The next morning, letters arrived at Old Creaky from both Asa and Ren, written two days after Clem had been reported missing in action.

Cynthia read out Asa's letter to the family, before passing it to Joy to keep.

Dear Mother and Father, and Joy, and everyone else,

You may have had a telegram by now that Clem is missing. I am pleased to say that he has now been found – he was injured and there was a mix-up and he was in a hospital tent all the while. He is alive but he's not well, and they are going to send him home, but he is alive. It was a very dicey time when we did not know what had happened to him, but I am told he is conscious and he hasn't lost any limbs.

I am well, but am not enjoying this bally war.

I have to go now, but am sending you kind thoughts. Joy, please kiss Rose for me.

Your loving Asa

Daisy knew that Asa was in a real stew about what had happened – he would never have repeated 'he is alive' twice in the same sentence otherwise, as he had always been a stickler for correct English and he hated unnecessary repetitions.

Ren's letter was longer.

Dearest Daisy

I thought I should write with all haste to tell you that your Clem has been found. I know Asa is writing too, but none of us know how much to trust the post these days, and you all seem so far, and so I thought if I wrote too, then you would definitely get at least one of our letters.

It was a rum do. Clem was beside me and then, suddenly, he was nowhere to be seen. But we had to keep going under bombardment . . .

There was a large bit redacted with a thick black line here, which told Daisy that the censor had thought what Ren was saying at this point contained sensitive information.

. . . and then later nobody could find him.

It was a terrible time as we waited for news, but at long last we heard he had been found in a hospital tent. He is being sent home – I don't know exactly what is wrong with him, but he must need attention he can't get here. I don't know whether 'home' means home-home, or just somewhere in England. I hope the former so that the family can see him.

We are all very glum that Clem is no longer with us as it feels as if our little band of brothers has been broken up most cruelly, and I feel this especially as he is my best friend. I would be very grateful for any news of him that you can pass on.

I think often of that party in the summer when the weather was fine and we were all so happy – in these cold and difficult days, it seems a memory from a distant world.

Yours truly, Ren Brewer

Daisy knew exactly what Ren meant about the party seeming an age ago. It really did. She felt a very different person to the playful and optimistic girl she'd been back then, and clearly Ren did too.

She was relieved to discover she didn't have the energy though to feel awkward about Ren getting in touch, when her thoughts were stuffed so full of those of herself and Silas.

This was a problem for another day.

A couple of hours later the doctor arrived to examine Marguerite, and then he drove her to the hospital in Canterbury in his own motor car, whereupon they admitted her.

Poor Marguerite was now very unwell with blurred vision, a pain in her stomach and her hands and feet were swollen; she had been sick too.

It all felt like too much, Daisy decided.

Frankly, she felt like going back to bed and pulling the covers up and over her head, hiding there until the war was over.

It was horrid and difficult, and there was no end in sight.

Chapter Twenty-three

The days lurched along in this dismal fashion. Marguerite remained in hospital and would stay there until after the baby arrived, and there was no further news of Clem, and no letters from Asa or Ren. Olive was now back in London, but would be transferring well before Christmas to the same hospital where Marguerite was.

Basil Brewer drove over to Old Creaky to say how sorry he was about what had happened to Clem.

He and Cynthia and Jared spent some time talking in the parlour, Daisy hearing Basil say as he took his farewells, 'If there's anything I can do, anything at all, you only have to ask. You know where I am, and any time night or day. I really do mean that. Anything at any time.'

Jared looked as if he might blub as he came to where she was in the kitchen, and Daisy had hastily to turn her eyes away as she couldn't bear the thought of seeing her proud father being reduced to tears simply because somebody had said a few kind words to him.

Cynthia walked Basil to his car parked in the lane, and Daisy watched as they talked beside the driver's door, before they shook hands and Basil climbed inside.

Basil Brewer had obviously remembered Cynthia's kind words when he'd been so upset at waving off his three sons on their way to war, on the train in August, and Daisy felt very touched.

People could be so kind sometimes, couldn't they?

It wasn't that long afterwards that Daisy's face finally felt less bruised and the doctor had been back to take out her stitches.

After looking at her reflection closely in the hall mirror, she decided that she'd healed enough that she could be seen in public again, especially as with her short hair it was easy to arrange a section to cover her still-swollen eyebrow.

Joy was in her element bossing everyone around in the teashop, and Rose seemed happy enough either in her pram, as her mother took orders from customers, or lying on her tummy on some cushions near a warm bit of the wall, and so Daisy took the opportunity to walk over to the photographic studio to see if Silas was at home.

But Briar had to break the news to Daisy that neither Silas nor Roscoe were based in Crumford right at the minute. Several days previously they had received sudden orders to leave for France, and Briar wasn't sure when they would be back.

They had had to leave very hurriedly, and there hadn't been time for Silas to come to see Daisy as he had had to carefully pack a lot of equipment, and the same had been true for Roscoe too.

Daisy was already feeling low, but this news crashed her mood down further.

As she walked back to Old Creaky, Daisy had a shock, although one more intriguing and perplexing than horrifying.

She'd taken a roundabout route for her return to the smock mill to give herself a little time to get used to Silas not being at close quarters any longer.

They had never seen each other very often, as Silas was so busy, but now Daisy realised that the knowledge that he was near at hand had definitely become a reassuring prop to her. She'd found it very comforting to think of him eating his lunch and supper, and going to bed, and taking his photographs, all within a mile of where she was.

Now she felt unfairly spurned and cast aside, and very much on her own, and this made Daisy feel even more jumpy and twitchy than she already was.

First Clem and now Silas, it was almost as if everyone she cared about was determined to show her that they might not always be there.

In theory she'd always known this, and about Silas especially, but now it was happening, it felt different, she discovered.

She must learn to be stronger and more resilient, Daisy told herself.

It was at this point that her attention was caught by something most peculiar.

She stopped in the lane and stood on tiptoe as she craned her head this way and that, trying to get a better view.

There was no way around it.

Daisy could see a corner of the bumper to Basil Brewer's distinctive shiny green automobile. She was certain it was his. There couldn't be too many people in this part of Kent who could afford a Rolls-Royce nor would want to park it in a gateway to an ordinary field.

Daisy wondered what Basil might be doing – it seemed such an odd place for him to be parked, and very out of character for a debonair businessman like him.

Very tentatively and as quietly as she could, Daisy crept forward a step or two, determined to get a better view, although hopefully without being seen or heard.

Then she almost let out a cry of surprise. For she saw she saw someone she knew very well get out of the car's passenger seat and then smooth her clothes down, as if they'd been badly ruffled up and now needed restoring to something decent.

It was Holly!

And the next moment, Holly turned round quickly and climbed back into the car so that she was kneeling on the seat she'd just vacated, in order that she could kiss Basil right on the mouth.

They kissed like this for what felt to Daisy like a long time, hungrily running their hands over one another. It was as if Holly couldn't get enough of this older man.

Whoa.

It was the last thing Daisy had expected to stumble upon.

Daisy was flabbergasted, and she shrank as far back into the hedge on the opposite side of the lane as she could. She really didn't want them to think she had been spying.

But she couldn't quite stop looking. The way Holly and Basil greedily caressed each other very much reminded her of her feelings when she was with Silas.

Holly and Basil Brewer!

Basil Brewer.

And *Holly*!

It wasn't that Daisy's shock was at Basil Brewer being old enough to be Holly's father, but more that he was almost old enough to be her grandfather.

So Holly being over at the brewery to work on the accounts so often was clearly a cover for something else.

But what on earth were the pair of them thinking right now, behaving in this way and in broad daylight too?

This was how scandals were made, thought Daisy.

At least she and Silas had had the good sense to keep what they had between themselves, she told herself prissily, ignoring what she had said to Olive.

And then with a rush of shame Daisy remembered how brazenly she and Silas had behaved out in the open on the birdwatching day, and how eagerly they had reached for each other. She hadn't been so sensible that time, had she?

Did this mean that love made fools out of everyone?

Daisy rather thought it did, although it was hard to believe that Jared and Cynthia had ever felt that passionate about one another, even though they had managed to produce seven children.

Silently, Daisy retraced her steps a little way, and then, crouching down, she hid behind the hedge of an adjacent field until she heard the sound of Basil's car reversing out into the lane, and driving away, followed by the dwindling sound of Holly's footsteps retreating as she headed homewards.

Goodness, but this was one secret that Daisy really wished she hadn't stumbled upon.

If indeed it were a secret, that was.

For all Daisy knew, Violet could be well aware of what Holly was up to, especially as presumably Basil or his car-owning cronies had given Violet the odd lift to Canterbury so that Violet, and probably Holly too, could spend time at the magazine. And her two sisters had been much closer of late, so maybe Holly had shared her relationship with Violet.

If Cynthia and Jared were to believe Silas was too old for herself at age thirty-four, should they ever find out what had happened, which had always been Daisy's assumption, then what on earth would they say about Holly, not yet twenty, and Basil Brewer, who was in his fifties?

Then Daisy remembered how impressed Cynthia had been with the way Silas had dealt with Flo Squires that awful day in the tea room. Perhaps this would mean that Silas did have points in his favour as far as her parents were concerned, although maybe not enough for them to believe Silas the right man for her.

Ren Brewer, her parents definitely approved of as a potential partner for their eldest daughter, Daisy knew, but Ren and Silas were as different as chalk and cheese.

She didn't think either man was necessarily better than the other, just that she was more drawn in an urgent, primal sense to Silas, even though she knew that it was unlikely to go anywhere long-term.

And unfortunately for Daisy, having experienced what she had with Silas, it meant the pitch had definitely been queered when it came to Ren, and so she would always think him well meaning but essentially a much more watered-down version of a lover than fundamentally she desired.

But what would her parents think about Holly and Basil Brewer?

Obviously if Holly and Basil were serious it wouldn't hurt that Basil was an immensely rich and influential, relatively recent widower.

Would this mean that her parents would believe Basil a good match for Holly, in large part because of his wealth and high standing in Crumford society, even though Holly would be younger than all his sons?

This wasn't inconceivable, Daisy had to acknowledge, as the Grahams weren't a particularly wealthy family even though their business turned a reasonable profit, and Holly would be unlikely to meet anybody else who could give her such a stable home as Basil. And any children Holly might have would be very comfortably provided for.

Cynthia and Jared would both be very aware of all of Basil Brewer's many advantages, and they had never made any secret of the fact that they were keen for all their children to make advantageous marriages.

In Crumford terms, it probably didn't come better than marrying a Brewer, although her parents' hopes were more likely for their daughters to marry the Brewer sons.

The way the two of them had smiled at each other, and the familiar way they had leaned forward, suggested that it might indeed be quite serious between them. Or to put it another way, it seemed obvious to Daisy that what she had seen wasn't the couple's first kiss or embrace.

Daisy wondered if Holly had realised that when she reached the age of fifty, Basil would be well into his eighties. While the age gap might not seem insurmountable to Holly now, it might very well be a different story at that point.

And what with Violet and her magazine, and now Holly and Basil, plus of course Daisy and Silas, and also nobody knowing what was wrong with Clem, it was hard not to think that Cynthia and Jared would be having some rude awakenings very soon, thought Daisy with a melancholy sigh as she opened the gate to Old Creaky.

As she made her way into the house a while later, she tried to plaster a happy expression upon her face, as she didn't want the family to know there was anything wrong.

Bad news, if it were going to come, would wing its way to her parents quite soon enough of its own accord.

∽

Olive came over the next lunchtime with news.

She had arrived at the hospital in Canterbury a little while previously, and as luck would have it, had been on night duty at the hospital where she would complete her nurse's training when Clem had been admitted.

She'd suspected, correctly, that the Graham family and Marguerite still hadn't received official notification as to Clem being transferred to the Canterbury hospital, and after she had been to see Marguerite in her ward upstairs to where Clem was to give her the news, Olive had made haste to Old Creaky the first moment she could in order to fill everyone else in on what she knew.

As Perry looked after the tea room and everyone else squeezed around the kitchen table in the mill house, Olive explained, 'From what I can tell it's not clear what is wrong with poor Clem. But he doesn't seem able to communicate properly and he can't do that much for himself. Well, anything for himself really. He has the mark of what to me looks like a horse's hoof on his brow, so I don't know if that is part of the problem. He's very jumpy too, at loud noises especially. He screamed when another nurse dropped a broom and it made a tremendous crash. His notes say he has nightmares most nights and he makes a terrible racket with yells and shouts, which disturb the patients sleeping near him.'

Cynthia and Jared clasped each other's hands at this point.

Olive continued, 'I told Clem that Marguerite is in the hospital too as she waits for the baby, and that I could wheel him to see her today, but he didn't respond at all. Various doctors are looking at him, but from what I see, they haven't yet decided on the best treatment.'

Jared and Cynthia stared at each other, their eyes brimming with unshed tears.

'Poor Clem,' whispered Daisy.

She also thought sadly about Marguerite, as if Clem didn't buck up, it could be that this poor young woman would end up caring for both a new baby and her husband.

Not long afterwards, Basil Brewer arrived with his car, ready to drive Jared and Cynthia over to the hospital, and Olive too.

The person who had driven Olive from the hospital to Old Creaky had gone on to break the news to Basil, on Olive's instruction, as she thought Basil would step in to help, which he had.

Daisy watched Holly carefully in the resulting flurry of activity that Basil's arrival provoked, and she spotted that Basil and Holly studiously avoided eye contact with each other, indeed in such an obvious way that Daisy was sure that everyone else must notice too.

Daisy looked at her parents, but they certainly only had thoughts for Clem.

She turned her attention to Violet to see if there was any sign that Violet knew what Holly was up to, but she was helping Cynthia and Jared get ready to go, and so there wasn't any clue there either way.

Daisy decided that since Holly and Basil clearly wanted it under wraps still, this had to be a sensible decision as the last thing their parents needed at this moment was more on their plates.

'Mother, I'll find your hat and gloves and coat so that you can be off,' said Daisy, thinking the best thing was to get her parents to Clem's bedside as quickly as possible. 'And tell our Clem that we all send him love and our very best wishes.'

Nativity

Chapter Twenty-four

December had almost arrived and everyone tried to paste on cheerful faces because the twins were excited about Christmas coming, and their roles in the play that Marguerite had written and that they had been practising for several weeks now.

In normal times, Christmas was traditionally a very jolly time in Crumford, and Daisy had always thoroughly enjoyed the Yuletide festivities.

Understandably, this year it seemed that all the adults at Old Creaky were somewhat jaded, even Holly and Violet, despite the other things going on in their lives. At any rate, Daisy definitely felt sorry for herself now that Silas wasn't around to lift her mood.

Cynthia made it very clear that despite the family's travails, they were all to make a real effort to give Tansy and Senna a good time, as it wasn't the fault of the young twins that Britain was at war. Cynthia adding that, religion aside, Christmas activities were really for the children anyway.

Although Daisy and her two oldest sisters agreed that they hadn't felt like children for a very long time, it was odd for each of them to hear a not very patient Cynthia close the door with such finality upon their own childhoods.

'Mother is not herself,' said Holly.

'She certainly has got out of bed on the wrong side,' added Violet. 'With her in this mood, I can't see her wanting us to put our stockings out.'

'Actually, I think we should all forget about our own stockings – it doesn't feel the right time. Have you noticed that Mother is looking peaky as well – I think it's the worry about Clem, and Asa too, and Marguerite and the forthcoming baby, that's taking a toll, and she's probably not sleeping too well. I've an idea.'

Violet and Holly groaned at the thought of one of Daisy's ideas.

Unbowed, Daisy elaborated, 'Why don't we offer to take over and do everything for Christmas and the New Year so that Mother and Father can have a bit of time to themselves, and maybe even put their feet up for a couple of hours?'

Her sisters didn't blink as they stared at Daisy.

She went on, 'If the three of us take over doing all the Christmas things, it can't be that hard, can it? Three strong women like us . . .'

The sisters thought about it.

Then Violet said, 'What do you mean by "everything", Daisy? I can't afford a lot of time, you know.'

'Me neither,' agreed Holly.

Daisy felt her sisters were being selfish, but she didn't want to argue with them as if that happened then nothing would get done, and so she thought she'd cajole them instead.

'Well, there'll be your birthday tea, Holly, as your nineteenth birthday is just before Christmas, and I'm sure you'd like us to mark that in some way, wouldn't you? And then there'll be the nativity play that the twins are in, and for that I had been planning anyway to give cast and crew a jolly in the tea room afterwards,' Daisy explained. 'I don't suppose there'll be a pantomime to go to, which will be a shame, but we can take the twins carol singing with lanterns, which will be fun, and we can decorate the house for Mother, and the tea room, and take over cooking Christmas dinner – she's already made the pudding and the cake, and there's no sugar so we won't have to ice the cake, and so that is part of the responsibility taken off us already.'

Daisy had to take a deep breath as she'd been speaking quickly so as not to lose her sisters' attention. She added then, 'Us three can each organise a game or two for after Christmas dinner – charades, sardines, squeak piggy squeak, up Jenkins, you know, all the usual culprits. And there'll be midnight mass on Christmas Eve and the supper when we get back from that, and perhaps we can think of something special too to do to mark New Year's Eve. And hopefully Marguerite's baby will be here by then and she'll be home, so we can live the spirit of Christmas by making up her food. And we'll go to see Clem too, of course. And as long as Tansy and Senna have stockings at the end of their beds, that's the main thing, and we can put those stockings together.'

'That does sound like quite a lot of work,' said Holly.

'And not much of a rest for us,' Violet said. 'I wonder though what Marguerite will call the baby, as she hasn't got first dibs on the name Holly?'

'Ivy, maybe, from "The Holly and the Ivy", or Carol, if she wants a name that reflects the time of the year?' said Holly. 'And for a boy, perhaps Joseph or Noel?'

'Let's hope she doesn't choose Ivy, as Mrs Lang will never let us forget it if she does,' said Violet.

'We're getting off the subject, you two,' sighed Daisy. 'I think Mother needs a rest more than we do. And I expect Olive will be around to lend a hand, and I thought that as Perry lives alone and his family is in Bristol we could invite him too – he's bound to want to help as he's that sort of obliging chap. Joy will be there too. And we can give the twins some jobs to do as well, and so it will be a case of many hands making light work.'

Her sisters looked at Daisy, and then rather reluctantly they nodded their capitulation to her plans with pointedly dramatic groans, with Holly adding, 'Oh be quiet, Daisy – you win. But please stop being such a goody-two-shoes about it as it's really irritating.'

Violet nodded in support of Holly, and Daisy thought she had best keep schtum, much as she wanted to say 'Irritating, *moi*?' and then to remind her sisters of everything that Cynthia and Jared had done for them all over the years, without a word of complaint (well, not too many words of complaint).

'We could ask Basil Brewer to join us for Christmas lunch, and I'm sure Olive would like it if we asked Briar too,' Daisy added, immediately forgetting that she hadn't intended to speak. 'We can have lunch on Christmas Day in the tea room, and then we won't all have to squash in together uncomfortably in the mill house.'

There was another short silence.

'Well, I suppose I could see whether Basil Brewer has already made any plans for Christmas Day,' Holly said casually.

'That's the ticket, Holly,' said Daisy, 'and if you have any Canterbury friends that you'd like to invite, Violet, then add them to the list.'

Daisy didn't dare look at the faces of either of her sisters and she quickly left the room so that she could tell Cynthia about their plans.

Chapter Twenty-five

The next day Basil Brewer drove Daisy to Canterbury so that she could visit Clem for the first time.

Even though Cynthia had taken care to explain to Daisy what to expect, she still wasn't prepared for the sight of her brother.

Clem was grey-skinned but with a garishly red mouth from where he'd bitten fragments of dried skin from his lips. He was obviously several stones lighter than when she had last seen him, and his hands trembled constantly, fluttering uncomfortably above the bedclothes, while he had a patchy beard growing upon his chin. She could hear his breath scratch, and his chest bubble. He looked briefly towards Daisy, but didn't give her any sense that he'd recognised her.

She went to hug and kiss him, but her heart felt as if it were breaking when he flinched and turned his head away before she got too close, his eyes tightly shut.

Daisy backed away at once. The Clem she knew had always been very tactile with others, him even teaching her some basic wrestling moves the previous Easter.

Now, Daisy found herself at an unhappy distance, reduced to chatting to him absurdly about minor goings on at Old Creaky, and how much they were all looking forward to having Marguerite and the baby back home, once the baby decided to arrive.

But poor Clem barely seemed to take in anything she said, and when he did, he had a very delayed response, which he showed only by turning his eyes to hers for half a second before glancing away again.

Daisy didn't know how she should respond.

She found herself groping for Olive's hand, who was standing beside her.

'Speak to him normally, Daisy,' said Olive, looking smart and professional in her nurse's uniform. 'You can hear, can't you, Clem? And you understand this is your sister Daisy?'

Clem turned his face to the wall and shut his eyes again. He most definitely didn't look as if he did want to understand.

'I think he needs to rest, Olive,' said Daisy, salty tears tracking down her cheeks.

This was so far from the Clem she had grown up with that it physically hurt Daisy to be near him.

Olive nodded.

'Clem, dear, I'll come and see you soon,' said Daisy, trying to make her voice as warm as possible as she sought things to say. 'I am going to go now and say hello to Marguerite. But please remember that we all love you very much indeed, and we want you home with us. Father needs help in the mill. How is he going to manage without you there at his side to lend a hand, as you've always done so well? And Marguerite will want you to learn how to change that baby's nappies, I'm sure.'

Daisy saw a large tear slide down Clem's cheek.

He would hate for her to see him cry, she knew, and so abruptly she turned on her heel and then marched as quickly as she could through the ward and out into the corridor, where she stood with both hands against the painted wall, and her brow pressed against the plaster as she breathed heavily and she tried to compose herself, leaving Olive to follow her out.

'Wait up, Daisy,' Olive said. 'I know it's difficult for you to see, and a real shock. But please remember that at least Clem is in one piece, which is a lot more than can be said for some of the other soldiers we have here that have been sent to us from the front. And all the doctors say that brains are remarkable things, and if we can get his chest better, and allow nature to take its course, then he might return one day almost to normal.'

An engine backfired outside and Daisy heard an anguished squeal that she just knew came from Clem.

Her heart tore in sadness for him. She didn't think it likely he would return to anything like normal, no matter how much Olive tried to convince her otherwise.

Her cousin seemed to understand what Daisy was feeling as she wrapped her arms around her, and said, 'There, there' as Daisy gasped in anguish, her shoulders heaving.

After a minute or two, Olive said, 'Right, Daisy Graham, that's enough of that. It's time to dry your eyes. Are you ready to visit Marguerite now?'

Damply, Daisy took a small step back and nodded at her cousin.

'I need to prepare you for a bit of a shock there too, I'm afraid, as she's not going to look like she did when you last saw her either,' said Olive. Daisy steeled herself for whatever it was that her sister-in-law might look like.

Poor Marguerite was indeed in a very bad way as she lay on her back, her belly huge, and her legs, feet and hands all preternaturally large, these extremities propped up on banks of pillows, presumably to discourage further swelling.

But as Olive gave Daisy a rapid touch on the arm to say goodbye as she had to get back to work, Daisy was relieved to find Marguerite alert and ready to talk, and while obviously plagued with debilitating physical symptoms, she didn't seem in herself to be anything like as poorly as Clem was.

'How are you feeling?'

'My head hurts like hell, thank you, Daisy. I think this will be my only baby. And if I don't go into labour soon, they are going to operate,' said Marguerite. 'Beached whales and me have a lot in common, other than they can move around more easily than I can just now.'

'How nasty,' said Daisy. 'It looks very uncomfortable. Is there anything I can get you?'

'It's ridiculous, and no, there's nothing I need, other than to get this damned baby out. They won't let me get up to go and see Clem, and he can't get to me, so it's a pretty parlous state of affairs.'

'I've visited him just now, and it strikes me he's very low, and – please don't be upset by what I am going to say – I suspect the sight of you at the moment wouldn't be much of a comfort. I think hospital may be too busy and too noisy for him,' said Daisy. 'I'm sure he's sending his love up to you though, even if he can't right now actually say as much.'

'Well, I agree as I know exactly what I look like, and I'm sending my love down to my Clem,' said Marguerite, 'It's true you can't get a moment's peace here, as the minute you fall asleep they wake you up to give you a drink or a bed bath. But now I want you to cheer me up. You can tell me all the gossip that is going on in Crumford.'

And so Daisy pulled up a chair and tried her best to do as Marguerite had requested, although she had to take great care to avoid any mention of Violet and the magazine, or Holly and Basil Brewer, in case Marguerite forgot she wasn't to spill the beans about either of these subjects when Cynthia and Jared next came in to see her.

Fortunately, a visit from Marguerite's colleagues in the Crumford branch of the Salvation Army band to provide afternoon 'entertainment' at the tea room the previous week, plus a hammed-up description of how the twins were getting on with learning the script Marguerite had written for the nativity play, proved a rich vein of gossip, and Daisy was pleased to be able to make her sister-in-law bark with laughter.

‿∞⌒

As Basil, who'd been waiting very patiently outside the hospital, drove back to Old Creaky, he and Daisy discussed an idea she had had as she had walked down the stairs from Marguerite's ward.

Basil proved to be a very good listener, and actually some of his suggestions were rather good too. For the very first time Daisy thought she could see a glimmer of the man who had entranced Holly so.

Neither of them mentioned Holly however, which relieved Daisy, as she really didn't know what she could have said.

She did however ascertain that Basil was very keen to spend Christmas Day at Old Creaky with all the Grahams, even though Daisy took great care to tell him that while it would be lovely to have him join them, it was best that he pulled back any expectations of high-quality festive fare that he may be harbouring to practically zero.

His laugh of genuine amusement rather endeared him to Daisy, and a bit to her surprise she found herself hoping that he and Holly would be happy together if they decided they were serious about one another.

Chapter Twenty-six

Daisy had a word with her parents, and the upshot was that Jared and Basil went to the hospital to request Clem be admitted into the care of the family, with Daisy moving into Clem's cottage to take care of him.

Now that Joy seemed at home in the tea room and was happy to be there for a little while longer, Daisy felt she could move temporarily across the grass to Marguerite and Clem's cottage to take charge of her brother. They could live quietly as Clem recuperated, him on a bed in the downstairs parlour, while Daisy could sleep in the kitchen next door on the camp bed from the journeymen's room in the mill house, to be close at hand should he need her.

'I think I should be in the cottage with Clem,' said Cynthia.

But Daisy said, 'Let me do it, Mother. Tansy and Senna need you here, and I would feel privileged to look after Clem, once I know exactly what I have to do. And I think he would take me looking after him, and washing him and so forth, better than he would if you did it as I suspect he would be embarrassed with you, now that he is a grown man. And this means I can feel useful and as if I'm doing my bit, which I've felt I needed to do since that time in the tea room with Flo Squires. And it frees you up for doing the nice things with Clem, like reading to him, and I am sure that would be of much more value to him in the coming months than you spooning him his morning porridge. And naturally I would run across and get you if *anything* happened out of the ordinary.'

'Oh, I don't know, Daisy . . .' began Cynthia.

But then Jared said, 'I think Daisy is right, Cyn, and that if she wants to look after him, then she should be allowed to. It will only be for a short time as Marguerite won't be in hospital for ever.'

'I need to think about this,' said Cynthia firmly.

But in spite of Cynthia's resolute words, it wasn't long before Basil Brewer was driving them – Jared, Cynthia and Daisy – back to the hospital in Canterbury, where they had had a conference with several doctors during which Daisy and Jared had it explained to them very clearly exactly what they needed to do to take care of Clem, and what they should expect.

Then Cynthia, who had been upstairs with Marguerite, and Daisy went to see Clem, and Cynthia explained very slowly to him that if he wanted – and he had to want to do this – then he could come home, and his father and Daisy would care for him, and she, Cynthia, would spend a couple of hours a day sitting with him to take his mind off things. They would make sure that everything was as quiet and as comfortable for him as they could.

Cynthia held Clem as silently he put his head against her breast, and he allowed Daisy to give him a brief touch of support on his nearest leg.

Leaving Clem and Cynthia to spend some time together, just the two of them while Jared smoked a cigarette outside, Olive walked with Daisy up to the ward where Marguerite was. Olive said, 'You're doing a good thing there, Daisy.'

Daisy stopped, and looked seriously at her cousin. 'I do hope so. To be honest though I'm not sure why, but it feels as if it's Clem who is doing the good thing for me, rather than the other way around,' and the two cousins gazed seriously at each other. Then Olive made Daisy laugh by breaking the tender moment with, 'And so begins the path to how one decides to train as a nurse and work in a proper hospital.'

Marguerite was thrilled after hearing Cynthia's news, although she joked to Daisy that once she was home, she still might not let Daisy move back to her bedroom at the mill house, as she rather fancied being a lady of leisure with someone like Daisy to wait on her hand and foot.

'You haven't tasted my cooking yet,' warned Daisy.

'True,' said Marguerite. 'But I daresay you are better than you are letting on.'

Daisy grimaced in reply, and Marguerite chuckled, saying, 'Poor Clem. But I know you'll be a tonic for him until I can get home.'

'I very much want to be,' said Daisy, 'I really do.'

∞

The next morning Jared and Perry heaved nearly all of the furniture out of Clem and Marguerite's small parlour and put it upstairs in the room that one day would be the baby's bedroom. All apart from a bookcase, and a chair for visitors. They brought down the bedside table from the main bedroom, although they had a bit of a tussle getting it out without damaging the plaster on the wall from beside the double brass bed, which took up nearly all the space in the small bedroom.

Then they moved Olive's single bed over from the mill house and placed it in the parlour, and Daisy let Cynthia make the bed up with clean linen as she knew her mother would have hated not feeling that she had helped get things ready for Clem.

Basil Brewer drove over and collected Jared to go to the hospital, who then came back in an ambulance with Clem. The ambulance men helped install Clem in Olive's bed.

Clem was alabaster white in the face, clearly exhausted by the process of moving, and his expression suggested that he was in great physical pain.

At the sight of this, Daisy had to wonder privately if her good intentions were destined to fail, as she couldn't help feeling that she might have bitten off more than she could chew.

But after Clem had had an hour to settle, when Daisy next went into his room she saw that he was listening to the creaks of the mill's sails turning and the grinding sound of the mill stones, giving a small but satisfied smile as he nodded gently along to the rhythm. The look on his face seemed to say to Daisy that he'd been waiting a long time for this but it had been well worth it now that he was back at Old Creaky.

Daisy smiled at Clem, who was still having difficultly looking directly at her.

She forced herself to ignore this, and instead made herself busy making her brother a hot drink and in ensuring there was enough coal on the fire in the parlour where he was lying.

∽

Several days later, Daisy received a note from Ren and one from Silas, dropped off at the same time by Big Tom, who gave Daisy a taciturn comment of 'Popular, eh, young lady?' which she didn't deign to respond to.

She was weary these days, and so she didn't feel particularly amenable.

Since Clem had returned, his frequent nightmares had resulted in her having bad dreams every night too, and the night before she had slept in a chair beside

Clem, wrapped in a blanket and holding his hand as they both tried to sleep.

He was now able to look her in the face though, and so Daisy was taking that as a huge improvement.

Daisy sat at the small table in Clem's kitchen, and hastily tore open the envelope from Silas, her heart thumping and her mouth suddenly dry.

Daisy Graham, I am so disappointed not to have seen you before rushing to leave Crumford, as myself and Roscoe — and goodness knows where he is now, as he's been sent somewhere different to me — were given two hours' notice before we had to go, and it took that long to pack my cameras and other bits of equipment. It seemed rude of me to leave without a goodbye, but that was simply because of the lie of the land, and it would have been very rushed and unsatisfactory as I had a lot to think about. Suffice to say, hopefully it won't be long until I am back in Crumford, and can make it up to you in person.

Until then, best thoughts!

Silas

As her heartbeat steadied, Daisy couldn't help but notice that Silas wrote a lot about himself in his letter, and not very much about her.

While she liked the hint she was in his thoughts and that he intended to see her upon his return, she was left disappointed, thinking he could have focused on her a bit more.

She sighed deeply, and decided two could play at that game, and so she wouldn't let herself dwell on Silas any more just now.

She poured herself another cup of tea before picking up Ren's letter.

But when Daisy began to read she found herself gripped.

His letter was short but was the stronger for that, as it described eloquently how hard the four of them who were left – Ren and his two brothers, and Asa – were finding it now that Clem wasn't with them, and how much Ren was missing home. He thanked Daisy on behalf of all of them for a box of scarves and vests that hailed from the VAD group Violet belonged to, and some cigarettes and matches, and a tin of the hard biscuits that she had sent to be shared out amongst them.

Daisy went to read the letter to Clem, but he was asleep with a more peaceful look on his face than she had seen previously, and so she crept back to the kitchen table, anxious not to disturb her brother.

She reached for her notepaper.

Dear Ren,

Thank you for your letter – I am so glad our package to you arrived safely. Mother has just sent another to

Asa, with playing cards and pencils and so forth, and so I am sure that will arrive soon.

I have exciting and welcome news for you – I am living in Clem and Marguerite's house currently, taking care of Clem!

He is asleep at the moment, but I know he would want you all to know this. He has been here just a few days now, and I can see an improvement, I think.

It is just the two us here in Clem's cottage as Marguerite is in hospital now in Canterbury until a few weeks after their baby is born.

Clem was sent to the hospital in Canterbury, where as luck would have it Olive was when he arrived – having transferred down from London – and subsequently if we hadn't stepped in, Clem would have been referred in time to a recuperation hospital.

But he was incredibly agitated by the noises on the ward, which was hideous for everyone, and so we asked if we could nurse him here in the peace and quiet, and we were allowed, but on condition that he goes back to hospital if things worsen with him.

I was able to do this for Clem as Joy is enjoying herself in the tea room at the moment, and it is working out quite well, as she can have Rose there with her as she serves people, and she can earn some pin money. Obviously if Rose were crawling or toddling the tea room would not a good place because of the boiling water, but by then

Marguerite will be home hopefully and will be able to take over looking after Clem, and I can go back to work.

Mother wanted to nurse Clem, but Father and I persuaded her that she will be better use keeping him entertained. I do not mind if Clem gets cross with me – which he has not, but I expect he will – whereas I suspect Mother would be terribly upset.

Clem is still not really communicating with actual words, although he does say the odd one, and he seems very trembly, and at the moment is more or less immobile, although the doctors say there seems to be no reason to suppose that any of this is permanent. He has had pneumonia and has lost an awful lot of weight, and he has not much of an appetite, which is a concern too.

But he has his wits, which is the most important thing and he certainly enjoyed Father giving him a shave and a good general wash and brush-up earlier, while I think that he is able to follow the news stories in the paper when I read them to him as long as we take lots of breaks.

It is mostly, I am sure, that he is exhausted and his brain needs to be quiet as he heals.

Your own father has been extraordinarily kind to us, by the way, and we are all getting rather fond of him.

Aside from helping us by driving us to Canterbury whenever we needed to go, he then went with Father to talk to the doctors over whether there was a possibility of Clem being released to us.

And then Mr Brewer yesterday brought a kitten over, a little grey and white one with the sweetest pink nose – and as I am always trying to think of things that may interest him, I told him (Clem, not your father!) to look at me seriously and to nod when I suggested a name that he thought suited the kitten, who was very boisterous when playing with me but extremely gentle with Clem.

And then I tried to come up with the silliest names I could think of. I wish I had a camera, as I would love to send you a picture of Wicket – yes, that is the kitten's name, as I had had to move on to sport by this point as I had exhausted my repertoire of men's clothing and types of Kent beer – sound asleep on Clem's lap as he was propped up in bed as me and your father sat beside him. And this morning I found Wicket on his pillow, as close to Clem as he could get, and they were both sound asleep.

We are all so appreciative of everything your father has done, and so I do hope you are as proud of him as he is of you, which is 'very'!

War is a terrible thing and I am sure you are seeing and experiencing the worst side of human nature, but it also seems to bring out the best in people too, and we simply could not have got to where we have right now without your father's help.

Still, I think it's going to be a long haul now we have got Clem back with us.

He seems tearful at times, and he definitely hates sudden noises, although I think the continual sounds of the mill's sails turning, and the grinding stones, and the seabirds, are soothing, maybe because he grew up with them all, and they remind him of the safe feeling of childhood. I have noticed already that Clem usually falls into a nap not long after the milling starts in the morning.

I read to him when he wakes up, and then give him lunch — and Mother comes in late in the afternoon after he has had another snooze, and Father comes over after supper and talks about grain and various farmers Clem knows, which makes my eyes heavy-lidded pretty quickly, and Clem's too, it seems!

We have only had Clem back here several days but we seem to be in a decent routine, at least for now. It's not much of a life for a young man, but we are all determined to do our best for him, and I would like to get him in the wheelchair and out in the fresh air for an hour every day.

Violet is coming in later this morning for an hour with him. I am sure Clem will like that as I think she always was his favourite sister.

It is hard to know what to write to you otherwise. You are not allowed to tell us what it is like for you,

329

and we wouldn't be able to imagine it anyway. Please
know however that we do think of you four every day,
and we long for the war to be over and for you all to be
safely home.

   With kindest regards

   Daisy

∽

Once Clem woke up, she read out Ren's letter to her, and she saw his hands tremble anew as he tried to pet Wicket.

'Oh, Clem, I don't want to upset you,' Daisy said. 'Is it too much hearing from Ren, dear, and how badly he cares that you are doing well?'

Clem gave an almost imperceptible shake of his head.

'I haven't sealed the envelope yet to my reply. Would you like to hear what I've said back to him? I've talked about you.'

Clem nodded, and as he softly nestled the kitten in his arms, Daisy read her brother all of the letter she'd just written, even the bit about her thinking it would be a long haul to get him better.

When she had finished reading, she said, 'Is my letter all right, Clem? I don't want to say anything about you that you aren't comfortable with. I can rewrite it to change anything you don't like.'

He shook his head as if to say no, this wasn't needed, and so after Daisy checked again that she hadn't upset him, she said, 'When you're feeling a little better and are up to getting out of bed, you can dictate your own letter to me and I'll write it down, and we can post it to Ren. I'm sure Asa and the others would love to hear from you too. Perhaps you and I shall be able to bundle up in coats and eiderdowns and talk about what we want to say outside, as I'm sure it would be nice for you to sit in the fresh air.'

She had deliberately given Clem two small goals to work towards – being out of bed, and him telling her what to say in a letter. The doctors had stressed the importance of letting Clem know what was likely to happen, but they had told Daisy not to make him do anything if the thought of it obviously upset him.

Daisy looked at her brother, who was staring at Wicket, the kitten's purrs clearly audible.

She decided that Clem didn't look beside himself over anything she had suggested, and although Daisy was pleased about this, it was almost impossible not to compare such a small triumph with Clem's endless energy and activity before he had left Crumford to fight.

'Wallet,' Clem said suddenly, throwing his head up to look at Daisy. It was the clearest thing he had said to her since being back at Old Creaky.

'Oh, you made me jump,' laughed Daisy.

He had arrived back at the mill from the hospital with a bag of possessions.

Cynthia had already taken out his muddied uniform to clean, while Jared had taken charge of his boots. But at the bottom of the bag Daisy found some cigarettes and matches, plus a rumpled hanky and a little loose change.

His wallet, the leather stiff from having been wet, was there too, and Daisy passed it over to Clem.

Achingly slowly, he tried to open it with his shaking hands as Wicket rolled onto his back so that he could reach for it better, and Daisy had to force herself not to offer to help. The doctors had been very insistent that they all had to let Clem do as much for himself as possible.

And eventually Clem managed it. He passed the wallet back to Daisy over the top of Wicket's flailing paws, as the kitten thought it was a game, the wallet's two sides flopped apart, with a shy smile of achievement on his face.

Inside a central pocket Daisy found some small photographs, presumably mostly taken by Ren on his Kodak Vest Pocket, all featuring the three Brewer brothers and Asa and Clem.

There were two very nice photographs that Daisy stared at for a while, her favourite being the one of Asa and Clem standing side by side, laughing at the photographer as Clem made his hands into bunny ears behind Asa's head. The other was of Clem and Ren standing more seriously side by side where they looked so alike they could have been brothers.

'These look like fun days. Try and remember them rather than all the other awful things you've been through, dear. Here, let me put these where you can look at them whenever you want,' said Daisy, and then very carefully she propped the photographs on his bedside table against a pile of books that she placed so as Clem could easily look.

Daisy helped Clem turn onto his side, and with Wicket snuggled tight to his chest, he lay there looking at the pictures.

Although she smiled bravely at her brother, she left the room with a huge lump in her throat, and had to spend quite some time out in the December chill as she tried to steel herself to go back inside.

Chapter Twenty-seven

Holly seemed like a bear with a sore head, being snappy and generally unobliging, although – sensibly – not when either Jared or Cynthia were around.

Daisy was busy allocating the final Christmas jobs to herself and each of her younger sisters. Holly's attitude was not helpful, especially as it was proving an issue deciding who should judge the charity children's drawing competition, as the role needed somebody who didn't know the children and so couldn't be accused of favouritism.

'Who do you think I should ask to be judge?' Daisy asked Holly one evening, when she and Holly were in the scullery doing the washing up after tea.

'Basil. Obviously.' Holly's reply was abrupt.

Daisy snapped. She had had enough of her sister being curt and rude. 'Holly, into the tea room right now,' Daisy hissed. 'No ifs and buts.'

It was bath night for the twins in the tin bath in front of the kitchen range, while Violet had gone to her knitting group, and Joy and Rose were back in their cottage.

Jared was with Clem, and so Daisy knew that she and Holly wouldn't be disturbed.

Sulkily, Holly followed her older sister out into the cold and across to the tea room, which was still pleasantly warm from Violet's ovens on the other side of the wall.

'Do you want a drink?' asked Daisy. 'I can easily pop across to the kitchen to heat some water.'

Holly let out the sort of huffing sigh that suggested a no, and so Daisy put down the kettle in her hand, and came and sat beside her.

'What on earth is the matter with you? You're really not yourself, Holly.'

Holly stuck out her chin as she looked defiantly at Daisy, who added in a much more conciliatory way, 'Holly, whatever can it be?'

Holly still didn't say anything, and so Daisy continued, 'You have such a lot going for you, as Mother and Father are always telling me what a head for business you've got, and Mother was only saying to me earlier today that you've been invaluable in costings and so forth with their hard biscuits, and if they get the army contract it will be very much down to you. And you're helping Violet with the magazine, and she's only had good things to say too. And Basil Brewer seems, um, to think a lot of you and how you've been helping him with his books, and I'm sure he wouldn't suffer fools gladly.'

It was the mention of Basil that made Holly's face crumple, and Daisy watched with alarm as Holly took a jagged and uncomfortable-looking breath inward.

Before speaking, Daisy had wondered if this would the case, which was why she had mentioned Basil in the way she had. Presumably Basil had come to his senses, and realised how young Holly was – she still wasn't yet twenty! – with the result that he'd ended things between them.

Daisy reached for Holly's hand, saying, 'Aw, try not to take on so, Holly. You don't have to see Basil, if you don't want to. He can get somebody else to do the books, and you wouldn't have to go to the brewery.'

'Stuff his accounts!' Holly mumbled.

'Yes, stuff his accounts,' Daisy echoed.

In spite of Holly's drive, somehow Daisy had always assumed her to be a little dim, and so it probably would be a relief for Holly if she stepped back now to something less challenging.

Then Holly looked at her with the type of sour expression that told Daisy her opinion of Holly's intelligence had been noted and Holly wasn't impressed, and as Daisy had the grace to look a little embarrassed, Holly said, 'It's not that . . . Daisy, it's that I'm pregnant. And Basil wants to marry me.'

Daisy could hardly believe her ears.

'Bugger the Boche!' was all she could think to say.

'Mother and Father are going to be furious,' said Holly. 'Basil wants to speak to them now, before I show. But I told him that we should wait until after Christmas, as it's going to be a horrible time for all of us over the festive period if he speaks to them before, and with the twins being small, and now we have Clem back, nobody needs that.'

'How long has this been going on?'

'Ages. I've always had a thing for Basil, even when his wife was alive,' Holly confessed conspiratorially. 'I don't know why, but there it is. However, it was only this summer that there were *developments*. In fact, he was the "romantic entanglement" I was alluding too when we had that chat in the tea room the day the church ladies came around. I threw you a thread to pick up on but, typically, you didn't notice it – I would have told you then. If you had asked.'

'Touché,' said Daisy, in acknowledgement that Holly was right to think that Daisy wasn't as smart as she liked to think she was. 'So it's been going on all this time?'

'It began properly in a quiet way the night of the party as when most other people were well into their cups, I realised that he'd noticed me. So when Rosen – who I do like, but just not in *that* way, disappeared for the end of Olive's cricket match – I took the opportunity to be alone with Basil and suggested that we could go to Father's desk and I could show him the accounts I was helping with,' explained Holly. 'And Basil seemed impressed with what I was doing, and that led to me hinting very strongly to him that I'd love to do some book-keeping more seriously in somewhere like a brewery, with a proper payroll and so forth, as I wanted to be a businesswoman and therefore I needed to learn how to be one by working somewhere very successful, *such as his brewery*. Basil tried to put me off by saying that our father's business was successful, and I said I knew that Father did well enough, but that I was feeling more ambitious than Old Creaky, and then Basil told me I was "remarkable". And that felt good, extraordinarily good in fact.'

Daisy nodded. She could completely picture how the discussion had gone between Holly and Basil.

Holly went on, 'And then, a few weeks later at the train station when we waved everyone off, I told Basil I'd been serious in what I said about working at the brewery, and eventually I managed to inveigle my way in. And almost the moment I started, I made myself *so* useful that after a very short while Basil realised that he enjoyed teaching me, and I was a quick and interested learner. And then it was impossible for him to resist me in other ways. I was very determined in catching his eye, you know.'

Daisy had always thought Holly to be the best-looking sister by far of the trio of older Graham sisters, and so it wasn't surprising that Basil had succumbed to her obvious charms. Daisy still found it hard to see in Basil whatever it was that had first snared Holly's attention, but Daisy certainly wasn't going to let her sister know that.

'Clearly. You've obviously seen Basil in a very different way than the rest of us. And you've been much more taken with business than the rest of us knew. I think you've been very clever at keeping things under wraps,' said Daisy carefully, trying her best to be diplomatic.

'You and everyone else have always underestimated me, Daisy, which isn't a bad thing necessarily. And it's obvious that Basil is older and all that. But when I think about him . . . Well, just "*but*".'

The tone of Holly's words was recognisable to Daisy in the way Silas had made her feel. She was impressed that Holly had been able to say more clearly what she wanted to her lover, much more so than Daisy had managed with either Ren or Silas.

'All right, Holly,' Daisy said, 'let's look at this another way. Taking Mother and Father, and Basil as well, out of the equation for the moment, what is it that *you* want? It's not a given you have to keep the baby, or that you should get married, you know? While it might be a bit awkward at first, people would get used to whatever you decide to do. And you won't be the only young woman in this position these days, I'm sure. I think wartime has made a lot of people live for the moment.'

Despite her fighting talk, Daisy knew that for Holly not to marry, or even if she decided to give her baby away, should Crumford society get wind of it, which they almost definitely would in such a gossip-hungry place as this, the consequences could be disastrous for Holly, and the other sisters too.

It could even affect the marriage prospects of Senna and Tansy further down the line, as they wouldn't be seven years old for ever. And when the time came for them to look for husbands, this would be as part of a man-short society because of the deaths of those fighting, a situation that would only worsen should the war go on for a long time.

It would mean that young single ladies would be in heated competition for the hands of any eligible young men; and for the twins to have someone with 'loose morals' in their immediate family, as nastier people would deem Holly to have, might well end up as a nigh on insurmountable black mark against them.

In any case, Daisy couldn't imagine Cynthia letting any Graham baby be brought up outside the family. Traditionally, everybody knew that mothers of young girls who found themselves knocked-up, pretended to be pregnant themselves, and then presented the baby as a sibling to its real mother. But realistically Crumford was too small and its inhabitants overly nosy for this to happen, with too many people constantly in and out of Old Creaky. There wouldn't be a plausible cover story Cynthia could spread around that would stand much scrutiny, and even if there were, Daisy wouldn't trust the confidentiality of the local doctors. And Daisy had seen Basil and Holly together in *that* way, and if she had, it was possible others had too.

Still, Daisy didn't need to tell Holly any of this. She was shrewd and would have considered all of this already.

'Oh, I want to marry Basil, Daisy, without a doubt I do,' said Holly confidently, 'and have our baby. I love him and he loves me. And frankly I want to run that brewery one day.'

'Well, that last thing might be something to keep to yourself for now,' said Daisy, 'else you'll be accused of being a gold-digger. Only outside the family, of course.'

'None of his sons have much interest in the business and Basil is worried about the brewery if none of them want to get involved, but I know you're right. Our most urgent problem is how we should handle Mother and Father.'

'It's tricky,' said Daisy. 'They are going to be very shocked if Basil comes and asks Father for permission to marry you out of the blue. But for him not to do this will make it seem as if he is running from his responsibilities, and so I don't think you can speak to either Mother or Father first to lay a few padstones to lessen the shock. Either way, they will be convinced that Basil took advantage of you, despite how helpful he's been to the family.'

'I know. And that won't be fair on him,' said Holly.

'Yes, I can see how problematic it all might be,' said Daisy carefully, 'with Father and Mother about to have a wake-up call, especially so close to what has happened with Clem, as that has really knocked them for six. And it will have to come out soon about Violet and her magazine. Mother and Father will feel their world has turned upside down in the last six months.'

Holly didn't need to know about Daisy and Silas, or that Daisy had already known about the relationship between Holly and Basil, or that when Violet came clean about the magazine, she might be blamed for encouraging her younger sister towards lewd behaviour as part of her quest for women's emancipation and breaking away from traditional roles.

The sisters stared at each other for what felt like quite a while, and then Daisy said, 'Have you two thought about eloping?'

'What do you mean?'

'Well, it might solve a lot of problems. I overheard somebody talking about it in the tea room a while back. Apparently, if you go to Gretna Green, you don't need a licence as it's under Scottish law, and that means you only have to make a notice of declaration before two witnesses, and you don't have to have bans read or anything like that, so it can take place immediately. From what I could make out the only requirement is that the bride has to be sixteen, but you're well past that.'

Holly looked interested. 'I suppose Basil could check this.'

'I think it's quite well known as an option,' said Daisy. 'It's a long way to go, especially from here up to Scotland. It's got to be close on four hundred miles away. But Basil has his own transport and it would mean you could go there and come back with the marriage already a done deed, and then Mother and Father wouldn't have to make any decisions over what they would allow you to do as, Gordon Bennett, you'd already gone and done it. They'd be cross for a while, certainly, but once the baby arrives, they'll forget all about that. And Basil carries such a lot of influence in Crumford society, that if you are out and about very publicly on his arm as his wife, no one will dare to upset him, and in time the gossip will move on to other things.'

'Do you really think so, Daisy?'

'What I think is that you need to talk it over with Basil. He has his three sons to take into account too, of course, and they might not take kindly to a stepmother younger than all of them, and so that might make a difference in a way that you and I can't think of right now. But elopement could be a way that would cause a furore, but one which would quickly heal itself, and whatever happens next, you're not going to be able to avoid a furore.'

Holly looked thoughtful.

Daisy added, 'You could maybe, the two of you, have to go to Durham or Newcastle for a few days for work purposes, after which you could say you both got carried away while you were there, and hopped over into Scotland to make the declaration, before you consummated the relationship. Mother would guess when the baby is born, of course, but then it would be to her advantage to pretend to us all that everything is perfectly above board.'

∞

Two days later, Basil and Holly were off to visit the Newburn Steelworks in the north-east of England to check out a potential supplier of huge and specially commissioned new vats that Basil was designing to speed up the fermentation of his beer, with Holly required to go too for the mathematics and should any general running around in a business sense be required.

'I'm amazed that metal is being diverted to this sort of thing when I thought they wanted everything for armaments,' Cynthia wondered the morning after the couple had departed.

Daisy knew her mother was correct, but she said, 'I suppose that Basil Brewer may have had the nod from army supplies that beer is going to be part of our troops' rations.'

'Oh, Asa will be pleased if they do that,' Cynthia cried.

'He certainly will,' agreed Daisy, and then quickly changed the subject to talk of the army prospects for Cynthia's hard biscuits.

Chapter Twenty-eight

Meanwhile Clem's health seemed to take a dip, with his chest being quite bad. Daisy had been expecting this as the doctors had said there would inevitably be setbacks along these lines.

Despite this, Daisy was determined to get Clem used to being in a wheelchair. She made him sit outside in it for a while every day, after she'd bundled him against the December cold.

It helped that Wicket enjoyed being cosy. Violet had knitted a balaclava that Wicket would happily curl up in on Clem's lap. He would sit for ages watching with interest the much bigger and tougher outdoor ratting cats that lived at the mill go about their daily lives.

Customers to the tea room began crossing the grass to say hello to Wicket as they seemed to find stroking the sweet kitten under the chin easier than speaking to an obviously still very poorly Clem.

Daisy noticed that although on the first day or two Clem felt very awkward about having people from outside the family approach him, soon he found it quite pleasant, and his speech began to improve as he passed the time of day with all manner of people. One visitor even made Wicket a little waistcoat to wear, which made people laugh.

Daisy placed a couple of chairs near to where she wheeled her brother and his kitten to encourage anyone who felt like it to sit down and talk for as long as they wanted.

While she liked seeing Clem settling into a routine, Daisy found herself more depressed than she had expected to be when looking after her brother, and it was a difficult feeling to shake.

This wasn't anything to do with Clem himself, but more that having to watch him battle every day with the smallest of jobs, when even doing up a button could totally defeat him, was wearing in the psychological sense. Daisy felt that what had happened to him was such a terrible waste, and it gave her a constant feeling of being angry and sad in equal measure.

Whatever Clem's future might be, it certainly wasn't what he would have chosen, Daisy knew, and she found it hard to be optimistic for him, although she took great care that nobody should notice this.

Marguerite wrote Clem notes that arrived most days, but there was still no sign of their baby.

'I'm sure this little one coming will be a boy – he's taking advantage of staying in a nice warm place,' Violet said.

Daisy asked Clem if he was looking forward to being a father, but all he could do was shrug his shoulders at her.

∞

Holly and Basil returned from their trip to the north of England, Holly looking bright-eyed. Once she had made sure she and Daisy were alone, she hoiked out a slender gold chain that was hanging secretly around her neck inside her blouse, to show Daisy the spanking new wedding ring hanging from it.

Then she whispered to Daisy, 'We've only bloody gone and done it! We drove from Newcastle across the country and up to Gretna Green. It was so romantic! Basil is going to write to his boys, although not until after Christmas, at which point we'll tell Mother and Father. We certainly don't want to be the centre of attention at the nativity play or midnight mass, or at the Christmas meal.'

'Congratulations,' Daisy whispered back. 'Have you told Violet or anyone else?'

'Not yet.'

'Right, while I've still got you at home here, there's no excuses for not throwing yourself into doing everything that's still left on my Christmas list. Deal?'

'Deal,' laughed Holly, and she set to doing everything that Daisy asked of her.

∞

All the Grahams, other than Jared, who was over with Clem, went carol singing a few days before Christmas, collecting a surprising amount of money for the war effort. This was very possibly because the twins insisted everyone went with swathes of paper garlands strung around their necks, which even Daisy had to admit worked rather well, not least because making the garlands had kept the twins occupied for nearly a whole weekend.

Then there was Holly's birthday tea party, which was limited to family and her pals from school, an afternoon that everyone seemed to enjoy.

And the Sunday before Christmas, the nativity play went off without a hitch in the ancient but draughty church, with Senna and Tansy looking incredibly sweet wearing their donkey headdresses that Violet had made. Nobody forgot their lines, and it was followed afterwards by a raucous tea party for all of the Sunday school children in the tea room, with Olive having posted to Old Creaky a box of sugared almonds that she had unearthed from somewhere in order to give the children a real treat.

At the end of the tea party, Daisy awarded the prizes in the charity drawing competition, as judged by Basil (although a day or two later he begged not to be asked again, should Daisy run another one, as it was 'very difficult, and he was sure to have upset someone or other'), with the photographer from the *Mercury* taking photographs, just as he had promised.

In the aftermath of the charity competition Daisy didn't have the heart to tell Basil that 'someone or other' didn't come close to the number of mothers who felt their children's drawings had been cruelly and unfairly slighted.

Daisy found the midnight mass on Christmas Eve to be incredibly moving, making her damp-eyed during 'Silent Night', and then as they walked home, she had to make a huge effort to look cheerful as she had noticed Cynthia eyeing her carefully.

The next morning, everyone watched the twins open their stockings as planned. Little Rose had a stocking too, although Joy had to help with hers.

Then all five Graham daughters shooed Cynthia out of the kitchen so that they could prepare a gargantuan Christmas meal for their family and friends that would be served at two o'clock.

Violet was kept very busy as she had to divide her time between the kitchen and her bread ovens, which were all powering away, as she had given nearly all the space over to roasting other people's Christmas meals.

Daisy had been up early, decorating the tea room, which was to host the Christmas meal, with boughs of evergreen and fir cones, and by the time everyone sat down to Christmas dinner in the early afternoon, there was a very Christmassy smell from all the greenery. Rose was particularly interested in clutching at the boughs and then pulling what she'd been able to grab towards her mouth, and so poor Joy was unable to relax for a moment.

Daisy had persuaded Flo Squires to join them for the meal, as she couldn't bear the thought of him having the first Christmas without Ainsley all on his own.

She'd visited him during the afternoon of Christmas Eve as she hadn't wanted to give him too much time to work himself into a tizzy over whether to attend or not.

Daisy took care to say that Perry would be there, but maybe Flo should know that Perry was a brave man who would be happy to be an ambulance driver behind the front, and indeed he was ready to go at the drop of a hat should he be required, and if Flo could make his peace with that, then it would be very special if Flo felt he could join them.

Flo was extremely contrite over his behaviour, saying to Daisy that he was ashamed he had hurt her. She told him not to trouble himself further about that as she was perfectly well now and she knew the loss of Ainsley had affected his behaviour, and it was an accident and that Flo hadn't meant to hurt her.

And when a mercifully sober – Daisy had been a bit worried about this – Flo Squires made his way bashfully into the tea room for the Christmas dinner he made a special effort to head over to Perry immediately to apologise, saying that he was sorry for the things he had said and the punch he had given Perry. Perry was saved from having to say anything in reply other than he understood and was glad to see Flo there, by Cynthia coming over and announcing to Flo that it was good to see him and, as she slipped an arm through Flo's and began leading him away, that she'd saved him a seat right beside her for the food they were about to enjoy.

Violet shocked everyone, other than Daisy and Holly, after the remnants of the roast meal had been cleared away by using the lull before the Christmas pudding came in to walk around with a basket on her arm so that she could hand out to all those who were there – even the men – a rolled-up copy of her women's suffrage magazine, finally named *The Daughter*, hot off the press just a few days earlier, with the roll of each magazine tied with a strip of jaunty green or purple ribbon.

As a nonplussed Cynthia and Jared stared on open-mouthed at what their second-eldest daughter had been up to as they clearly were as surprised about the existence of *The Daughter* as everyone else, Violet lapped up the attention.

Cheekily, she had dyed two of her old petties, one to green and the other to purple, which she wore on top of a white one, and so she took delight in lifting the hem of her skirt and kicking her foot out in order to show them off as the three official colours of the suffrage movement.

Holly stood up to lead the hip-hip-hoorays for Violet's achievement, which everyone threw themselves into with tipsy gusto as Basil Brewer had brought a lot of beer over with him, as well at several bottles of both sherry and brandy. Significant inroads had been made into these.

He and Holly took care to sit well away from each other, Daisy noticed.

'I'd like to make a toast,' said Holly, and Daisy realised that if one knew what to look for, there was now a small swell showing beneath her waistband.

For a moment Daisy froze as this didn't seem the right time for Cynthia and Jared to learn about Holly and Basil being married.

'What many of you don't know—' Daisy held her breath as Holly looked coquettishly around the room '—is that on the day of the summer party we had here at Old Creaky my big sister Daisy did something extraordinary.'

Daisy had no idea what Holly was talking about.

'She managed to crash Mr Basil Brewer's brand new Rolls-Royce, a momentous event I think we ought to acknowledge!'

'And she nearly ran me over into the bargain, the naughty girl,' called Cynthia.

Daisy felt herself go very pink as everyone roared, and then raised their glasses to Holly's cry of 'To Daisy's unequalled driving skills!'

Then Holly stayed standing as she whipped out from under the table two copies of the magazine that Silas had photographed Daisy for, and waved them around.

'Joking aside though, this is my Christmas present to Daisy, who arranged this lunch for everyone, and to our dear little Rose. It is some early copies of the magazine that Silas Grover photographed them for in the latest London fashions. I had to move heaven and earth to get them – they won't be in the Crumford newsagent's until after New Year,' announced Holly proudly. 'See how amazing they both look.'

As the guests looked at the magazine, at last Holly was persuaded to sit down.

Even though Daisy had seen the pictures before, seeing her and Rose on the front cover for the first time was extraordinary, even though it made her feel Silas's absence keenly once more, with a twisting pain within her ribcage.

Daisy wondered what he was doing at that very moment, and she hoped he was all right.

Then, Violet and Rose's thunder about her magazine was diluted massively by the abrupt arrival of a telegram.

A panicking Daisy had caught the eye of her mother and father at the sight of the telegram girl peeking around the door to the tea room, but then Daisy saw that the girl was smiling and so it didn't seem as if it were bad news.

It was good news. Marguerite had, that morning, given birth to a healthy baby boy.

And after Jared stood up to announce that he was now a grandfather for the second time, Daisy filled up a schooner with a little brandy for Clem to toast his son's arrival, and then she filled a second.

Perry was with Clem now in the cottage   they were all taking it in turns to look after Clem as he hadn't felt he was up to the party – and so Daisy ran across to tell him that he was now a father, and that the brandy was so that the Clem and Perry could wet the baby's head.

She promised her brother that she and Cynthia would go with Basil Brewer to the hospital after everyone had finished eating, so that they could see mother and baby, and then they would then come back to Clem with first-hand accounts.

'Thank you,' Clem managed to say as Daisy waited patiently for him to form his words. 'Marguerite, well done. Kiss the baby. She must name him.'

This was the most she had heard her brother say in one go since he had been home, and she clapped.

∞

Several hours later, Daisy was back in Clem's room, breaking the news that his wife wanted their son to be called Star, in view of arriving on Christmas morning, her belonging to the Salvation Army and it being the time of the nativity, and also because she liked to think of Clem having had a star guide him home to Old Creaky.

There was a silence as Clem tried to absorb this with a somewhat horrified look on his face.

'It's not *that* bad,' said Daisy. 'I mean, Star is very close to Stan. If you think about it. When it's written down.'

She and Clem looked at each other and then he grinned.

Naturally, the baby was called Stan at Old Creaky from that moment on, with even Marguerite agreeing a few weeks later that he should be known as Stan to everyone after she had been given a quizzical look once too often for her choice of name.

Phew, thought Daisy. It wasn't that Star was a ridiculous name for a little boy, especially given Marguerite's reasons for choosing it, but more that it was the sort of moniker that would get him roundly teased at school in a few years.

Then it seemed in the blink of an eye, it was the last day of 1914.

And this was the day that Ren surprised everyone by arriving at Old Creaky.

Chapter Twenty-nine

Daisy was wheeling Clem, who was feeling stronger and his speech improving in leaps and bounds, down the lane towards Crumford with Wicket bouncing alongside.

Each day since Christmas she went a few yards further to acclimatise Clem to being in a new place. She was hoping that she would be able to get him as far as Crumford before too long.

Then, unexpectedly, Basil Brewer's Rolls-Royce hoved into view.

But it wasn't Basil who was driving. It was Ren! He pulled the car over and leaped out, giving Daisy a quick hug, and then shaking hands warmly with Clem.

Ren was the last person Daisy expected to see, and although her heart didn't jump in a romantic way, she did feel warm and distinctly fuzzy at the sight of him.

Clem didn't say anything, not even when Ren bent over to tickle a surprised Wicket under the chin, with a 'So hello there, Wicket Graham.'

'Ren! What a lovely surprise,' cried Daisy. 'You should have let us know you were coming.'

'What? And miss the shocked looks on your faces,' laughed Ren. 'All three of us Brewer lads are back for two days, but I had to see you both as soon as I could. You've no idea, Daisy, what a tonic your letters have been. And Clem, what a sight for sore eyes you are!' Ren's voiced cracked as he spoke to Clem. 'Asa has had to stay across the Channel, unfortunately, but he should get a break at some point.'

'Let's get Clem back into the warm,' said Daisy. 'Why don't you make yourself useful and push his chair, Ren? I'm sure the car will be fine if you leave it where it is.'

Clem's eyes were shiny, and Daisy thought he'd perked up no end at the sight of his friend.

She scooped up Wicket, and once back on Old Creaky's turf Daisy ran to the mill and then the mill house to say that they had a very special visitor.

Annoyingly, nobody was at home and the house was silent.

The tea room was closed, and so was the bakery, and Jared and Cynthia were out making a few social calls in Crumford. Everyone had decided to take the day off.

Daisy had no idea where Violet and Holly were, but she couldn't find them. The twins and a group of their Sunday school friends had been taken out into the fields for a nature table competition, and so even they weren't around and Joy and Rose had gone with them to make sure Tansy and Senna stayed out of trouble.

Daisy ran back across the patch of grass, Wicket still in her arms. It was at this moment that she saw something through the window to Clem's parlour that stopped her dead in her tracks.

For Clem and Ren were embracing each other.

It wasn't just that they were embracing, but they began kissing passionately.

These kisses were hungry and all-consuming, and nothing like the half-hearted kisses that she and Ren had shared that night of the summer party.

Daisy realised immediately that it wasn't she that Ren had feelings for, and indeed nor had he ever, but it had always been her brother Clem who meant the world to him.

And Clem clearly felt exactly the same way about Ren. There was something about the way they looked at each other that made Daisy quite sure of this.

As Daisy stood transfixed, she realised she had never thought for a moment that two men could be attracted to one another.

But it was obvious now that they could.

Daisy wasn't sure what to do. She had to go back into the cottage, otherwise they might realise what she'd seen and she really didn't want that. The moment between Ren and Clem looked so precious that she didn't want to do anything that might spoil it.

If ever somebody deserved a precious moment it was these two men, Clem especially.

Instead, Daisy called over her shoulder, in a voice that would carry to the men inside, as if speaking to someone at the gate, 'Oh, I'm terribly sorry but we're not open today. Yes, thank you – everything back to normal tomorrow.'

Daisy marched past the parlour window without glancing inside, past Clem's wheelchair in the porch, and then she opened the door to the parlour, saying in a cheerful voice, 'As luck will have it, nobody's here, Ren.'

The two friends were quite far apart now, Clem sitting on the edge of his bed and Ren standing up, saying, 'I can't stay long, I'm afraid, as I promised Father it would only be a flying visit.'

'I'm so sorry that it's only us to welcome you, Ren. Everyone would have been here if they had known, of course. Clem, you take Wicket, and Ren, will you put some more coal on that fire please as it's looking slug-gish?' said Daisy, moving the chair for Ren to sit in, and managing to pull one of the curtains halfway closed, as she was a bit anxious what Joy might see if she chose that moment to bring Rose back if she were grizzly. 'Anyway, I'm going to go and pop the kettle on, and then nip across and see if Mother made any biscuits first thing. I'm sure your father will want to spend every second with you that he can, Ren, but before you go, you must have a cup of tea at least. I'm sure you and Clem have lots to catch up on, and so I'll leave you two to reminisce for a few minutes.'

Daisy went to the kitchen and deliberately took a while dealing with the kettle and tea things.

She hadn't known she had it in her to be such a good actress.

⚬⚬⚬

Ren went home, but later returned with his brothers and Basil, who all came over for tea. This time Clem joined the party.

It was a jolly hour and they toasted Asa, although the tone turned more thoughtful as the three Brewer sons described a remarkable Christmas.

'On Christmas Eve—' Ren held the room in thrall '—we could hear the German soldiers singing and playing mouth organs. It was a lovely night, frosty and with a clear half-moon, and so a lot of the mud froze hard, and because there were no guns going off, this made the sound carry to us. Then the next morning Fritz shouted across to us, "Merry Christmas" and asked if some of us would go halfway to meet them. And we did – we exchanged cigarettes and buttons and chocolate, and shook hands.' Ren's voice shook with emotion, but he didn't stop. 'Not a shot was fired all day, and we walked around together on top of our trenches, and when a hare broke and ran for cover, we all chased it as one, Englishmen and Germans running pell-mell side by side, and when the hare got away we all cheered and clapped each other on the back. It was most astonishing, and none of us would have missed it for the world.'

Alder and Rosen nodded and agreed that the unofficial truce and temporary ceasing of hostilities had been extraordinary.

And then Briar, whom Olive had invited to come with her to the tea, reached into a coat pocket and pulled out that day's newspaper to show everyone that it had a photograph taken by Silas of British and German soldiers kicking a football around together, pointing out Silas's name appearing in tiny type underneath the picture as a photographer's credit. The Germans had won by three goals to two.

Daisy, whose heart had leaped uncontrollably when Briar mentioned Silas's name, couldn't help but think it might have been possible that exactly when she had been thinking about Silas on Christmas Day and wondering what he was doing, perhaps at that precise moment he had been taking this very picture.

Daisy showed the photograph Silas had taken to Ren and his brothers.

Both she and Ren had made a good show of being pleased to sit beside each other for the rest of the tea. Ren smiled at her in a sympathetic and friendly way that just for an instant made Daisy wonder if it was in part Ren working up to letting her know the depth of his feelings for Clem, or that somehow he knew about Silas and that was OK with him, or maybe it was just because he was genuinely happy to spend a little innocent time at her side.

Daisy smiled back at Ren, trying to put into her smile, but without daring to say out loud what she knew, that she hoped he and Clem had something special.

Olive, painfully observant as ever, smelled a rat, and when Daisy stood up to take around the teapot once more, indicated she wanted a private word, and so the two slipped out into the passageway, and then outside.

'What's going on?' said Olive bluntly as she sparked up two cigarettes, passing one to Daisy. 'You and Ren are both doing a marvellous job of putting a good face on things, but it's not washing with me. And I don't mean about you two pretending to be together, as I know there's a big fat shadow of Silas Grover in the way. It's more that something else has changed between you two. Am I right?'

'You have no idea,' answered Daisy, once she had stopped coughing. She had never tried smoking before.

'Spill then, as we can't be long.'

'Ren and Clem don't know this, but I saw them kissing this morning. Kissing very deeply, you know, in the way a husband kisses a wife.'

'Gawd, that would be two years' imprisonment and that's if the judge were feeling lenient,' muttered Olive, who didn't seem shocked in the least, 'so they really mustn't be careless like that.'

'It's illegal? I didn't even know it happened, a man with a man,' said Daisy, her voice very soft. She hadn't even thought about how the law might stand over something like this.

'Wise up, Daisy, you are unbearably naive at times. I reckon Clem and Ren have been involved with each other for years,' said Olive. 'I've had my suspicions for ages, and I thought you'd twigged.'

'No. No, I hadn't.' Daisy didn't mind about her cousin calling her naive as she knew it was the truth.

'I tried to give you clues, Daisy, in case you'd not noticed. But I didn't want to say outright, as once something is out in the open it's there for all time with possibly hideous consequences,' Olive told her. 'Obviously it's different now you know.'

'Well, you didn't try hard enough with your hints, did you!' hissed Daisy.

But then she added, her brow wrinkled into a confused frown as she tried to work it out, 'But Clem is married and a father now, and Ren kissed me, so how can that be?'

'No, that's not very fair of either of them to behave like that. But if you imagine being in their position, what else can they do? It's not as if they can ever be together, other than in snatched moments, and what bigger diversion away from where their proclivities lie can there be as far as everybody else is concerned, other than a family and marriage and children? You'd do the same if you were them, I'm sure.'

'I suppose so. They don't know that I saw them. Nobody must find out, especially Mother and Father. You can't say *anything*, Olive, not that you would, but you understand,' said Daisy. 'I thought Holly and Basil Brewer were shocking enough, but that's kids play compared to this."

'What do you mean, Holly and Basil?' Olive forgot to whisper.

'Sssh, Olive! Holly and Basil eloped and got married at Gretna Green. It's because Holly is pregnant. None of Basil's boys know yet, and actually nobody else besides me, I don't think.'

'Goodness, I leave Old Creaky for a few months, and you all start behaving like loons!' laughed Olive, her hand on the doorknob to go back inside. 'Well, it might be a bit unfair to loons, but you know what I mean.'

'You've very probably not even heard about Violet's suffrage magazine yet. She announced it at the Christmas meal, and it's all been top secret. It's called *The Daughter*. She'll be giving you a copy before you go back to the hospital, you mark my words!'

'Her *what*?' said Olive. 'Oh, forget it, Daisy. I can't take it all in!'

They put out their cigarettes, with Daisy saying she wasn't sure about smoking, and Olive telling her confidently she just needed more practice and she'd grow to love it.

And when Olive opened the door back to the tea room, it was just in time for the two cousins to hear Basil call the group inside to order with an authoritative clap of his hands as he stood up.

As Olive and Daisy crept back into the room Basil started speaking. 'Holly, come and stand by me. I hadn't planned for it to come out like this as it had seemed sensible that we wait until the New Year for our announcement. But with the unexpected delight of having us all here together, with my lads back in Kent, and Clem, the good man, enjoying his first social outing, it seems the ideal time to tell everyone our delightful news.'

Basil looked around at everyone as he spoke, and then he said in a very proud voice, 'Holly and I got married at Gretna Green the other week. Please allow me to introduce to you, Mrs Basil Brewer!'

Basil hoisted Holly's hand nearest to him aloft, and the couple stood there beside each other, beaming happily.

'*Our* Holly?' said Cynthia incredulously.

'Mother!' Holly cried, as she handed Basil the wedding ring from the chain around her neck.

Dropping to his knees before her, Basil slipped the ring on to Holly's finger right in front of everyone, before standing up and kissing her quickly on the lips so that there could be no doubt in anybody's minds that this marriage most definitely had a physical aspect.

Everyone was silent, transfixed by what they were seeing

Basil, unhelpfully, then tried to be funny, adding, 'I think you'll find, Cynthia, that a more accurate description of my lady wife would be *my* Holly . . .'

As attempts on lightening an atmosphere go, this was a damp squib.

However, if Daisy thought the awkward moment of silence after Basil's words was the embodiment of a pregnant pause, it was nothing to the silence after Holly broke the quiet to screech, 'Listen, everybody, I'm *so* excited to be Basil's wife. It's as if all my dreams have come true. And our good news doesn't end there – I'm thrilled to say we're going to have a baby!'

Daisy understood at this point that the saying 'you could have heard a pin drop' really was true.

In fact, it was so intensely silent in the room that Daisy was pretty certain she could have heard a pin drop all the way over in Crumford.

And then Daisy, who didn't dare look around her to see what everyone else's reactions were, raised aloft her teacup, and in a very loud voice said a little shakily, as suddenly she really wanted to laugh at the bizarre turn the tea party had taken, 'Congratulations to the happy couple!'

There was a beat of silence, and then almost everyone raised up their teacups too and called out, 'Congratulations.'

∞

Much later, once all the fuss had died down and Clem and Daisy were back in the cottage on their own, Daisy said, 'I didn't quite see our simple tea party going that way.'

After she'd made a bank of pillows on the bed for Clem to lean against, she poured them each a small brandy.

Clem looked exhausted, but managed, 'Entertaining.'

'And how. So indescribably but rather deliciously awkward!' Daisy said, taking a sip. 'I expect Mother and Father will calm down eventually, in a decade or so. Ren and his brothers will be talking about it right now, I bet. I don't think I have ever seen three young men look so shocked. And Holly going back with them . . . Oh, to be a fly on the wall at the brewery house right now!'

Clem blinked, and then he gave a nod.

Daisy laughed. 'If Olive goes on to marry Briar, at least he's already had the baptism by fire of the Graham way of doing things.'

They listened to the crackle of the fire, punctuated by Wicket's squeaky purrs that made him sound like the feline equivalent of Old Creaky.

For the sails of the smock mill were making their usual creaks and groans and whistles as they turned, but neither brother nor sister paid any attention as these noises were so familiar that they had long ago ceased to hear them.

'Clem, please don't be offended or get upset or frightened, but I saw you and Ren today – in here, before I came in. I think you know what I mean,' said Daisy carefullyy.

He breathed in sharply and in shock at her unexpected words sloshed over Daisy most of the brandy that she had just poured him.

Daisy reached for her brother's hand so that he would know she wasn't cross or shocked with him, and she looked at him earnestly as she quietly asked, 'Do you care for each other very much?'

Sadly, Clem gave the smallest of nods.

'Yes, I thought so; it looked like love. Here, have a little more brandy, dear.' Daisy topped up Clem's glass, and then gently touched her own against his. 'It must be very difficult for you both.'

Clem stared at her for a long while, and then he managed to say, 'Hate me?'

'Not for a minute, not even a single second,' insisted Daisy. 'I never could and I never will. Ren and I aren't right for each other, and I felt that before I knew about you two. I'll never tell anyone, I promise. Olive has guessed but she is the only one, I'm sure, and she'd die rather than ever say anything. I'm just sorry that the world is the way it is for you two, and that we're all having such a miserable time. I saw how cherished you are to each other, and I envied you.'

She climbed onto the bed to lie beside her brother, and they held each other tightly, Daisy realising after a while that they both had tears in their eyes.

Daisy thought Clem was upset like this as he and Ren could never be together, and because of this he had married Marguerite and now he was responsible for a wife and a baby, neither of whom he could ever be honest with. Although he would love Stan dearly and be immensely fond of Marguerite, at the same time he would feel he was being very unfair in regard to them both. And because he was ill too, and might never again be the vigorous and happy-go-lucky Clem who went off to war.

Quite what she was in turmoil about herself, Daisy wasn't sure. Because she didn't feel happy or settled maybe, or perhaps because she was very probably in love with a man she didn't really understand and whom she suspected would never be as involved with her as deeply as she cared for him. Or was it the sight of her poor brother beside her, trapped as he was between the proverbial rock and a hard place?

All things must end though, and after a while both Clem and Daisy stilled their thoughts and they relaxed against one another.

It was nice lying together in the dimly lit room, calm before the warm fire and with a content grey and white kitten with a bright pink nose draped across their legs, lying on his back in total surrender.

Daisy peered out at the clear night sky through a chink in the curtain. She could see a single very bright star.

She turned to Clem, and broke their companionable silence by saying, 'Look at that star, dear. It looks so encouraging and pretty – perhaps it's the promise of good things to come.'

Clem moved his head around until he could see the star. 'Stan,' he said.

Daisy laughed, and said, 'Yes, it's a Stan. I do love you, Clem! It's not midnight yet, but I'm going to wish you Happy New Year for 1915 now. Bugger off, 1914!'

'Nineteen fourteen,' echoed Clem as he managed to flip up the first two fingers of his wobbling hand to show the regard with which he was saying goodbye to the year. It was a slow flip, but he managed without too much trouble, which was a huge achievement for her poorly brother.

Daisy liked it that she could see Clem more in control of his body than previously, and how at the same time he was demonstrating a bolshy attitude that surely had to auger well in his recovery.

And as Daisy turned her head once again to stare up at the star high in the velvety blackness outside, she fancied that it shone that bit more brilliantly, offering a glimmer of hope and salvation for both her brother and herself.

She closed her eyes for a second or two, and when she opened them again Daisy was sure the star so far away was shining even brighter.

Acknowledgments

The biggest debt of gratitude must go to the inspiration for this novel, White Mill, a real-life smock mill that's close to Sandwich in Kent, and is what Old Creaky is based on. Do visit – it's riveting: https://whitemillheritagecentre.org.uk/ I recommend some fascinating YouTube films that detail the current restoration work and the incredible feat of removing the mill's cap.

Huge thanks must go too to my editor at Bonnier Zaffre, Claire Johnson-Creek, and of course the rest of the team. They've tried hard to save me from myself, and so any errors will be wholly my own.

And the final thank you is for my agent Cathryn Summerhayes. She's a gem.

·MEMORY LANE·

Welcome to the world of Anna Cliffe!

Keep reading for more from Anna Cliffe, to discover a recipe that features in this novel and to find out more about Anna Cliffe's inspiration for the book . . .

We'd also like to welcome you to Memory Lane, a place to discuss the very best saga stories from authors you know and love with other readers, plus get recommendations for new books we think you'll enjoy. Read on and join our club!

·MEMORY LANE·

www.MemoryLane.Club
www.facebook.com/groups/memorylanebookgroup

Dear reader,

It's such a solitary experience putting words down that it becomes almost impossible to imagine the final result will be read by anyone else. So thank you very much for making it this far at least! As I wrote, I admit to falling in love with sisters Daisy, Violet and Holly, and I hope you will too.

I wanted them to seem like young women we'd like to have as friends today, but also to be thoroughly characters hailing us from 1914. This was a time when women had few options over their lives. They never suspected that when war was declared that many would discover a big world waiting for them outside the family and the home. And once that had happened, life changed.

What I tried to do as well was to show how naïve most people were when war was declared. Almost a century before we can have news through a few taps on our mobiles, 1914 was a time when news travelled slowly and the words of those in power were believed simply by virtue of the speaker's position. Society supported Britain going to war, and young men were thrilled to volunteer en masse with no idea of what they were racing towards.

The more I imagined my three sisters blossoming into their womanhood at the same time as living with the worry and uncertainty of a world tipped suddenly upside down, the more I realised there were stories I could tell of how three resourceful sisters might regard their own selves in this challenging period of history, stories that wouldn't skirt the horror but that would show, too, positivity and humour, and how even in the darkest of days there can be hope and that life will always go on.

It's been a pleasure to write this novel, and I can't help wondering what Daisy, Violet and Holly will discover in the next instalment of their adventures? One thing I'm certain of is that they will very much tell me their stories as I write! In fact, I can almost hear them right now, calling to me from across the years . . .

With very best wishes, and much appreciation of your interest in *The Flour Mill Girls*,

Anna

Cynthia's Simple Shortbread

Daisy brings some of Cynthia's freshly baked short-bread along while visiting her sister-in-laws. This simple yet delicious recipe is perfect for sharing with friends over a cup of tea and a chat, or even curled up along with your favourite book!

Makes approximately 20 biscuits

Ingredients
- 180g plain flour
- 125g unsalted butter
- 55g caster sugar, plus extra for finishing

Recipe

1. Preheat the oven to 190°C/gas mark 5.
2. Beat the butter and the sugar together in a mixing bowl until smooth.
3. Slowly stir in the sifted flour and combine with a wooden spoon to get a smooth paste.
4. Turn the dough onto a floured work surface and gently roll out until the dough is at least 1cm/½in thick.
5. Cut into shortbread rounds or fingers and place onto a greased baking tray.
6. Sprinkle with caster sugar and chill in the fridge for 20 minutes.
7. Once chilled, bake in the oven for 15–20 minutes, or until pale golden-brown. Set aside to cool on a wire rack.
8. If you're feeling adventurous, why not try adding orange zest or chocolate chips into the dough in step 3?

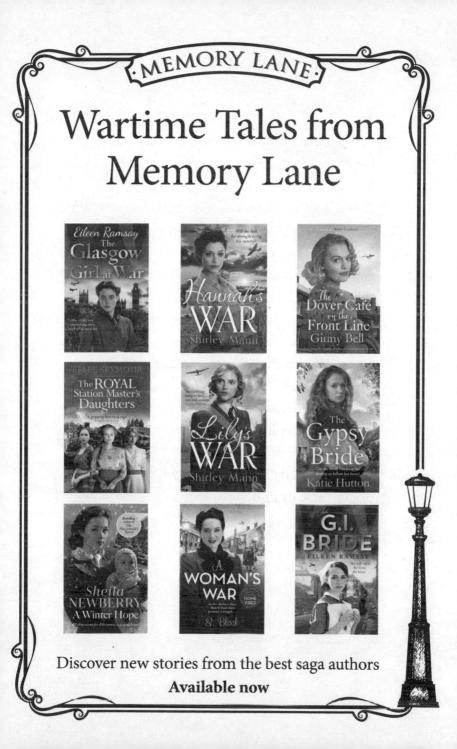

Tales from Memory Lane

Discover new stories from the best saga authors

Available now